Kind of lonesome out here, isn't it?"

The deep timbre of the voice, though soft-spoken, leaped out of the darkness at her. The simple unexpectedness of it was enough to make her heart hammer, and the edge of fear was enough to hold her quiet. Though it was too dark to see the man clearly, she nonetheless felt his weight on the log as he stepped onto it.

In the face of her silence, he spoke again, gentle reproof in his voice. "It isn't safe to wander off too far alone."

The fear crept closer, but one thing she'd learned from her father's years of absence was that a woman had to keep her head and not be easily intimidated. So thinking, she mustered some calm and strained her eyes, trying to make him out in the darkness.

"I'm not alone," she said, priding herself on the even tone of her voice. "I'm with a band of travelers. We're camped beyond the trees. My father and brother'll be along shortly to help me back with the wash."

"You're Miss Rachel, aren't you? We met earlier."

Adam Hawk! She should have recognized those soft southern syllables. He was close enough now that she could make out his slouch hat, the fringed buckskins. "I thought you'd moved on, Mr. Hawk." Rising from a less than graceful pose, she felt the rough bark of the tree beneath her tender feet, flinched over a sharp jab in her instep, and nearly lost her balance.

Confidently he covered the distance between them and steadied her. In the instant it took his hand to fall away, her uneasy feeling returned. His hand and his towering height held strength. Should she thank him for saving her from a spill in the creek, or scream the trees down?

Cries the Wilderness Wind

SUSAN KIRBY

of the Zondervan Publishing House
Grand Rapids, Michigan

A Note from the Author:
I love to hear from my readers! You may correspond with me by writing:

Susan Kirby
Author Relations
1415 Lake Drive, S.E.
Grand Rapids, MI 49506

CRIES THE WILDERNESS WIND

Serenade/Saga is an imprint of Zondervan Publishing House,
1415 Lake Drive, S.E., Grand Rapids, MI 49506.

ISBN 0-310-47571-6

Edited by Nancye Willis
Designed by Kim Koning

Printed in the United States of America

87 88 89 90 91 92 / EP / 10 9 8 7 6 5 4 3 2 1

To Margaret Kirby
with love

He walks upon the wings of the wind;
He makes the winds His messengers,
Flaming fire His ministers.

Psalm 104:3–4 (NASB)

chapter 1

EARLY EVENING CLOSED IN as the band of weary travelers made camp. The trees along the banks of the creek, tight-fisted with buds, were dark towers against the amber sky. After weeks on the trail, the group knew that spring had settled in with a promise. A baby cried, a mother crooned, and the livestock milled about, eager to be fed.

The scent of campfires hung in the air when the stranger rode in. Rachel Whitaker paused from nursing her fire and spared him a glance as he hailed the camp. A tall man on a dark, trail-worn horse, he had a resolute set to his broad buckskin-clad shoulders. Beneath the brim of a slouch hat, his eyes were a dauntless blue; a livid scar spanned his left cheek, standing out upon a field of razor stubble. His appearance said he was better suited to these wilderness surroundings than the travelers he surveyed.

"Headed west?" Rachel heard Francis ask the stranger.

"Going back when I've taken care of some business," the stranger replied, still on his horse.

"You're welcome to step down and rest a spell," Francis invited. He nodded toward his campfire. "We'll be eatin' directly. Care to join us?"

Rachel missed the man's reply, but moments later, as he joined them around the fire, assumed he'd accepted.

Rachel's stepfather shook the man's hand, introducing himself, then his family. "I'm Francis Pierce. My oldest son Samuel's feeding the stock. This is Philip."

At seventeen, Philip was sunny of nature and easy to befriend. "Howdy," he greeted, then offered to care for the man's horse.

"Much obliged," the stranger accepted.

Hearing the soft sound of the South in his voice, Rachel glanced his way as Francis finished introductions, saying, "And this here is my stepdaughter, Rachel. Rachel, meet Adam Hawk."

Rachel murmured, "Pleased to meet you." Finding herself the object of scrutiny from those brilliant blue eyes, she turned her attention back to the sputtering fire.

Francis made note of the smoke and weak flames. "We made camp awhile ago, but it 'pears like supper could be a spell. My wife's not been well," he added, beckoning toward the wagon. "Rachel here's been doing the cooking. Lacks Clara's experience, but she's learning," he said with customary bluntness.

Rachel's pride smarted at his words. Privately she thought she was coping well enough, all circumstances considered. Aloof beneath the stranger's watchful glance, she bowed her head and went back to fanning reluctant flames.

Across the camp came a welcome voice. "Miss Rachel, Miss Rachel, here's your surprise. Close your eyes tight now and don't peek!"

A smile graced Rachel's lips at the sight of copper-skinned, blue-eyed Dorie Ferguson flying toward her. The eight-year-old tried, as she ran, to conceal the contents of the bowl in her hands.

"You're peeking, Miss Rachel!" Dorie accused.

Wishing they could dispense with the "Miss" that made her feel older than her twenty-two years, Rachel closed her dark eyes.

Aware of the stranger's unwarranted attention, she played along with Dorie's surprise, opening her mouth on command to taste the substance Dorie spooned in. Bland, unseasoned, but not unpleasant. "Greens, isn't it? You fix these yourself, Dorie?"

The girl's untidy braids whisked from side to side. "Mom-Julia did. But I gathered them. All day I watched for them. It's curly dock and pepper grass mostly. Mom-Julia wouldn't put in bacon rind. She says we have to be thrifty if we are to have food for the rest of the trip."

Thriftiness had never been one of Rachel's strengths, yet she didn't fault it in Julia Ferguson. She and George were good people. The burden of caring for a young family had wrought a maturity in Julia that Rachel knew she herself lacked.

Dorie's round eyes were anxious. Her eager-to-please manner touched Rachel's heart. "These are about the best greens I've ever eaten—and to think you watched all day! Your hard work makes the surprise all the more special."

Dorie's smile deeply defined the dimple in her chin. At the beginning of the journey, she'd been aloof, but now, certain of Rachel's love, she was like a puppy wanting its ears scratched. Touched by the child's attachment to her, Rachel was always quick to oblige.

"The whole dish is yours," Dorie said, when Rachel tried to return it. "I cut enough for everyone, but Billy and the twins wouldn't eat them. That leaves plenty for you. Maybe you could give your ma some. Could be they'll help her feel better. It must grow tiresome, lying in the wagon day after day."

Seeing the earnest blue eyes cloud with sympathy, Rachel felt the weakness creep in. She drew a deep breath, then leaned down and pressed a cheek against Dorie's, whispering, "I'm sure it must. Mama tries to be brave, but at times she grows so weary. You're a good child to think of others. Thank you for caring."

The smooth brown cheek grew warm against hers, but beneath the child's embarrassment at being sincerely complimented, Rachel sensed pleasure. She gave her an affectionate pat, then straightened to see Francis leading the stranger off a few yards to introduce him to the other men.

Briskly changing the subject, she said, "It appears everyone's eaten but us. I'm still all thumbs when it comes to cooking."

Dorie caught a handful of her skirt and tugged gently. Lashes sweeping upward, voice imploring, she asked, "Your ma's going to get better, isn't she, Miss Rachel?"

Rachel's eyes grew misty and she tried to swallow the lump that clogged her throat. Mama was dying. They all knew it, had known even as they began the long journey. A knife turned in her heart at the thought of burying her mother somewhere along the trail. Yet she had to admit the possibility.

The travelers had taken her mother's health into consideration as they made plans. They'd kept the group small to heighten the possibility of finding accommodations as often as possible. That way Mama wouldn't be subject to foul weather both day and night. Bonded in the beginning by a common destination, the ties tightened in their kind concern for Mama. Each night they gathered for evening devotions, sending up prayers for her. Prayers that always ended, "Thy will, not ours, be done, Father."

Of late, Rachel had wanted to cry, "Don't say that! Pray for healing!" She'd never said the words aloud. It was wicked enough to think them.

Vowing to be less selfish, more faithful and brave, Rachel covered Dorie's hand with her own. She held back her tears, speaking soft words. "We'll keep praying, Dorie. Your thoughtfulness, and that of all these people is an encouragement to Mama. To me too."

Blushing again, Dorie lowered her gaze to her dusty toes. "I'd better get back," she whispered. "You can return Mom-Julia's dish tomorrow."

Rachel thanked her again. As the girl turned, one black braid caught in a button midway down the back of her dress. Rachel delayed her to untangle the strands of hair from the button, then drew Dorie into her arms and held her close. Her black hair held the smoky scent of the campfire and her thin arms, as they closed around Rachel, were surprisingly strong. Marveling at the unspoken closeness, the warmth, the healing balm of a simple hug, Rachel kissed the top of her head. Huskily, she said, "Better run on now, precious."

Wiping her eyes, watching the girl cross the campsite in coltish strides, Dorie caught a second glimpse of Adam Hawk. A head taller than Francis and Samuel, he stood in the midst of talking, gesturing men. The hat cast his unshaven face in shadow, so it might merely be a trick of light, but it seemed to her that, as he studied Dorie, his expression seemed even to alter, the hard line of his mouth gentling. His big hand trembled as he removed the hat from a thatch of chestnut hair and slapped it against fringed buckskins.

As Dorie disappeared around the Fergusons' wagon, he turned abruptly and caught Rachel watching him. Samuel too turned from the group. Seeing Rachel had taken Hawk's attention from the circle of men, his mouth turned sour, and Rachel could feel his displeasure across the open ground that separated them. Resentment swept through her; lately Samuel had been a watchguard of her every movement. She glowered back at him until he stalked off in the other direction.

Adam Hawk, hat still in hand, strode toward her cooking fire. Rachel fed it another stick, aware he'd paused beside her.

"I won't be staying for supper, ma'am. The boy who took my horse—"

"There's plenty," Rachel cut in, echoing her stepfather's hospitality.

His look told her he knew that wasn't true, knew even better than she that the scarcity of food was one of the larger problems looming ahead of the travelers. "All the same, I'll be going," he murmured.

Rachel turned toward the trees where Philip stood grooming the dark horse. "I'm afraid my brother's unsaddled your horse."

He followed the direction of her gesture, and with a nod, said good-by. She watched him go, curious why he'd hailed their camp if it wasn't a meal he was looking for.

Her fire soon recaptured her attention. Healthy flames were heating the flat stone she'd placed beneath her wood. She raked it out and placed the bowl of greens upon it.

Mush and milk. She turned up her nose at what had become frequent fare and stirred the lumps out of the cornmeal mixture. Perhaps Mama would perk up at the sight of Dorie's greens. Their meals of late had been sadly lacking in variety.

As the men finished caring for the animals, Rachel waited, still uncertain how to judge when the fat in her skillet was hot enough to pour in her batter. Boston born and bred, more recently removed to her stepfather's farm near Utica, New York, she still found camp cooking a difficult art. Neither the scent of wood smoke wafting on the spring breeze nor the cracking embers could drive away her yearning for the comforts of home. Uppermost in her thoughts was her mother's cookstove—not that she was particularly accomplished on it—it just made the chore more tolerable.

She winced and nursed a grease-splattered finger. Francis had promised the cookstove, along with their other bulkier furnishings, would arrive safe and sound in Oquawka, Illinois, the nearest point to Galesburg on the river. The furnishings, which would travel by sailing vessel to New Orleans, then by steamboat up the Mississippi, would be fetched from Oquawka by wagon.

Exhausted by another day, another twenty miles of walking alongside the wagon, Rachel wondered, and not for the first time, if they might have been more comfortably transported by waterway. A steamboat would have been a luxury compared to this!

But her mother wouldn't have considered boat travel even if they could have afforded it. She'd burst into tears at the mention of crossing the Niagara River at Queenston. Knowing her to be a reasonable woman in every other respect, Francis had given in and agreed they'd travel overland the complete way.

"Stranger must have had a change of heart," Philip interrupted her thoughts. Straddling a nearby stump, he hooked his thumbs in his suspenders.

"It would appear so," Rachel murmured. Always glad of his cheerful company, Rachel tossed him a smile and stooped to stir the coals in her fire.

"Could be you scared him off—you with your cookin'." He cast a stone into her fire, scattering embers as he teased, "Get that grease any hotter 'n we'll be setting up the bucket brigade."

"Hush up, Philip, or you'll find yourself frying this mush instead of my doing it!" Cautiously, she turned the frying mush, pleased to find it nicely browned on one side.

"What? And rob you of all the glory? Lookin' fine. Really, it is!"

he added with more sincerity when Rachel shot him a warning glance.

Philip took out his knife and began sharpening it against the rim of the large crock which held fresh milk. "Philip!" Rachel objected. "Who wants to drink milk with bits of this and that floating in it? Can't you sharpen your knife later?"

He chuckled, but put his knife away. A companionable silence fell between them as Rachel finished frying the mush, her thoughts straying once more to her mother's fear of water.

Though not in agreement with it, Rachel could sympathize. Her natural father, an officer of a seagoing vessel, had been lost at sea the year Rachel turned sixteen. Now, six years later, she wondered that she'd missed him at all. He hadn't seemed like a real parent, rather like a stranger who reappeared on occasion to present her with lavish gifts.

"Ought to be crossing into Illinois within the week," Philip mused. "Wouldn't admit it to Samuel, but my thoughts are sometimes too small. I never supposed this country of ours could be so wide across."

Rachel murmured agreement. New York itself had seemed vast. Finding an occasional arrowhead along what had once been the Iroquois Trail, passing a lichen-covered boulder that had witnessed the soundless tread of countless moccasined feet had driven home the realization that less than a century ago, these had been the homelands of the mighty Iroquois. The trail, then a mere forest path, had linked together the Five Nation network of fierce and ruthless warriors. Following the Shore Trail along Lake Erie through much of Ohio, she'd found her thoughts turning to the French traders who had once walked these woodlands skirting the lake. The further they pushed across Indiana, the more sparsely populated the country. Fewer taverns were to be found, and the quality of those they'd encountered lately was so poor as to make the least efficient New England housewife shudder!

Daily the roads worsened. Sighing, thinking of the weeks of hard travel behind them, Rachel hardly dared speculate the on quagmire paths, the dismal rains, the hardships that lay ahead.

A hot coal popped, the smell of scorched fabric jerking her to the problem at hand. She dished up the last of the mush, called Samuel and Francis, then bent to inspect the latest bit of damage to her brown woolen skirt.

"A hole the size of my finger," she muttered. "My clothes will be rags by the time we reach Galesburg."

Samuel settled on the tailboard of the wagon to eat. Philip eased down beside him. Handing Francis two plates, Rachel said, "Tell Mama that Dorie Ferguson provided the greens. She's a sweet child, worrying about Mama."

Samuel sopped his mush in milk. "Good Book speaks of the futility of worry. Better to leave trouble in the Lord's hands."

Rachel bit back a quick retort. His lofty manner, more than his words, needled her. Sinking down on the stump Philip had vacated, she poked at her supper, then paused to reexamine the new hole in the hem of her skirt.

Philip wiped his mouth on his sleeve. "Stop fussin' over it. When you get to Galesburg, make you another'n. Sewing's no trouble for you. Why, you could make enough skirts to open your own shop in less time than it takes Samuel to harness the team."

Ignoring the teasing nature of the comment, Samuel said, "Don't be planting *that* idea in her head. It's just the kind of notion she'd delight in."

"And why not?" Philip asked, clearly enjoying the prospect of a good-natured argument. "Wouldn't be a stranger to the business, now would you, Rachel?"

Rankled anew by Samuel's proprietary manner where she was concerned, Rachel sided with Philip. "I hadn't given any thought to a shop, but you're right, Philip. It'd be a way to earn money on my own. 'Pin money' as the Beacon Hill ladies used to call it. Nothing so demanding as our Hanover Street shop, though. It'd leave me time for nothing else."

Samuel sniffed. "Galesburg'll be a far cry from Beacon Hill, so don't be letting Philip drop frivolous ideas to take root. Be plenty for you to do without some tomfool notion about your own shop."

Bristling, she watched him swallow the last of the supper she'd prepared. "There's nothing frivolous about the idea at all, Samuel. Mama and I did quite well with our shop back in Boston. It paid for my education with enough left over to hire a day girl to do the cooking and cleaning in our home."

Rachel did not mention the fact that the shop had been their only means of support after Charlton Whitaker's death. Though she wasn't yet as skilled with a needle as her mother, Rachel had shown a flair for design that'd kept the Beacon Hill society girls badgering their fathers for the means to consign the Whitakers to attend to their wardrobes.

"Woman ought to do her own cooking and cleaning," Samuel groused. He cast her a sidelong glance. "You'll acknowledge a little know-how in that direction wouldn't hurt you any. How many times have I fetched sand for you to scour the black out of the bottom of that skillet there?"

"I won't ask you again, so don't bother your head about that!" Rachel rounded frostily.

Philip gave her a broad wink. "Any sand you need, I'll do your fetching, Rachel."

"Thank you, Philip. And any mending you need done, just ask." Her glance lingered pointedly on a three-cornered rip in Samuel's shirt.

"You don't have to take that attitude," Samuel protested, a slow flush creeping up his neck.

Feeling her crossness justified, Rachel ignored him and began entertaining Philip with stories of the young ladies who'd graced their Boston shop. Modestly hinting that her aptitude for adding personal touches to the fashions found in such periodicals as London's *Court Magazine* and Philadelphia's *Lady's Book,* coupled with Clara's skilled needle, made her equal to any challenge, she told of evening dresses, morning dresses, riding habits, ball gowns, and dinner and carriage dresses that would have done London royalty justice.

"The nicest thing about the shop was that it was always a place of laughter," she continued. "Girls blushing and giggling and whispering about well-heeled young men." She sighed, thoughts roaming over happy memories.

"One afternoon, a red-faced evangelist strode in. He'd found himself in the embarrassing situation of being due to preach at a revival at Hanover Street Church and in need of either a new pair of pants or a quick needle."

Samuel's disapproving glance bounced off her. She tipped her chin and laughed. "You can't imagine how out of place he felt in that shop. But Mama was a marvel with customers. She fixed his pants and put him at such ease, he returned the next day to buy a shawl for his wife. And while he was there, he invited Mama and me to attend the ongoing revival."

"Which is where your mother met Father," Philip filled in the part of the story he knew. "He'd gone as a layman in training. Left Samuel in charge at home. The longest four weeks of my life, I tell you!"

Samuel ground a boot heel in the dirt at the implication. Rachel picked up the story again.

"It might have seemed forever to you, but I don't think it did to Mama and Francis. They were growing to love each other."

Samuel made a disapproving noise. Both Philip and Rachel dissolved into laughter. Having accomplished his goal of getting under his brother's skin, Philip nudged him and teased, "You surely didn't think Father'd marry a woman without coming to love her first."

"I don't think it's any of my business. Or yours, either," he snapped, his gaze including Rachel. "Ought to be wiping the dishes instead of wasting your time chattering. I'll get you a bucket of water, Rachel."

Rachel sprang to her feet and snatched the bucket from him. "Don't trouble yourself. I'll get it." Turning, she asked, "Philip, did I ever tell you about the time I attended the theater?"

Philip fell in step with her, a willing party to invoking Samuel's disapproval. Always happy to hear anything Rachel wanted to report, he took the bucket from her hand.

As Rachel talked, the flavor of Boston, its harbor, its flourishing manufacturing district, its blend of diverse people and occupations came to life. She spoke of the excitement generated by the shop clientele who chattered incessantly of balls and dinner parties, of musical clubs and art coteries and lectures at Yale, and in so doing, made herself a little homesick.

But Boston was long behind her. Rural life in the Mohawk Valley was in her past as well. Perhaps it was anxiety over what lay ahead that made her too quick to react to Samuel's stuffy, overprotective manner. Galesburg might well be near the edge of western civilization, but that didn't mean she needed a keeper!

A half-mile upstream on the opposite bank of the creek, Adam Hawk cleaned a rabbit and fixed the rabbit to the spit he'd fashioned. Hand more patient than his thoughts, he turned his supper over the fire and gazed toward the west, staring until his eyes lost focus in the sunfire gilding the earth.

An ember sizzled, a woodpecker tat-a-tapped while overhead the breeze sighed through hardwoods waiting to burst into leaf. Already the redbuds and wild plum were in bloom. As they knew the time of awakening, Tall Horse would know he'd found her. Restless, in need of another glimpse of her, he left his supper cooking over low embers and angled downstream.

chapter 2

Not a graceful Conestoga prairie schooner, nor even a fleet, lightweight Dearborn, but a lumbering farm wagon with a canvas top stretched over hoops had become a sickroom on wheels. Having taken the chill off the water, Rachel bathed her mother, then herself.

Clara was curled up in quilts, thumbing through the pocket-sized *Gazeteer of Illinois*. Published in 1834, it was three years old; yet the maps and information contained in the travel guide were as current as could be obtained. Watching her, Rachel asked, "Has the ride been hard today, Mama?"

Clara put the guide aside and flashed a pale smile. "Much the same as yesterday. Supper was good, Rachel," she drew the conversation away from her fragile health. "You're mastering open-fire cooking."

Her mother's appearance put Rachel in mind of the fragile petals of a faded summer rose. Rachel tried to inject a note of cheer into her voice. "That Dorie Ferguson certainly is a sweetheart."

"I doubt that Julia or George ever regrets taking her in."

"And why would they?" Rachel said quickly. "She's a good child. Quick-witted, obedient, and kind."

Expression tempered by the wisdom of her years, Clara admonished, "You can't ignore her Indian blood, Rachel. As young as she is, it marks her as different. Sometimes the children—"

"Children can be cruel," Rachel cut in. She'd heard the occasional taunts, too.

"It isn't something that's going to go away," Clara said matter-of-factly. "Perhaps growing up in Galesburg will make it easier. A Christian community has a duty to all its citizens."

Rachel didn't want to talk about Galesburg just now. It often was unimaginable to her, though Francis had been there and spoke glowingly of the founder, George Washington Gale, as well as the efforts underway. Gale wasn't a novice at laying plans and seeing them through. He'd tried equipping men for the ministry in exchange for manual labor first on a farm near the village of Western in upper New York, and, having succeeded on a small scale, had gone on to found the Oneida Institute of Science and Industry.

Unable to account for her personal doubts, Rachel kept them to herself and smoothed a fresh petticoat down over her hips. "Dorie has a dignity that serves her well, Mama. Julia says she's been shifted around a bit."

"Yes. I'd heard she's been passed around. I'd imagine it's difficult for a child to keep transferring affections. No matter how good Julia and George are to her, it may be in the back of her mind to doubt that it's permanent."

Without questioning the affinity she felt with the child, Rachel whispered a prayer for Dorie's future happiness. She dipped into a small trunk that held her favorite Boston dresses. They'd been ridiculously out of place on Francis's farm and were even more so here on the trail. That was why she'd made the two practical skirts for travel.

Tonight, though, no one would see her. She was in need of the lift pretty things gave her. Was it frivolous, as Samuel seemed to think, to appreciate fine fabrics stylishly done? If so, it was a harmless enough fault, Rachel decided as she dug down to the blue-green brocade with its exquisite rosettes on the bodice and repeated pattern on the cuffs of the leg-o-mutton sleeves.

Surprise apparent, Clara said, "It's nice to see you dressing up for devotions. I wish I could go."

Feeling devious, Rachel finished dressing, then kissed her mother's cheek. "Perhaps soon you will be feeling well enough to, Mama. We're all praying."

Her mother touched the rich fabric with a wistful hand. "That's a sweet dress, dear. Becoming to your fair hair and dark eyes. Wear it for my funeral, Rachel? And remember how much I enjoyed making each tiny rosette."

Heart hurting, Rachel pleaded, "Please, Mama, just try. Don't give up. What will Illinois be without you but a dreadful backwoods prairie without roads or fit houses or a breath of culture?"

It sounded selfish, even as she said it. Yet her mother's touch was gentle as she lifted a hand to her flushed cheek.

"Log City is only temporary, just until fit houses can be built within Galesburg. There won't be a single log cabin within the city. Francis said Gale himself made that stipulation. As for culture, what could be more sweet than a society of Christian friends and neighbors?"

Did her mother believe in Gale's dream? Or did she echo Francis out of loyalty? It was a private matter, and she respected her mother too greatly to ask. All the same, she couldn't imagine settling down to a new life without her mother's sure presence.

"You might as well come to terms with it, Rachel," her mother said softly. "We're all born, we all die. It's a natural thing. The fear comes from fighting it."

"But I don't want to lose you!" Rachel gripped the hand that caressed her cheek.

"You won't be losing me. Not for all time. We'll be reunited by and by; you know that, Rachel."

Hanging her head, Rachel murmured, "I know, but it's hard."

"Run along to devotions and don't be late," her mother urged. "Sing full and clear, Rachel. Sometimes I can pick your voice out of the group."

Rachel held back a smattering of tears. Perhaps for her mother she'd postpone the washing. But no, the odor of too many days' wear made it a must. With her back to her mother she made a tidy bundle of her underthings, wrapping them inside her cream blouse, then using her brown skirt to conceal them all.

"Would you like the lantern lighted?" Rachel asked before leaving.

"No, dear. I'm fine. Run along now," her mother insisted.

Rachel stepped carefully around the bucket in which her mother's favorite rosebush was being transported. One brier caught at her dress, and she dropped her bundle out of the wagon before carefully pulling the thorn away from her skirt.

"Is it budding yet?"

Guiltily Rachel shook her head. The poor bush looked dead. She hadn't been giving it the water and sunlight it needed to flourish.

Her mother exhaled a little sigh. "Charlton brought it from England, you know. He helped me plant it in front of the shop. It looked half dead, I never expected it to revive, but it did. It certainly did."

The mention of her father caused Rachel's feeling of kinship with Dorie to slip into place. Dorie was waiting, just as she had waited each time her father set out to sea. Only Dorie's was a child's wishful thinking; a reunion would never come for her. Shaking loose of the thought, Rachel murmured, "Next time it rains, I'll set the bush out."

Clara made a sound of agreement. Rachel climbed out of the wagon. People were gathering around Reverend Clark's fire. Even in the open air, his voice carried along on the light wind.

Rachel caught snatches as his voice rose in enthusiasm, discussing the orderly, pious community of which they'd be a part, a community where the cause of Christ's kingdom outshone all others, where success was measured by souls won and by the outreach of the ministers they educated.

Making certain she was unseen, Rachel picked up her bundle of clothes and slipped into the cover of trees. Twilight gilded the sky, touching the treetops with an orange torch. Stepping quietly along, she measured the distance to the creek in footsteps, thinking of the return trip to the camp under a curtain of darkness. A slight depression in the grass had been made by the livestock as they'd been led down to drink. It was the same path she'd followed earlier with Philip.

The sound of Reverend Clark's voice faded. It was good to be alone for a while, to let her mind wander, sampling here and there, but making no commitment to troublesome worries.

Twigs snapped beneath her feet. A few sleepy birds let the day go with an unrehearsed chorus of song. She paused beneath the branch of a redbud tree and tugged it low to smell the fragile pink-purple blossoms. Disappointed over their lack of scent, she walked on, shaking out a shower of blossoms that had caught in her hair.

On the path, green struggled for life amidst last fall's shedding of leaves, now dark and dank and decaying. The evidence of the cycle of life saddened her mood when she wanted nothing more than to have her drooping spirits lifted.

Giving her head a shake, she said it wouldn't be long before wildflowers bloomed in cheerful confusion. Had the light been better, she was certain she could have found an early Spring Beauty or two.

The stream showed itself quite suddenly. Its waters brimmed to the banks, coursing along, chuckling and gurgling. The current would make her job easier.

Rachel walked upstream a bit and stopped where a fallen tree made a natural bridge across the water. Would her chore be easier accomplished from the spine of the log? She removed her shoes and clean stockings, hiked her skirts, and sat down on the log, keeping the slick brocade beneath her and away from the water.

Her feet protested at the chilly temperature, but she had no choice but to let them dangle in the creek. She suddenly realized she'd forgotten to bring along her cake of soap. Oh, well, she'd just have to wash without it. She dipped the first stocking, squeezed it out, then dipped again. In the fading light, it was difficult to tell whether the stocking *looked* any fresher, but it smelled better.

Rachel wrung it out, draped it over the log, then reached for its mate. Her chemise was next, then her petticoat. By the time she'd done her best by them, her toes were numb. She drew her knees to her chest and rubbed some warmth into her aching feet.

"Kind of lonesome out here, isn't it?"

The deep timbre of the voice, though soft-spoken, leaped out of the darkness at her. The simple unexpectedness of it was enough to make her heart hammer, and the edge of fear was enough to hold her quiet. Though it was too dark to see the man clearly, she nonetheless felt his weight on the log as he stepped onto it.

In the face of her silence, he spoke again, gentle reproof in his voice. "It isn't safe to wander off too far alone."

The fear crept closer, but one thing she'd learned from her father's years of absence was that a woman had to keep her head and not be easily intimidated. So thinking, she mustered some calm and strained her eyes, trying to make him out in the darkness.

"I'm not alone," she said, priding herself in the even tone of her voice. "I'm with a band of travelers. We're camped beyond the trees. My father and brother'll be along shortly to help me back with the wash."

"You're Miss Rachel, aren't you? We met earlier."

Adam Hawk! She should have recognized those soft southern syllables. He was close enough now that she could make out his slouch hat, the fringed buckskins. "I thought you'd moved on, Mr. Hawk." Rising from a less than graceful pose, she felt the rough bark of the tree beneath her tender feet, flinched over a sharp jab in her instep, and nearly lost her balance.

Confidently he covered the distance between them and steadied her. In the instant it took his hand to fall away, her uneasy feeling returned. His hand and his towering height held strength. Should she thank him for saving her from a spill in the creek, or scream the trees down?

Before she could decide, he said, "You're doing your wash? Kind of late for that, isn't it?"

Refusing to be ruffled, she lifted her shoulders in a small shrug. "I forgot my cake of soap."

"Not much point in washing without soap. You could go back for it."

She shook her head. "It's getting too dark. Anyway, by the time I went back for it and returned to wash again, I'd be missed."

"I've got soap you could use."

To his disappointment, she said, "I couldn't possibly accept, but thank you for offering."

"A cake of soap doesn't make you beholden. Come along now," he demanded, scooping up her bundle, "and I'll show you how to do this job right."

Alarmed at her sudden loss of control of the situation, and with as much authority as she could muster, she cried, "Here now, you! Bring back my wash!"

"Better put your shoes on," he warned. "There's briers growing along the way."

She could go back to the camp and bring help. Oh, wouldn't Samuel like that! Immediately, she discarded that idea.

Maybe she should forget the clothes, write the whole thing off as a lesson in wilderness survival. Or she could put on her shoes and show enough pluck to go after him. The thought of losing her cream blouse was the deciding factor. The blouse had seen enough service to be relegated to everyday wear, and still it was a favorite. She'd fashioned it from a picture in a Paris fashion magazine but a month before they'd left Boston. Cut high at the throat, the front was laid in diagonal pleats from shoulder to waist like a fan and the sleeves were full, tapering to a lacy cuff at the wrist.

Retracing her steps to the other end of the log, she called out, "All right, I'm coming. But I don't have much time, you hear?"

Ignoring the discomfort of a wrinkled stocking and hastily buttoned shoes, she carefully picked her way to the other side of the log. Fluctuating between trust and mistrust, she accepted his hand down from the log, then pulled free, saying, "I can make it now, thank you."

He held a branch from snapping back in her face, his southern drawl growing familiar as he slowed his pace and fell to talking in a way that soothed the nervousness she couldn't dismiss.

"I understand you're headed for Illinois. It's good country, fertile soil. Well watered. Shouldn't have any trouble farming there."

"Francis has been to Galesburg. His reports were enthusiastic." So much so, her mother had willingly traded the comforts of their farmhouse for a rattling deathbed on wheels. Her private resentment of Francis, never once voiced aloud, stole in unexpectedly. She pushed it from her as he went on to ask, "How long have you been traveling?"

"Eight weeks." She punctuated the statement with a heavy sigh.

"Emigration not to your liking?"

She wondered with sudden ill-temper how *he'd* fare out of his element. Say a ballroom in Boston! She stared at his dark shape. Lean-waisted, narrow-hipped, he wore buckskins well. Hopelessly outdated. Nobody in the East wore buckskins. Nor had she forgiven his implication that she was a weak sister, failing to embrace this emigration adventure wholeheartedly. Ignoring his offer of help, she cautiously felt her way along.

"In *Boston,*" she said with emphasis, "gentlemen don't snatch a lady's wash and go marching off with it."

"Don't reckon they do at that."

Falling back a step, she noticed he moved with assurance, right at home in the dark. Not a good omen. What was it the Bible said about those who love the darkness? They love it because the light shows up their bad deeds. She shivered as she trod along behind him. She shouldn't have let disgruntled feelings over Samuel's protectiveness sway her reasoning. If this wasn't pure folly, then a cat didn't have whiskers.

She ventured, "Isn't one spot as good as another? Just drop my things and go get your soap."

Throwing words back over his shoulder, he kept walking. "I noticed a place earlier that'll work out fine."

For him, perhaps. She was doubting more strongly her careless decision. Resolving it was foolishness to follow him any further when each step she took led her further away from the safety of Reverend Clark's party, she came to a standstill. "I have a pebble in my shoe."

"It's just ahead here," he beckoned. "Smell the campfire?"

What she smelled was the beginnings of fear. Stooping, she felt around on the ground for a good hefty stick. Her hand settled not on a stick, but a rock. She concealed it in the folds of her skirt.

chapter 3

THE GLOW OF HIS CAMPFIRE was visible around the next bend. Rachel clung to her rock as they moved forward. A horse blew a soft greeting. Adam murmured a reassurance in response as he dropped her bundle of clothes.

Rachel watched as he crouched near the fire. His supper was skewered over low burning coals. The fire sizzled and sent up a pleasant aroma. Rabbit, Rachel judged. Nearly done, too. Her stomach rumbled. Mush had a way of not staying with a person long. No wonder he hadn't been interested in taking supper with them. Though game was fairly plentiful, Samuel and Francis hadn't much interest in hunting. Philip, who could usually be counted upon to take his rifle out and come back with something, hadn't had much luck the last several days. Except for fresh fish, they hadn't had a truly filling meal since staying at a tavern three nights ago.

Forcing her gaze away from the tantalizing food, she covertly studied Adam, curious about where he had been, why he was here, and where he was traveling. The flicker of firelight revealed little. He was older than she, of that much Rachel was sure. How old, she couldn't judge, since a good deal of his face was covered by several days' growth of whiskers. His head was bent as he worked over the fire, eyes hidden by the wide brim of the hat. But she hadn't forgotten their blue brilliance or the fine lines engraved in the sun-cured skin framing them. Nor had she forgotten her disquieted feeling when those eyes had followed Dorie's movements with such intense interest.

"Hungry?" he asked.

"No," Rachel denied quickly. "I'm short on time, so—"

"Get on with the lesson?"

His grin, exhibiting a sudden flash of white teeth, caught her unprepared. "It isn't a lesson I need, just a piece of soap."

He rummaged through saddlebags she'd overlooked in her swift scrutiny of his camp and came out with the soap. "Grab your things," he said, gesturing that she was to follow.

Rachel lifted her bundle, hiding the rock within it as she followed him to the creek. The shallow shoreline, only yards from his campfire, was better suited to washing than the log she'd selected.

Along the way he scooped up a flat rock, much larger than the one concealed in Rachel's bundle, and settled back on his heels, soap in one hand, to wash its flat surface before reaching for her bundle.

She dropped it beside him, trying without success to retrieve her rock without his noticing. He shifted his hat back on his head and glanced up at her. "Right idea, but not near big enough for the job."

She felt heat rise to her face, and she felt foolish, as if her cautious mistrust did him an injustice.

The shallow water lapped gently at his feet as he remained crouched at the water's edge, rubbing the cake of soap against the fabric of her skirt, then rubbing the skirt against the stone.

"Your supper will burn," she murmured, squatting down beside him and reaching for her skirt. "Thank you for your help."

Nodding, he turned the work over to her, straightened to watch her a moment, then sauntered back to his campfire.

A bush grew nearby, and as Rachel washed and rinsed each article of clothing, she draped it over the outspread branches. When the chore was complete, she gathered all her garments together and made as compact a bundle of them as possible. Rock forgotten, she retraced her steps and returned his cake of soap just as he was sliding the rabbit off the skewer onto a tin plate. She thanked him again and prepared to find her way back to Reverend Clark's camp.

"Might as well have a bite before you go," he offered. "Rabbit's done and I've got bread fresh from a farmer's table where I had breakfast this morning."

The mention of fresh bread was a strong temptation. Even as she prepared to decline, her mouth watered and her stomach raised a stormy complaint. "I really should be getting back. Devotions will soon be over and I'll be missed. But it's kind of you to offer," she added, anxious he not be offended by her refusal.

On the contrary, he ignored it entirely, drew out a second tin plate and divided the rabbit and the bread between the two. "It's not much. Won't take you long to eat. Never have cared much for eating alone."

Resolve weakened by his sincerity, Rachel changed her mind and accepted. "This farmer," she asked, "did he pass along any news? I haven't read a newspaper in weeks."

"Can't say any of it'll interest you." He pushed the plate into her hand and motioned for her to sit on the log he'd vacated. After one bite of the bread, Rachel was glad he'd made the decision for her.

With a bit of coaxing, he went on to share the farmer's news while she ate. "The farmer was feelin' discontent with his worn-out soil, and wantin' to know about Oregon Country, if it's true the earth is rich and black, better even than Illinois dirt. And he was mighty interested in the ball Old Hickory started rollin' before leaving office."

"Settling the northwest?" Rachel licked one finger for want of a napkin.

He nodded. "Farmer's wife was of a more cautious nature. Said she wasn't packin' up and going nowhere until she got news the first wagon train that started out in March made it safely through. Then maybe she'd take it under consideration."

"Wise woman." Rachel chewed carefully. All the rigors of the trail were fresh in her mind. A trip to Oregon Territory was unthinkable to her.

"But the farmer couldn't think of anything but those two hundred acres, free for the takin'. Jackson knew the right bait to dangle, a man has to give him credit for that."

"You disapprove?" Rachel watched him closely, interested in his response.

He tossed a rabbit bone into the fire and watched the flames lick the grease from it. "It had to happen, I guess. But the Indians have been pushed further and further west. There's a limit to how far they'll be pushed. They aren't going to cotton to settlers plowing up their hunting grounds and disrupting the natural course of things. And it'll deal a death blow to the fur trade."

"You're a trapper?" she asked, already knowing the answer, and then assured him, "I for one won't be filling up your northwest. I was content in Boston."

"What brings you west?" he asked.

Getting past the difficult truth of her mother's impending death, Rachel finished by saying, "I thought if Mama could face the journey, coming along to ease her discomfort was the least I could do."

"Not a conviction you had to be a party to filling up Illinois?" he said with a trace of quiet humor.

"No, certainly not that," she assured him.

Stretching his feet toward the fire, he leaned back on his elbows. "Tell me more about this town Galesburg."

Surprised at his interest, Rachel told him of George Washington Gale's dream of a manual labor college where young men who wished to train for the ministry could receive an education in exchange for farm labor.

He squinted as the breeze shifted, blowing smoke his way. "So the town'll exist for the purpose of the college?"

"Mr. Gale thinks farmers' sons in particular are suited to the ministry because they're used to hard work and humble means. But they find the cost of college too staggering to consider, which accounts for some poorly educated, yet perfectly sincere itinerant preachers roaming the countryside preaching their own brand of Christianity."

Adam Hawk chuckled softly at her words. Scratching his chin, he asked, "And Mr. Gale thinks he's got the solution to the problem?"

"If he can build up a community of Christian people who share his concern for the college, yes."

"Folks who'll also have to share his doctrine, I'd reckon. That part might be a tall order to fill."

"Mr. Gale and subscribers to his idea bought nearly eleven hundred acres of land at the government's price of $1.25 an acre. Some of the land's been set aside for the town and the institution grounds. But the rest is being laid out in farm tracts, available at five dollars an acre."

"*Five* dollars?"

"It's fertile land, well situated between the Mississippi and Illinois rivers with the Rock River to the north," Rachel repeated Francis's justification of the price. "With river travel opening gates all over the country, the farmers who settle there will have ready markets for their crops. The profit from the sale of the land will pay for the college. It isn't to be some sort of Utopia, closed but to a limited few. It's open to anyone."

"Anyone who can afford five dollars an acre," Adam corrected her.

Rachel added, "I suppose it would be accurate to say those who are going understand the religious ideal behind Galesburg. But that isn't to say they aren't calculating on making a better life for themselves. Financially, I mean."

He tossed a pebble at the fire and sent up a scurry of sparks. A touch of approval in his voice, he commented, "Sounds as if you've got a fair understanding of the place. Hope it turns out to be what you're counting on."

Warmth crept up her neck at the realization she'd misrepresented herself. Yes, she understood the dream behind Galesburg and the actions setting it into motion—had perhaps expounded upon it to a degree some would find unseemly in a woman. But as for her hopes, her expectations—she was too preoccupied with worry over her mother, and with quiet resentment over Francis's having uprooted her when she most needed rest, to work up any genuine enthusiasm at the thought of being a part of Gale's Christian effort. Never having admitted it, she wasn't going to start now. Coming to her feet, she thanked him for the meal.

Adam moved to block her path and said carefully,

"I've not been entirely honest with you, ma'am. Not about my reason for bringing you here."

Her chin shot up, and she shot him a quick darted glance, but he plunged on. "Earlier this evening a little girl came to you."

"Dorie?"

Again, her gaze flashed over his face, cautious, but less surprised. He nodded and asked, "She's traveling with the Fergusons?"

She frowned and nodded. "Why?"

"Her grandfather sent me."

She was shaking her head. "*Grandfather?* You must be mistaken. Dorie's an orphan. Fergusons got her from a mission school six months ago."

"He wants to see her. He sent me to bring her to him," he said.

Caution, then doubt ruled her reaction."How can you be sure this is the child you're looking for?"

"I know," he said. "There's no mistake."

Rachel's senses whirled as she thought of the girl's attitude of waiting and for one moment, it seemed believable. Dorie had a hard-to-define quality that made Rachel think it might be possible the child could, without really knowing why, *know* someone would eventually come for her.

Rachel shook her head as reality came crashing home. She was again playing that old game with herself; only this time, Dorie was the child, overjoyed at the long-awaited reunion. This man, this Adam Hawk—whoever he was—came out of nowhere. And he claimed authority, power over Dorie, over her future—power to make her dream come true, or more likely, to crush her with disappointment. Perhaps worse.

"Do you have letters? Papers? A description?" she asked, pulse fluttering in her throat, half fearing he would produce them, then fearing he wouldn't.

He shook his head.

"How do you expect anyone to believe you? To turn her over to you? How can you *know* she's the child you were sent to collect?" she demanded.

"She has a birthmark on her foot."

"And you saw it? Today, you saw it?" Her doubts were growing. Dorie'd been barefoot, but how could he have—

He said, "No. But it's there. I've spent too many months looking to make a mistake. She's the child."

"You're willing to let a birthmark rest as proof?"

"It's no ordinary birthmark." He stooped to draw in the ashes of a campfire left behind by some other wayfaring soul.

By moonlight, she saw it was a heart he'd drawn, one side fuller than the other. He'd marked a line like an arrow slashing through it.

"It's on the bottom of her left foot," he said, rising to tower over her again.

He seemed sure. Rachel chewed her bottom lip, grappling with uncertainty. She had no idea whether she'd find a birthmark on Dorie's left foot or not. And even if she did, what did that prove? Beginning to tremble from within, she asked, "What is it you want exactly?"

"I'm going to take her to see her grandfather. I gave him my word."

He made it sound so simple! "Doesn't it matter whether or not she wants to go? Mr. Hawk, do you realize what you're about to do?"

In silence, he met her incredulous stare, and held it until she shifted her bundle, the first to lower her lashes. Trying to reason with him, she explained, "Dorie's lost her parents, she's been shuffled from one set of guardians to a mission school to another set of parents. And now you intend to sweep her off to see some grandparent who suddenly has a great interest in her?"

"I gave him my word."

He said it with such simplicity! Rachel wanted to stamp her foot and rail at him. "Where does Dorie's welfare enter into all of this? What if she doesn't want to go with you to meet this mysterious grandfather? What if she's content where she is?"

"I thought of that," he said. "I don't want to be forced to take her against her will. It'd be better if she goes eagerly."

"You *can't* just take her!"

"I don't want to," he said again. "But I will if it's the only way. So do you want to help me or not?"

"Help you?" Rachel said, washed in disbelief. "I don't know how I could if I wanted to. And I don't. No, Mr. Hawk. The more I think about it, the more it seems to me Dorie's best off where she is."

"If that's the case, then I'll bring her back. Fair enough?"

She didn't know him, had no reason whatsoever to trust him; yet his quiet tone commanded belief. Her thoughts scattered every which way and refused to be neatly gathered.

He eased out a sigh. "I told you I don't have a lot of time and I don't. But I'm willing to give her a week to get used to the idea of going. I think you could help her."

Against her better judgment, she asked, "How?"

"She thinks something of you, I saw it in her eyes. Unless I'm wrong, you care about her too and wouldn't want to see her hurt."

"I do," she admitted. "That's just why I'd have to be firmly convinced you're who you say you are before I'd even consider encouraging her to believe that something good could come of a meeting with her grandfather. And even then, I'm unsure uprooting her would be in her best interests. The Fergusons are good people. She's being cared for, loved."

His silence, a sort of passive stubbornness, seemed a further indication he'd do as he planned, with or without her approval. Frustrated, Rachel cried, "What if I think encouraging her is too much like filling her with false hope? What if I tell her in plain words she's better off staying with the Fergusons where she knows what she's got? What then, Mr. Hawk?"

The moonlight picked hollows in the burnished scarred plane of his cheek. A muscle flickered alongside the hard line of his mouth. His gaze was solemn, unwavering. "Then I'll talk to the Fergusons at first light. By the time your teams are hitched, we'll be gone."

What was an eight-year-old child's happiness to him? *"His word"* he'd said. As if it were some noble deed he was doing. Horsefeathers! His word no doubt had been paid for in cold hard cash. In the silence between them, her thoughts dropped like water splashes on hot oil, spreading flames of helplessness and anger. Her arms ached from the weight of the wet bundle and the front of her dress was damp through.

"What's it going to be?" he broke the silence between them.

She shouldered past him, thoughts continuing to race as the light wind combined with the dampness and the dread to send a chill through her. If she refused, he'd take Dorie just as he said. If she agreed, she might at least buy some time, feel out George and Julia, see what light they could shed on the possibility of Dorie's having kin still living. And Dorie herself—it was unthinkable that he would just spirit her away.

"Tomorrow morning, I'm going to take a look at Dorie's foot. Then, I'm going to have a talk with Julia Ferguson. If it seems probable you're telling the truth, I'll talk to Dorie and see how she feels about a grandfather who's let months and years pass without contacting her, letting her be raised by whoever's willing to take her in, not seeming to care whether she's alive or dead. Depending on *how* she feels, I might decide to help you."

On her last words, she spun around to face him, expecting at least a mild defense for the man he said was Dorie's grandfather.

But all he said was, "Fair enough."

He took the wet bundle of clothes and stepped around her, leading the way. His step was quiet, but Rachel crashed along, mindless of the noise she was making, or the underbrush snatching at her skirts.

"Apparently he didn't buy your loyalty along with your services," she tossed words at his back.

"Ma'am?" he questioned.

As if he didn't understand perfectly well! Smoldering, she said, "It's just that I would expect you to offer some sort of explanation as to why the man has let years pass—why he's suddenly interested in finding his granddaughter. How much is he paying you to take her, anyway?"

"Nothing."

Uncertain whether or not to believe him, Rachel silently wrestled with the question of his reasons for so doggedly searching for Dorie. If not for money, then what? Loyalty? Perhaps. He had the look of a man who'd be just that loyal.

Ahead of her, he angled to the right and approached the log that made a path across the creek. He stepped up on the log and glanced back at her. "It wasn't until a few months ago that anyone had reason to believe Dorie was still living. It's a big country. Lots of folks lose touch with their kin."

"But to think she was dead . . . what reason did he have to believe such a thing?"

When he reached the middle of the log, he pivoted to face the bank where she stood. Ribbons of moonlight rippled the water, an owl hooted, and off in the distance a coyote loosed a lonely cry. For a moment, he seemed as much a part of the moon, water, and forest as the night sky. She shivered, caught wondering who she was to challenge him. The wind shifted, blowing a shadowy cloud past the moon. The silvery light dimmed; he continued his way across the log, the spell broken. She let out a caught breath and followed.

Waiting for her on the other side, he picked up the story again. "Dorie's mother was a missionary. Smallpox swept through the village where she and her family were living. Many lay sick and dying, too sick even to bury their dead. Grief, confusion, some crazy with fever," he said, his words short, clipped, as if he wanted the telling behind him. "Those unaccounted for were assumed dead."

Measuring the probability of his words, that a child *could* disappear and be mistaken for dead in such a tragic set of circumstances, Rachel's anger faded. It was news to her that any women had been allowed to accompany missionaries who had journeyed into Indian Country, yet she wasn't particularly knowledgeable about such things. "You're saying her grandfather thought she died with her parents?"

He resumed walking, and Rachel took his silence as an affirmative response. She felt a little numb. Dorie's mother—a missionary. Then the Indian blood . . . it didn't seem decent to ask. The village he spoke of *must* have been Indian. She'd heard of smallpox and other diseases being carried to the Indian by white man, just as she'd heard of missionaries going to Indian villages to spread the word and never returning. Sadness for Dorie, for the fate of her mother, softened her view of Adam Hawk as well as the man on whose behalf he'd come. She paused at the sound of the night wind carrying singing voices. "You don't have to come any further; I know my way." She swallowed hard. "If I've been harsh or seemed uncompromising . . ." She accepted her bundle of clothes and began again. "I have a better understanding now, Mr. Hawk. Let me think it over. If you meant it when you said you'd return her to the Fergusons if she isn't happy with her grandfather, maybe I can help you."

chapter 4

THE WAGON WAS SMALL and cramped with belongings. Having made space on the floor for her blankets, Rachel tried to sleep. Yet her thoughts sloshed around like cream in a butter churn. Restless, she twisted and turned, the wagon creaking with each small movement.

The night air was cool, her blankets a comfort. Beneath the wagon, Philip ground his teeth and mumbled in his sleep. Thinking of the men sleeping in the open air, nothing but a blanket between them and the ground, she chided herself for minding her own minor discomfort.

She couldn't dismiss Dorie from her mind. What would it do to the child to be uprooted once again? Again, she wondered about Adam Hawk—what had motivated him to search for the child? And again, she drew the conclusion he must have taken on the task as a favor for a friend. It seemed the only plausible explanation. What sort of man would this make Dorie's grandfather? A rough frontiersman sort, it was likely. Like Hawk himself. Not a trapper, she prayed, or a scout or trader or any other kind of wanderlusting soul. Wanderlusts didn't make good parents; she knew that from personal experience. She'd make it her business to find out what sort of man he was, because she certainly couldn't accept Dorie's grandfather's making his living wandering about in the great Northwest!

Of course, if he were a rover, wouldn't he have come after the child himself instead of sending Hawk? The logic of that thought calmed her some. She wanted to believe he was a farmer or rancher with a pleasant house near a village where Dorie could go to school, make friends, grow up safe and secure in her grandfather's love.

Across the camp the Fergusons' dog barked. Rachel sat up, heart in her throat. Hastily crawling around obstacles, she made her way to the canvas flap and poked her face out, afraid of what she'd see. But no man on a dark horse was riding off with a frightened child—there was only a silly mongrel howling at the moon. George Ferguson gave a harsh command and the dog went quiet.

Rachel lay down again, telling herself Ferguson was more than capable of looking after his children. Anyway, Hawk had given his word and somehow that seemed to mean something with him. She willed herself to relax and closed her eyes. Half-formed prayers rose from her heart. Bothersome sounds of the night faded as she drifted off to sleep.

The following morning Rachel fetched water and fixed breakfast, catching no sign of Adam Hawk. Across the camp, Dorie stood with stoic patience as Julia braided her hair. Smiling, Rachel waved and called out a greeting. Dorie lifted her hand, but Julia, in the process of talking to the twins, paid no heed. Rachel started toward them, intent on returning the bowl, but when Julia's voice rose in a sound scolding, she frowned and retraced her steps. Her friend was usually patient and soft-spoken. What had upset her? Again, she thought of Adam Hawk.

Samuel was busy hitching the team. He and Francis took turns trudging alongside the horses, encouraging them over the stump-riddled road. Few in their company rode the wagon boards. It was an unnecessary addition of weight for their horses to pull. Francis was fortunate in that he had extra horses, but even then, he was frugal, and tried his best to spare his team undue hardship.

Repentant over her crossness as well as her teasing of Samuel the previous evening, she paused to talk to him a moment, then hurried to finish packing away the dishes and the spider skillet she'd used to fix breakfast. As they prepared to move out, she paused at the tailboard to pet her mare's neck, and croon a few words. Because Francis had shipped her saddle, pointing out to bring it along would take up space they couldn't afford, Sada hadn't been ridden once on the trip. She could have made the argument that if Sada were saddled each day, the sidesaddle wouldn't have created a space problem. However, with her mother to care for, she'd doubted she'd have many opportunities to ride. Now, with the advantage of hindsight, she thought wistfully of the saddle, and glanced down at her worn shoes.

Early in the day, the children in the group were high-spirited. They raced ahead, laughing and entertaining themselves with games and races. As the day lengthened, the smallest ones rode in the wagons and napped. The older children, with the help of the Fergusons' dog Blue, found a fox hole to investigate. Dorie, who was at ease only with the Ferguson children, backed off from the group now that the twins were riding the tailboard of the family wagon.

Dorie's lonesome expression squeezed at her heart. On impulse, she called out, "How'd you like to ride Sada awhile?"

Interest kindled in her fine blue eyes, Dorie came running. "You mean it? You'd let me ride your horse?"

"I don't see why not. She needs the exercise," Rachel said with a smile. "That is, if you're willing to try it bareback. And you have to promise not to get careless. I wouldn't want you to fall off and get hurt."

"Oh, I'd never fall!" Dorie assured. "I can ride like the wind; you'll see. You're so good to me, Miss Rachel," she whispered shyly. "Angels couldn't be any better."

Coloring at the high praise, Rachel gave her an affectionate pat. "I'd imagine I'd size up pretty poorly next to an angel," she said with a little laugh. Rachel untied the lead rope that kept Sada plodding peacefully along the lumbering wagon. She pulled her off to one side and stroked the blaze on her face. "That's my pet, you'll be good for Dorie now, won't you? None of your naughty tricks, you hear?" she crooned, as the rest of the caravan left them behind.

"She does tricks?" New interest shone from Dorie's blue eyes.

Rachel chuckled. "She tries to eat as she walks if you give her her head. She isn't above taking you under a low branch, either. Smiles when she does it, too. She thinks it's a fine joke."

"She won't do it to me," Dorie vowed, a firm note in her young voice.

The dust had settled from the last creaking wagon. The sounds of plodding hoofs and jingling reins were well ahead of them now. Rachel linked her hands saying, "Come on, I'll give you a boost up."

Dorie slipped her left foot into Rachel's hands, grabbed Sada's mane and pulled herself astride the horse. Feeling a counterfeit, Rachel dusted Dorie's narrow foot with the fringe of her shawl. "This poor little foot's walked a lot of miles; look at the calluses," she said, her voice gently teasing.

Dorie squirmed and giggled. "That tickles."

Rachel let go of her foot. Conflicting emotions caught her in a grip of confusion. Beneath the morning's layer of dust, she'd glimpsed the birthmark. Red in color, it did at a glance resemble a heart with a line slashing through it. So it was there, just as Adam Hawk had said it would be. Striving for a normal tone, she said, "Are you ready?"

Dorie protested, "You don't have to lead me." She overtook Rachel, grabbed the lead rope from her hand and with an expectant smile, turned the horse back down the trail they'd just covered. She commanded, "Watch!"

Rachel's heart leaped to her throat as the girl pressed her knees into the mare's sides, sending the animal into a quick trot. Not satisfied with that, Dorie gave a curt command, and with her heels, urged the horse into a loping gallop. Rachel cried after the departing figure, "Dorie, do you know what you're doing?"

It was clear she did. She rode with a natural grace, her braids slapping her back, her firm brown legs hugging the horse. The smooth gallop soon took them out of sight.

Standing alone, Rachel listened to the sound of horse hoofs fading on the beaten path. The Indiana woodlands skirting the road and the overcast sky were a witness to her troubled thoughts. Here she stood worrying over a short ride that took the girl out of sight for a few moments, when Adam Hawk planned to take her into an entirely different life! He was asking a lot, requesting she help prepare Dorie. And for what? For a big kettle of doubts, that was what! She could dig in her heels and refuse. But even as she considered such a course, it didn't seem fair, for Dorie deserved a chance to at least meet her grandfather. She let out a discouraged sigh. What a dilemma!

A light breeze whipped at her hair. Untying the strings of her sunbonnet, she swept her loose hair back over her shoulder, pulled up the bonnet and tied it securely. The sun peeked from behind a cloud long enough to spread a beam of watery sunshine.

What had become of Hawk, anyway? She'd fully expected him to make an appearance before now. He surely didn't expect *her* to break the news to Dorie, did he? or Julia and George? If he did . . . well, she wouldn't. That's all, she *wouldn't.*

Ears alert, she heard Dorie coming back. Her cheeks were flushed, her eyes glowing. Rachel couldn't help smiling. Gently, she scolded, "You rascal, you. You worried me, running off like that."

Instantly repentant, Dorie lowered her eyes. "I'm sorry, Miss Rachel. I just wanted to show you. Sada's a beauty, isn't she? She runs like the wind. Where'd you get such a fine horse?"

Walking along beside horse and rider, Rachel told how her father had returned from a long voyage when she was twelve or thirteen. Miffed because he'd been gone so long, she'd remained aloof. He'd gone out that very afternoon and bought Sada.

Dorie's eyes glowed. A frown worried her mouth. "How come you weren't glad to see him?"

"Oh, but I *was* glad. But I was mad, too. And hurt that he could stay away so long."

Dorie asked no more questions. Her expression was impossible to read. They moved ahead in a companionable silence until Dorie stopped the horse, cocked her head to one side and looked upward. "Listen! Do you hear that?"

Rachel paused to listen. The sound came on the wind like the cry of gulls winging over the sea. Shading her eyes, she looked to the sky, too. "Geese!" she cried. "Returning north. See, Dorie?" She pointed out the ragged *V* formation.

Dorie rubbed her stomach wistfully. "Wouldn't a goose taste good for supper? Suppose someone else will see them? Maybe I should ride up to the wagons and tell Papa-George."

"They'll be gone before anyone can get off a good shot," Rachel told her a bit sorrowfully, for she too could imagine the mouth-watering treat.

"My papa was a good hunter," Dorie said, catching Rachel by surprise.

She darted her a quick glance, unable to keep back the question: "You remember your father, Dorie?"

Dorie chewed the inside of her lower lip, her face a study of concentration. "No, I guess not. But I know he was a good hunter. He could bring down the buffalo."

Rachel had heard stories of how the Indians followed the buffalo across the western plains. To think that Dorie's father had been a part of that distant culture, where life consisted of simple survival, where tribe warred against neighboring tribe, where unspeakable things were done in the name of revenge. Heathens, some said. Yet Dorie's mother had gone to these people as a missionary, lived among them, even married one of them. It was almost beyond comprehension how she could of her free will do such a thing. Unless, of course, she hadn't married, if she'd been taken and used, with Dorie the result of that abuse. Rachel had heard those whispered stories, too—the sort that struck terror in the heart. Finding the possibility too ugly to dwell upon for any length of time, Rachel spotted a patch of violets just beginning to bloom. It didn't take much persuasion to interest Dorie in picking a bouquet. While they tarried, the weak sunlight played peek-a-boo with the clouds that continued to gather.

After a time, Rachel noticed the clouds seemed to be winning the tug-of-war. "We'd better go, or we're going to get caught in the rain."

Both Dorie and Sada, who'd been enjoying the violets, were reluctant, but Rachel gave Dorie a boost up and led the way with a quick step. The breeze was cool and brisk, smelling of rain.

"You'd better climb up behind me," Dorie said. "We're going to get wet if we don't hurry." Rachel was about to decline when the first raindrop splatted against her cheek. Reasoning that no one could see, she lead Sada to a fallen log and used it for a mounting block. Straddling the horse was unfamiliar as well as unladylike, yet the awkwardness wore off in a while.

A gentle rain began to fall as they plodded along. Rachel draped her shawl around Dorie's shoulders, and the child, spirits high in spite of the rain, began to sing. Rachel listened intently to the rollicking lyrics and when she reached the chorus a second time, joined in. Before long, she'd sung herself out of breath.

She laughed in a winded voice. "Where'd you learn such a song?"

"The Frenchman taught me."

"Who?" Rachel asked.

Dorie was silent a moment, a troubled dignity chasing away her lightheartedness. "The Frenchman, Jean-Claude. He came to see me at the Murphys'. He told fine stories and sang lively tunes. It was he who took me to the mission where I went to school. It was a long trip, like this. One horse went lame and for a time, we rode double, like we're doing. I worried that we were too heavy, and he told me of a time he and my papa rode double through a terrible storm. He said my papa was much bigger than he and I put together and it didn't hurt the horse. I saw then that he was a small man. It was my shyness that made him seem large."

Rachel took note of the change in her mood. She asked, "You were afraid of the Frenchman?"

Dorie sat very still and straight. "He fed me well, and never spoke harshly. But yes, sometimes I was afraid. He told stories of the Northwest, adventures he and my papa had shared, but there was bitterness in his voice, coldness in his eyes. I wondered . . . I worried . . . I was afraid he'd killed my papa."

Dorie's father hadn't died in the smallpox epidemic? Or had the child been too young at the time to clearly remember? Rachel wanted only to comfort. Gently she said, "If he had . . . harmed your father, he would have had no reason to be so kind to you, would he, Precious?"

"I don't know," Dorie admitted. "But something bad happened to my papa, or I wouldn't have had to go to the mission. He would have come to the Murphys' to get me."

With childish simplicity, the girl failed to see what difficulties her Indian father's presenting himself at the Murphys' to claim his child would have caused! And this Frenchman—what part had he played in Dorie's young life?

On a hilltop some distance away, Adam Hawk finished cleaning his rifle. He tied the legs of the geese together, then slung them over his saddle horn. Skittish to the scent of fresh kill, the horse tossed a nervous head. Adam spoke softly and patted the gelding's neck as he swung into the saddle.

Tugging his hat down, sheltering his face from the misty rain, he gazed down at the valley below, spread out like a miniature print. A farmer hurried to plow another strip of field—he would probably provide shelter for the travelers if they'd ask. The weaving line of the wagons rolled along single-file, and trailing by a half-mile, Dorie and the woman. He urged his horse closer.

Planning to slip off the horse before anyone could catch her riding astride, Rachel was keeping an eye peeled for the wagons. A lone rider seemed to materialize out of thin air. Alarm skated across her nerve endings, soon followed by recognition. The blue eyes beneath the brim of the stained hat burned hot and quiet. Dorie spotted the man too and fell silent.

"Whoa, Sada," Rachel called. She greeted him with a nod of her head, but his attention was on Dorie. Something in his gaze prompted the need to tighten her arm around the child. A moment passed in which she gathered her composure and began introductions. "Dorie, do you remember Mr. Hawk? He rode into camp last evening and visited with some of the men awhile. Mr. Hawk, this is Dorie Ferguson."

Adam tipped his hat and murmured, "How do. That's a nice horse you got there. Where's she bent on takin' you?"

The hard ice of his eyes melted some as he spoke to Dorie. The child relaxed against Rachel. She returned the man's scrutiny with frank interest, then totally surprised Rachel by offering a quiet, "Pleased to meet you, Mr. Hawk. The horse is Miss Rachel's. We're catching up to the wagons."

"Gettin' a mite wet in the bargain, too," he put in.

Dorie seemed to be warming up to the man. She gestured to the geese slung over his saddle horn. "Those will be your supper, then. Miss Rachel and I saw the flock overhead."

Adam said, "I wouldn't mind sharing, if someone was to invite me to supper."

"Mom-Julia and Papa-George would," Dorie said promptly.

His eyes darkened with an expression Rachel interpreted as self-congratulatory. He'd obviously neatly wrangled the invitation. And for his own questionable purposes. She steeled herself against the now-familiar conflict of emotions at the thought of Dorie's being taken away by this man and united with her grandfather.

"It looks like you have plenty," Dorie was growing bolder by the minute. "Miss Rachel'd be pleased with a roasted goose for supper. Her mama's been sick."

A smile altered his expression, further gentling his eyes and mouth. His teeth flashed white against his tanned features. He promised, "I'll take it under consideration. Why don't you catch up with the wagons while I have a word with Miss Rachel?"

Uncomfortable about Dorie's having almost begged her supper, she told him, "You can keep your goose, Mr. Hawk; we're in no danger of doing without."

"Didn't think you were," he replied, unruffled by her cool tone. "Just wagerin' fresh fowl'd taste fine after a cold, damp ride." Turning to Dorie again, he swung out of his saddle saying, "Why don't you take the geese, Dorie? Drop one by Miss Rachel's wagon if it pleases you."

Rachel prepared to dismount, ungraceful though it might be.

Adam's hands, warm and firm on her waist, added to her discomfort. Straightening her skirts, she stepped away from him and started out on foot as Dorie rode off to rejoin the wagons. Adam led his horse, falling in step with her.

He drew a deep breath and said, "I had a talk with George Ferguson this morning when he brought the horses down to drink."

Before daylight—operating under the cover of darkness seemed his normal practice. Almost afraid to ask, she murmured, "What did he say?"

"Surprised him some. Said he'd prefer to see some legal documents, but when we got down to it, he admitted he doesn't have legal documents, either."

"I thought they'd adopted her." Seeing him shake his head, her flicker of hope dimmed.

Adam stepped wide of a forming puddle. "The mission let them take her. Someone there must have been satisfied they'd give her a good home."

"And they have," Rachel said quickly. When he made no response, she admitted with reluctance. "I saw the birthmark. It's as you said, Mr. Hawk. Still I have doubts as to what's best for Dorie. What sort of man is her grandfather? You failed to mention that."

He was a long time in answering. "Those who know him respect him. His word is sound. He expects the same from others. He's proud; he's fair. In his younger years, he was a leader."

"Is he a trapper?" Rachel phrased the idea forming in her mind.

"No, he doesn't trap. Nor does he hunt much anymore. But he makes do."

His reply struck her as purposely vague. Annoyed he wouldn't be more specific, she frowned. "If the man is elderly, can he care for a young girl? I would think—"

Seeming suddenly out of patience, he interrupted, saying, "Beggin' yore pardon, ma'am, but it doesn't make much difference what you think. The girl's going with me with or without your help."

Rachel tilted her chin and met his stubborn stance. "We're

talking about a child's future, Mr. Hawk, not the price of a beaver hide. I find your attitude high-handed and insufferable," she added in starchy New England accent.

His blue gaze was steady. Seeming neither surprised nor moved by her flash of temper, he asked, "Does that mean you aren't going to help the girl get used to the idea of going?"

"I haven't decided." Lifting her skirts to sidestep a puddle, she marched ahead. Behind her, saddle leather creaked as he mounted his horse. Without a glance in her direction, he plodded past, his horse's hoofs splintering the puddle, sending the dirty spray up on the hem of her skirt.

Glowering at his broad back, she called after him, "And you can keep your goose! I don't want it."

chapter 5

BY THE TIME RACHEL caught up with Francis's wagon, Sada was tied to the tailboard and Dorie was nowhere in sight. Nor was Adam Hawk.

Stepping lively, she asked Samuel, "How's Mama getting along?"

"See for yourself, if you've a mind to," he said, stopping the team.

Rachel climbed up on the wagon seat and peered through the opening to find her mother resting on the cot. Clara offered a wan smile. "Dorie brought us a goose. Did you see?"

The thing was at her feet. Rachel shot it a disparaging glance as her mother went on to say above the squeaks and groans of the wagon how thoughtful it was of that pleasant Mr. Hawk, and what a nice addition he was to the party.

Bursting to discuss "that pleasant Mr. Hawk" with her mother in private, she coaxed Samuel into letting her drive the team for a short while.

Before sauntering off, he warned, "Pay attention to what you're doing; we don't need a breakdown. If this rain worsens, the trail'll be sucking at our wheels tomorrow, so we'd best cover as much ground as we can today."

Impatiently, Rachel waited until he'd marched off through the drizzle to join Philip. "I don't know why Samuel has to be such an old man," she said over her shoulder to her mother.

"Rachel!" her mother reproved. "The only thing wrong with Samuel is that he tries too hard to prove himself to you. He knows no other way to do it than to show he's responsible. Anyway, he was simply repeating what Francis said a bit earlier when Mr. Hawk told him a homestead is nearby, where we might find shelter for the evening. Francis was obliged, but he and the Reverend thought it best we keep moving for a couple more hours."

Well, at least Mr. Hawk wasn't calling all the shots yet. Samuel would have scolded her heartily if he'd known how little attention she gave the team as she carried a running conversation over her shoulder with her mother. When she'd told Clara the whole story of why Adam Hawk had joined them, her mother only said, "Could be for the best. If the girl has reliable kin of her own, she should be with them."

"I agree. Except who's to say Mr. Hawk is capable of judging whether or not this grandfather of hers is reliable?"

"He's giving us time to form an opinion on that subject," Clara pointed out. "He could simply take Dorie and go. He'd cover the miles more quickly on horseback. Where is it you said he was headed?"

"I don't know, but it must be in the same general direction we're going. Otherwise, he'd be heading out regardless what anyone had to say about it."

Her mother spoke again, exhibiting her simple faith in God's guidance. "We'll pray on this matter, Rachel, and let the Lord do the leading. His love and concern for Dorie is much greater than ours can possibly be. If it doesn't seem to be his will that Dorie go with Mr. Hawk when the time comes, I guess he'll simply be prevented from taking her."

"How, Mama? Adam Hawk has a dangerous determination about him. He's a man who does what he says he'll do."

Her mother reproached her gently. "Rachel dear, there's one of him and twenty-two of us. I think the men in this party are capable of looking after Dorie's best interests."

Wishing she could feel as confident, Rachel thought on the

wisdom of her mother's previous suggestion and whispered a prayer for Dorie. Having done so eased some of the burden. Her mood had improved by the time Samuel came along.

Stopping the wagon, allowing him to help her down, she asked, "How much further?"

"Another mile." Rachel fell in step with him as he led the horses along, telling her, "There's a splendid place to spend the night. The Lord does provide." Relieved her mother could find rest in more comfortable conditions, Rachel found herself in agreement.

They made camp beneath the trees, to cook their suppers, do chores, and have evening devotions before sleeping. After setting her mother's rosebush out to soak up the gentle rain, Rachel cleaned and cooked the goose. The savory aroma soon weakened her will, and she forgot her stubborn notion about not eating a bite of Adam Hawk's charity. Even Samuel, who'd taken a dislike to Hawk, remarked it was tasty.

The mists lifted as evening waned. Clean-up completed, Rachel crossed the camp to return Julia's bowl. Billy Ferguson and the twins, Matt and Mark, were under the wagon, tearing apart what was left of the goose and feeding it to their dog. When she peeked under the wagon, calling a greeting, Billy informed her, "Mr. Hawk says bird bones can choke a dog, so we're givin' it to Blue in little pieces."

"Little pieces," one of the twins echoed and nodded solemnly, lending the impression Adam Hawk had three new admirers.

Rachel circled the wagon to find Adam dipping dishes into a pot of hot water, then wiping them dry. Finding no sign of Julia, George, or Dorie, Rachel's pulse quickened.

Glancing in her direction, he dipped another dish and called, "Evening."

"Good evening." Mildly ill at ease, she looked past him and shifted from one foot to the other. "Where are the Fergusons?"

Resting back on his heels, he jerked a thumb toward the woods. "They wanted to be alone with Dorie when they told her. Mrs. Ferguson thought it'd be better if they did it themselves."

"She's probably right," Rachel had to admit. "She'll take it better coming from them."

Some emotion beyond her understanding twisted his mouth. He lowered his gaze, hands completing the chore of stacking the dishes for Julia to put away. "Might as well sit down if you're goin' to wait," he offered less than graciously.

Bending a little, she sat down. "The goose was delicious. Thank you."

"No bother," he brushed her thanks aside. The silence stretched out again.

"Have they been gone long?" Rachel finally asked.

His smile went out. "Awhile." His eyes darkened as they caught her gaze and waged an unspoken argument. "They got three fine children."

"Four," she corrected.

"She isn't really theirs." His mouth was strained.

Rachel ignored his soft-spoken words. "They're fine children because George and Julia are good parents. Anyway, Mr. Hawk, you don't grieve any more or any less over the loss of one child just because you've got three left, if that's what you're intimating."

"I wasn't," he said, his voice flat.

"You know, Mr. Hawk, if I didn't know better, I'd think you have some doubts yourself about taking her."

His face grew even more grim. "You're dead wrong there."

Rachel watched him stir the fire and reach for another log. "Not much point in building it up. Evening devotions will be held soon."

She could have bitten her tongue, for his expression led her to believe he found women, meddling ones in particular, a trial. He put the log into the fire, saying, "Reckon I'll stay put."

Misunderstanding, she adopted a brisk tone. "Don't be silly. You're traveling with us. Tonight, you've shared game. In return, let us share our evening devotions. Worship is open to everyone."

His look was assessing. He stretched his legs toward the fire, taking his time in answering. His voice held a hushed quality. "Why is it then, some folk keep tryin' to bottle it up like their own homemade concoction?"

She whirled away and crossed back to her own wagon. Later, during evening devotions, she stole a glimpse of him standing apart from the Fergusons and felt ashamed. His sentence sermon had been as meaningful as any she'd heard.

Some time later, stretched out on her pallet, Rachel's thoughts turned again to Adam Hawk. His words echoed in her mind, causing her considerable discomfort. She couldn't stamp them out, nor ignore them; she was forced to look inward and see a glaring fault. Christianity was not some sort of club with an exclusive membership. Christ's love excluded no one. And neither should she.

Her mother's even breathing had a tranquilizing effect. Her eyes drooped heavily as moonlight etched the shadows of swaying branches on the canvas wall. Yes, she reckoned there *were* mountain-men who knew him—trappers and traders and sailors, and perhaps even a handful of Indians, hard as that was to imagine. But the Word had been given them by people like Dorie's mother.

For the first time, she saw Galesburg and the plans regarding it in a broader light; she saw what Mr. Gale, Reverend Clark and Francis, too, had seen all along. Galesburg was a noble ambition, with long tentacles that would stretch out from both the community and the college and have far-reaching effects. She closed her eyes and prayed a heartfelt prayer for the venture.

chapter 6

Adam's easy posture in the saddle belied his wariness.

Because the trail was rain-drenched and slow-draining, the possibility of wagons' becoming stuck in sloughs was reason for concern. It was apparent to Adam that the trail would worsen with each wagon that passed, and equally apparent that Clara Pierce was in no condition to bear the discomfort of her wagon's being jerked, pried, and jolted out of mudholes. He suggested that the Pierce wagon be at the head of the line.

Adam Hawk had the qualities of common sense, drive, and ingenuity—a man capable of dealing with hardships and unforeseen circumstances. Just the sort of man the Lord would be expected to send when the burden of many difficult miles seemed almost too much for one man to bear. Instinctively trusting the man's judgment, Clark passed the word along that any instructions Hawk gave were to be obeyed.

But Adam gave no instructions. Seemingly unaware of his sudden change in status, he simply offered a few suggestions. Then he turned in the saddle and glanced back to see Samuel walking alongside Rachel, deep in earnest conversation. Heads bent, shoulders touching, they picked their way around a low spot.

"I don't trust that man Hawk," Samuel was saying, reluctantly releasing Rachel's arm when the ground beneath their feet became firm again. "He rides in here on some errand for a mystery man, and before you know it, he's all but taken over. Look at him there, riding on like some mighty self-appointed wagon master. Hope he keeps right on riding. Suit me fine if we never saw the likes of him again."

Rachel, too, was a bit disgruntled over the way Hawk quietly but firmly took charge. But it went deeper than that, right down to bedrock. The man was always so . . . so . . . so right! Being ruled more strongly by emotion than logic, she didn't pause to decide what was so unforgivable about that. She excused herself to check on Clara.

Finding her mother sleeping the deep, sound sleep of exhaustion, Rachel braced herself against the rocking motion of the wagon and touched her lips to Clara's cheek. Cool, dry, like a piece of thin parchment, her mother's skin seemed nearly translucent. She whispered a silent, pleading prayer, then quietly took her shawl from the trunk. In slipping out of the wagon she was struck with the thought that something was missing, something she'd spent weeks sidestepping. Before she could chase it down in her mind, Francis interrupted her thoughts, asking, "How is she?"

He too seemed older than he had at the beginning of the trip. His face more deeply lined, eyes dark and sad, showing the strain. Rachel's fondness for him caused her to soften the truth. She murmured, "She's just tired, I think. Maybe when she wakes up, she'll feel like eating something." Wishful thinking on her part, but it seemed to cheer Francis.

He remarked, "Adam Hawk suggested we stop at noon. If she's hungry before then, Philip's finished the milking. A cup of milk—"

"The rosebush! *That's* what's missing!" Rachel interrupted him with a cry of distress. "Francis, I left Mama's rosebush! I set it out in the rain last night and I left it behind. Maybe I should go back for it." Growing more agitated by the minute, she wrung her hands. "I really think I should. Mama loves that bush. Not that she'd scold me for forgetting it. But it'll hurt her inside; I know it will."

"Rachel, it's too late to be thinking of that. Anyway, it's just a bush. More dead than alive, last time I looked at it. Don't upset yourself over it; Clara'll understand," Francis said with a finality that should have ended the conversation. "Mr. Hawk advised us to put in as many miles as we can today. No, you're not going back."

It was pointless to argue further. Disheartened, Rachel trudged ahead. Stupid of her to have mentioned going back to Francis. She should have known he'd forbid it. But if Adam Hawk had kept his advice to himself earlier, Francis might not be so dead-set against it. If only she hadn't said anything . . . if she'd simply turned back . . . but to do so now would be wrong. She stepped briskly along, so preoccupied she hardly noticed when Dorie, small brown feet in shoes for a change, fell in step with her.

As if sensing Rachel's inner turmoil, Dorie slipped a hand into hers, but said nothing. They walked in silence, each wrestling with her own deep concerns. But the time came when silence passed and a rush of words spilled out into the open like the watery sunshine floating down from above.

"I left Mama's rosebush," Rachel began, but stopped short when Dorie's words raced over hers: "Mr. Hawk's taking me to my grandfather."

Shame pierced Rachel as she gazed down into the brown face, so pinched with intensity. How could she have been so tied up in her own worries? *Lord, forgive me,* she prayed, heart burning within.

Dorie's hand in hers, Rachel drew her off the path toward a low stump. Sinking down on it, feet settling in a nest of blooming violets, she drew Dorie down on her lap. "Tell me, Precious, do you want to go? Because if you don't, no matter what Mr. Hawk says, I won't let him take you. There's only one of him and many of us. He hasn't any papers, any *legal* papers to prove you have to go with him."

"I must go," Dorie said quietly.

"Because you *want* to?"

Dorie chipped at a broken fingernail. Her blue-black curtain of unbraided hair drifted over one shoulder to hide her face. "Because I always knew I would."

Puzzled, unable to fathom how the child could have known, Rachel asked, "You mean, you've just always had a feeling—"

"No, I *knew,*" Dorie insisted. "Just like I knew without anyone telling me I wouldn't always be with the Murphys."

"Precious, you were so young! How could you know? You said yourself when the Frenchman came, you were afraid."

"Yes. But not surprised."

Rachel mulled over her words and the certainty with which they were spoken. Who could understand what went on in a child's mind? How much was fantasy, wishful thinking, dreams confused with reality? Rachel wondered what she could say to reassure the child. "You don't *have* to go, Dorie. Of course, you want to think it over carefully before making up your mind."

"I'm going," Dorie said simply. "You don't have to worry about me, Miss Rachel. Mr. Hawk said he'd return me to Mom-Julia if I couldn't be happy anywhere else. I think I can believe him."

Thoughtfully, Rachel murmured, "Perhaps you can. For all of his rough exterior, he does appear dependable."

Sliding off Rachel's lap, sinking down on her knees to let her fingers pick and choose among the violets, Dorie confided, "I'm not afraid of Mr. Hawk. He isn't like the Frenchman. His words and his eyes are true."

Not entirely certain she understood the girl's words, Rachel nonetheless saw Dorie had not only made her decision, but she was at peace with it. Feeling an inexplicable wrenching within, she touched the child's head. "I'll miss you, Dorie. You've been a good friend."

"I'll miss you, too. It's the hardest part of leaving." Turning her face up to scrutinize Rachel's, she asked, "Would you ever have a reason to visit Independence, Missouri?"

"Independence, Missouri! Is that where he's taking you?" The startled gasp and the words were out before she could recall them. Quickly, she added, "I'm sure Independence is a fine little town. And with your grandfather there, well . . ." She trailed off, still aghast at the thought of Adam Hawk's taking the child to the very edge of western civilization, only a few miles from Indian Territory! But no one in his right mind would take a young child into Indian

Territory, even if she did have ties there. And, whatever else Adam Hawk might be, she was certain he was in command of all of his faculties.

"Miss Rachel?" Dorie's hand stole up to rest upon her knee. "What was it you were saying about your mama's rosebush?"

"Hm? Oh, that. I set it out in the rain last night, and this morning I forgot to put it back in the wagon."

"Is your mama going to be sad?" Dorie asked, dark eyes full of concern.

As Dorie began to question her, her attention was diverted to the fourth wagon. Its team strained with all its might, but the wagon settled like an awkward ark deeper in the mud. The brown water washed nearly up to the bottom of the wagon. The driver gave up urging his horses on and stood back to survey the sucking mess and see what could be done.

"They'll have to pry that one out. Perhaps hitch up another team to help pull, too," Rachel mused. "Even then, they're going to have a time of it. Come on, Dorie. Let's see if we can do anything to help out."

Though it wasn't yet noon, it was decided the women would build a common fire and fix something hot. Clearly, they were going to be delayed awhile. Once they got the wagon out of the mire, three more wagons remained to pass through.

Philip cheerfully commented, "Mr. Hawk should have done more than warn us this one was coming up."

"What'd you expect him to do—ferry us across?" snapped Samuel as he began stripping a branch of twigs to help pry the wagon out of the mire.

"Oh, I don't know but that he couldn't have come up with something smarter than this. 'Pears to me he's a man who keeps his wits about him." Philip caught Rachel's eye over the top of his brother's stooped back and gave her a broad wink.

Straightening and whirling around in time to intercept it, Samuel thumped on Philip's shirt front and demanded crossly to know just where was the fine Mr. Hawk when they needed him.

"Off huntin'," Philip replied. "Asked me along, but I couldn't go, bein's I had to tend the stock. Which reminds me, Samuel, seems I've been doin' more than my fair share of that."

Losing interest in their quarrel, Rachel went to their wagon to peek in on her mother. Finding her awake but weak and pale, Rachel assured her a good meal would put her to rights. Hurrying, she gathered what would be her contribution to the common meal and went to join the rest of the women.

chapter 7

MIDAFTERNOON WAS UPON THE PARTY bound for Galesburg before it was able to continue on its way. The woods thinned, giving way to open spaces, relieving after the deep woods. Rachel ambled along, thankful she'd picked up plenty of firewood early in the day.

Preoccupied with how she was going to break the news to her mother that she'd left her rosebush behind, Rachel pushed Adam Hawk and his purpose for coming out of mind. She hadn't seen him since he'd ridden off that morning. Nor, she realized, as she paused to rest a moment, had she seen Dorie in some time.

Looking back over the jostling procession of wagons, Rachel felt uneasy. Dorie wasn't to be seen. She shaded her eyes and looked ahead to where the livestock were being driven by Philip, Billy Ferguson, and another boy, out in front of the wagons. Dorie wasn't with them, either. Quickening her step, she caught up with Billy, and unease turned quickly to deep concern when Billy, purposely evasive, muttered, "Must be around somewhere," and religiously avoided meeting her questioning gaze.

Catching his sleeve, Rachel pulled him out of the earshot of the other two boys. "You know something you aren't telling me, Billy Ferguson! If you fellows have played a trick on her, and she's lagging behind, feeling hurt, just tell me. I won't tattle; you can trust me."

His eyes widened, his expression one of innocence in the face of unjust accusations. "We fellas didn't say nothin' to her, honest. Papa'd skin me alive if he thought I'd teased her. She went off, all right, but not because of me! It was to—"

Suddenly, he clamped his mouth shut, and looked around to make certain no one had overheard. "Go on," Rachel urged. "It was to *what?*"

"I promised not to tell unless it got dark before she got back," he mumbled miserably. "You wouldn't want me to break my word, would you, Miss Rachel?"

"I could ask you a question or two, and if I happened to guess, that wouldn't be going back on your word, would it?"

"Well . . ." Billy paused and stubbed a toe into the damp, packed earth.

Seeing him weaken, Rachel pushed her advantage. "Give me three guesses. If I guess wrong, shake your head; if I guess right, you don't have to say a word." Before he could refuse, she launched her first guess: "Mr. Hawk came back without anyone seeing him, and offered her a ride."

Billy's expression was blank. "I ain't seen Mr. Hawk all day," he said.

Puzzled, Rachel tried again. "Did Dorie go *looking* for him? Are you sure her disappearance doesn't have anything to do with Mr. Hawk?"

He shook his head. "Nothin' at all," he claimed.

"Then, what?"

"You already asked three questions, I don't have to answer anymore."

"Billy Ferguson, your sister could be in danger. You'd better tell me what you know and you'd better tell me right now!" Rachel lost her gentle touch. "Because if you don't, I'm going straight to your mother and—"

"She ate a bite, then lit off the way we come. Said we hadn't gone that many miles. Said she could get the rose . . ." He ground his runaway words to a halt, realizing he'd broken his word about as thoroughly as possible.

Why had she ever mentioned the bush to Dorie? Rachel tried to reassure him. "You did the right thing telling me, Billy. I'll go after her on Sada. We should be back before dark. If not, then you'd better mention to Philip where we've gone."

"But keep quiet until then?" Billy asked.

Rachel hesitated a second. Raising an alarm would throw the whole party into concern and confusion, and she'd be obligated to make a lengthy explanation. What harm would result from her simply going after Dorie alone and returning her with none but Billy the wiser?

"If anyone presses you, you can confide in them," she said at length. "Otherwise . . ." She measured her words with care, all the while holding the young boy's earnest gaze. "You're a busy young man with an important job. A fellow who's busy herding livestock doesn't have a lot of time to stand around chattering, now does he?"

He grinned from ear to ear, pleased with her portrayal of his importance. "Reckon you're right, Miss Rachel. You can count on me to keep a tight lip."

Untying Sada's lead rope from the tailboard of the wagon proved the easy part of slipping away unnoticed. Her short initiation in riding bareback the previous day wasn't enough to stand her in good stead. Once the wagons were well ahead of her she looked for a makeshift mounting block. A rotting log had to suffice. She climbed aboard, wishing for her familiar sidesaddle.

In the East, riding astride was unacceptable for a lady. Oh, the farm girls were inclined to do so, but in the upper crust of society, it was considered common, vulgar.

Pushing all that aside, she drew a deep breath and made up her mind to make the best of it. Minus the advantage of reins, she prayed for help, not only in finding Dorie, but in handling Sada.

The ride was awkward at first, but she soon gained confidence. Convinced her mistress knew what she was doing, Sada soon gave up trying to turn back in the direction the wagons had gone. Adapting herself to the horse's movements, and making use of what she had observed of Dorie's handling of Sada, Rachel realized to her surprise that though she felt as if she had less control, she was more finely in tune with the animal. Following the trail into the woods, she unconsciously lifted her eyes toward the heavens and thanked God for his faithfulness. Much ado about nothing, this riding astride.

It was with a heart of gratitude that, sometime later, she spotted a small familiar figure trudging along, a wave of black hair swaying between her shoulders. "Dorie!" she cried as she rode out of the woods.

First startled, then wary, Dorie waited as Sada closed the distance between them. Rachel slid off Sada's back and embraced her. "What a scare you gave me," she admitted. "Who'd dream you'd do such a thing. Precious, that rosebush isn't nearly important enough for you to take such a risk. Why, when I stop to think what might have happened if . . ." She held Dorie close, smoothed straying tendrils off her polished cheeks, and felt a sense of unworthiness. Such deep loyalty shone from the little girl's eyes.

She hugged her again, then took her hand. "Come. We'd best start back before we're both missed and stir everyone into a tizzy."

Finding a fallen tree from which to mount again, Rachel arranged her skirts as modestly as possible, then offered Dorie a hand up. Straddling the horse behind her, Dorie asked softly, "Can't we go on after the bush? It can't be much farther, Miss Rachel."

"I suppose it couldn't." Rachel hesitated, debating the wisdom of losing more time when the afternoon sun was beginning to grow pale. Concerned more with Dorie's feelings than with the rosebush, Rachel finally agreed.

Early twilight was falling when they came upon the spot where they had stopped the night before, easily recognizable by the churned-up earth and down-trodden undergrowth. Rachel pointed out the tree, beneath which was the bucket containing the rosebush. Wordlessly, Dorie slid off the horse's broad rump and ran to fetch it.

Transporting the wooden bucket by horseback was no easy task. Rachel kept switching it from arm to arm, the weight of it seeming to increase in proportion to her weariness. She tried to make a lighter burden of it by letting it rest between her thigh and Sada's shoulder, but even then, it was necessary to keep a firm grip on it.

Darkness came swiftly, tree-shrouded, hauntingly eerie, and with it, Rachel's heightening anxiety to rejoin the group. Her heartbeat quickened at the rustling of small creatures in the underbrush, the lonesome complaint of a whippoorwill. Determined not to transmit her growing concern to Dorie, she initiated a companionable conversation, all the while wondering if she could trust Sada to stay on the right path, or if they might by accident take a wrong turn. They also had to pass the deep slough, and it was all too easy to picture Sada tossing them headlong into its murky depths.

Numb now to the discomfort of the bucket chafing her leg, Rachel suddenly grew rigid. Dorie stiffened too, her slim arms painfully tight around Rachel's waist. Covering the child's linked hands with her own hand, she strained in the darkness to see—was that a tree shadow or the shape of a man? Before Rachel could fend off sudden paralyzing fear and form a plan of action, a deep clear voice pierced the night air.

"'Foolishness is bound in the heart of a child,' so says the Good Book. Reckon I expected better'n that from a grown woman, though some's slower to learn than others."

Accusation, anger, and yes, the hint of reprisal carried the soft southern syllables. On the heels of recognition came relief, then resentment that Adam Hawk's anger should be so unjustly directed at her. Determined not to be cowed by him, she found her own voice and called, "Good evening, Mr. Hawk. Are you by chance going our way?"

chapter 8

ADAM TRANSFERRED DORIE FROM SADA to his own mount and curtly informed Rachel she should be glad it was he who'd come looking for them, not the whole company of men as her zealous stepbrother Samuel had urged.

Stung by his tone, Rachel replied, "We weren't lost—just a little late in catching up."

"*A little late?* Pardon me for noticin' but it appears to me you're miles from camp on a dark muddy road with a stand of timber, a broad piece of prairie and a swollen creek to cross."

Put that way, some of her indignation ebbed away, replaced by concern over the creek he'd mentioned. He seemed displeased even with her silence, for he got in the last word, saying, "A dozen crossroads to choose between, too."

Rachel kept quiet, determined not to make matters worse by quarreling with him. He struck out in the lead, a tall straight shape in the saddle; Dorie a little camel's hump behind him. Rachel followed, letting Sada pick her way along. Never fond of being in the wrong, she found it harder to bear in the face of his condescending disapproval.

"What's in the bucket you're lugging along?" he asked as he paused on the path.

"A rosebush," Rachel said as Sada drew abreast of his horse.

He muttered something and nudged his horse out in front again. Behind him, Dorie said softly, "Will we be there soon? I'm hungry."

His response to the child was far gentler, explaining they weren't out of the timber yet and that, once beyond it, they still had a fair bit of riding ahead of them.

A silence fell, stiff and unfriendly, as the trees began to thin, and the moon peeked out from behind clouds. The fresh breeze, cool enough to make Rachel shiver, yet lacking the musty scent of the timbered miles behind them, blew some of the starch out of her, leaving bone-deep weariness to settle in.

As the path grew more level, less pitted and mud-slickened, he picked up the pace. Rachel urged Sada ahead, not completely confident he wouldn't leave her to fend for herself. The stars came out, and she could see from Dorie's limp posture, her cheek resting against Hawk's broad back, that she'd fallen asleep. Poor little mite, trudging back like that. And all for her, lest Mama be saddened by the loss of the bush.

"Creek's just ahead," Adam called back to her, his voice in the stillness of the night a startling reminder of the empty space around them. "Wagons made it without much trouble, but the current's swift, so take care you keep your horse to the ford. Strong swimmer, is she?" he asked, almost an afterthought.

"She's crossed her share of water," Rachel replied, unable to completely quench the resistance she felt toward him.

He shrugged. Not a good omen, she decided, and wished she'd spoken less defensively.

By the light of a few stars and the pale crescent moon, she watched him ford the stream. Midway across, the water at its deepest lapped at his stirrups. With a snort and a shake, his mount was out of the water and up the opposite bank.

Rachel dragged in a deep breath, and, thankful for the cover of darkness, tucked a good portion of her skirt beneath her. Less than confident, she urged Sada into the creek. The horse whinnied and resisted, but Rachel dug in her heels and insisted until the mare moved ahead. Clinging to the cumbersome bucket with one hand, and lead rope and a handful of mane with the other, she sensed Sada's nervousness as the water deepened. "We're almost there, girl," she muttered, comforting the horse and herself at the same time.

Later, she couldn't have said whether it was the water tickling at Sada's belly or the unexpected mournful cry of a nearby wolf that panicked the horse. One moment she was safe and relatively dry, the next the current was pulling at her as Sada, belly-deep, shied sideways and strayed off the ford.

No longer in contact with the creek bottom, the horse thrashed around a moment, then began to swim. The water billowed up, drenching Rachel to the skin. A million cold arrows of shock pierced nerve endings as, with a death grip, she clung to the bucket as well as Sada's mane. With the waves of shock came the sound of Adam's shout from the far bank.

"Don't panic; she'll swim out. Hold on with your knees and thighs, and don't let go of her mane!"

The bucket, buoyed by the water, was difficult to manage. Its weight dug into her cold hand, but she clung to it stubbornly, refusing to let the waters take it. It was hard to hold her seat, growing harder by the second as the swift flow of the swollen creek dragged at her trailing skirts. In a hard-fought endless moment, it seemed as if she would make it. But it wasn't to be. The force of the water and the weight of her skirts swept her off Sada's back and sucked her down.

Merciless cold needles pierced her flesh. She let the bucket go, came out of the water, caught a quick breath. "Help me! Adam—"

"Grab her tail," he shouted from the bank.

Belatedly she lunged for Sada's tail. But the momentum of the rushing creek widened the distance between her and the horse. She plunged under a second time and came up coughing and spitting. Panic set in as the currents lashed at her and jerked at her heavy skirts.

"Keep your head! Kick out of those skirts, they're pulling you under! Swim!" He yelled, sounding angry rather than frightened.

What did it take? Didn't he realize, as he watched, she was all but drowning? Would he stand on the bank, shouting orders until the waters claimed her?

Anger diminished her panic and refueled her efforts to rescue herself. The next time she went under, she let the waters carry her. Instead of fighting the current, she held her breath, yanked off a button, and kicked out of her skirt. Numb fingers jerked at the tie on her petticoat, until, with lungs screaming for air, she tore at the waistband, snapped one tie and swam out of the petticoat as well.

The anchor of weight gone, she angled toward the bank, confidence growing as it drew nearer. Dimly she made out the branches of a fallen tree stretched across the creek, and set her sights on it.

Cold to the bone, arms aching, breath coming in fluttery gasps, she reached for the limbs of the fallen tree. One hand closed around a wet, flimsy branch. Kicking to keep herself afloat, she drank in great gulps of sweet night air. Above the pound of her racing heart, she heard the rush of footfalls, muted by the damp ground.

Exultation swept over her. Shivering, she was, and drenched from head to foot. But she'd made it, made it with God's gracious help, for no way, except by his watchcare could she have survived such an ordeal. Trembling more violently, she trod water, saving strength to pull herself up out of the water.

"Look out!" The cry of warning jarred her out of her false sense of security. She swung around in the water, but too late to avoid the empty wooden bucket. It careened into her head, bringing a brilliant explosion of lights, then a void.

Rachel awakened to find herself enveloped in a scratchy wool blanket and propped against the spine of a tree. Water trickled from her hair, down her cheek. Something unyielding—the source of her pain—was pressing against her temple. She moaned and lifted a hand to encounter another hand, this one warm and dry as it held a cloth there.

As if from a great distance, she heard Adam say, "She's coming around. Bleeding's near stopped. Another bit of cloth, Dorie. And a long strip to secure it. That's a girl."

Rachel's head began to clear, and with the clearing came a stir of alarm. She'd nearly drowned! And when she'd thought herself safe, something had—the bucket! It'd knocked her out. Her head throbbed. The sensitivity seemed to go right down to the roots of her hair. "You dragged me out?"

"Sit still," he ordered. "It's not too late to toss you back. Let the waters have you, like that fool rosebush you clung to with such resolution."

Dorie searched for her hand. It was a comfort, in the shape she was in—half-drowned, head splitting, frozen to the bone. She squeezed Dorie's hand and tried to murmur something reassuring as Adam made a knot of the cloth he'd tied around her head.

Under the pale night sky, she saw him rock back on his heels and survey her. "Best I can do for you. I'll get you back to camp quick as I can. Can you ride?"

She would, or die trying. Not in any way did she intend to impose further upon his sympathies. Water squished in her shoes as she tried to rise. The blanket tangled in her feet. She started to cast it aside, only to remember her skirt and petticoat had gone the way of the creek. Belated modesty imposed itself upon her. She clung to the blanket with a vengeance, a trembling in her bones uniting with the chattering teeth to heap upon her more discomfort and misery. Unaided, she made it to her horse, then stood looking about for a mounting block.

Standing close by as if to scoop her up when she fell, Adam muttered, "I don't think you can ride, not in the shape you're in. Tenderfoot like you's got no business—"

"I'm fine," she interrupted wearily, then bit her trembling lip as a hot tear stole down her cheek. "Once I get up there, all I have to do is hang on."

"All you had to do in the first place." he pointed out. With Dorie holding Sada's head, he helped Rachel mount.

Anything but steady, Rachel grabbed a handful of mane. She was trembling violently; the ache in her head sent a piercing pain down her backbone and spread throughout her body. She prayed for the strength to stay aboard and clung to her blanket as Adam tossed

Dorie up behind her, saying, "If she pitches forward or passes out, sing out, Dorie. It's not far now."

Dorie's arms tightened around her. She whispered, "I won't let you fall. We'll make it just fine, Miss Rachel."

True to her word, Dorie's grip remained firm all the way back to camp. They made a quiet entrance in time to hear Reverend Clark tie up evening devotions with a prayer for their safe return.

Wanting only to escape from the stir their arrival was certain to cause, Rachel softened her disgruntled view of Adam when he purposely kept to the darkest of shadows and delivered her to her stepfather's wagon without arousing attention.

Her mother, exhausted by worry, gave a cry of relief as Rachel stumbled into the wagon and stripped out of her wet drawers and chemise. Feeling her way around the dark, cramped confines of the wagon, Rachel found dry clothes in the trunk. As she changed, she explained what had happened, admitting the trouble could have been avoided if she'd only remembered the rosebush early that morning.

When she at last fell silent and snuggled down in her blankets, her mother gave a weary sigh. "Sometimes you seem grown up, Rachel, and I thank God for a daughter who is all a young woman should be. Then you turn around and do something so foolish, I can scarce believe it! You surely couldn't have thought that rosebush meant more to me than your or Dorie's safety."

Rachel's head, which a moment ago had seemed much improved, throbbed with fresh pain. She was hungry, too, and her entire body ached from the buffeting it had taken. In a small voice, she apologized. "I'm sorry I worried you, Mama. It was an unfortunate mix-up. You can be sure I won't get into such a tangle again."

"I certainly hope not! You had everyone in this camp worried sick." Lecture ended, Clara asked kindly, "Are you hungry? Philip cooked supper. He saved some venison for you. It's wrapped in a clean cloth next to the trunk. Can you find it?"

Tired and too hungry to wonder where the venison had come from, Rachel rose to her knees and felt around until her hands settled on the piece of wrapped meat. Biting into it, she heard voices outside the wagon, then felt the motion of someone climbing up on the seat.

Sounding distraught and shrill, Samuel demanded through the flap that closed out the night air, "Are you all right, Rachel? Hawk said you'd received a nasty blow to the head."

Wearily, Rachel assured him a night's rest would put her to rights. Reassured, he launched into a reproach she cheerfully could have done without. Taking her resentment out on the piece of tough meat, she chewed with great industry and by so doing, resisted the temptation to inform Samuel she neither invited nor welcomed his opinion of her tendencies to embrace misguided adventures.

Philip was the next to inquire after her health, followed by Francis. Each conveyed the concern of the others in the group, and the prayerful thanksgiving of her safe return.

So everyone and his dog knows all the details, she thought as she curled into her blankets again. Gingerly cradling her head on her arm, she imagined Hawk had relished relating the tale. Little good it did for him to let her slip unseen into the wagon if he then turned around and made a public meeting of his rescue account.

Just when she was about to drift off to sleep, a whispering sound came from the foot of the wagon. Dragging herself back to the land of the wakeful, Rachel heard her name whispered again. Warily she asked, "What is it, Samuel?"

A wheel creaked as he rested his weight against it and spoke softly through the canvas: "I can't sleep. Too much on my mind," he said abruptly. A small pause, then a rush of words: "Under ordinary circumstances, I'd wait for a better moment. But the circumstances aren't ordinary and I'm afraid if I don't speak up now, something'll happen to make it impossible for me to do so. Rachel, do you know what I'm trying to say?"

He sounded uncomfortable, yet determined. Rachel's misgivings grew. "Samuel, whatever it is you feel compelled to say, can't it wait until morning?"

"Yes, Samuel," her mother chimed in. "We're all in need of a good night's rest."

Reluctantly agreeing, he murmured something about taking a stroll to clear his mind.

Rachel waited until she was certain he was gone, then squeezed her mother's hand. Initiating a whispered conversation, she said, "Thank you, Mama. I was afraid he was going to suggest marriage just to keep me out of trouble!"

"I believe he was, Rachel, but not for the reason you seem to think."

Uneasy and a shade defensive, Rachel tried to inject a bit of levity. "Ironic, isn't it? Samuel's all ready to offer to look after me, going even to the lengths of marriage, while Adam Hawk seemed to resent the imposition of having to pull me, half-drowned, from the creek!"

"Rachel!" her mother reproached her gently. "You do both men an injustice. Samuel loves you; you can't be blind to that."

"Oh, Mama, please don't say that. Samuel is fine as a brother, but . . . he just isn't the sort of man I'd want to spend the rest of my life with." In the dark safety of her blankets she pulled a face at the very thought!

"And Adam Hawk is?"

Rachel sat bolt upright. "Of course not! Whatever made you say such a thing? More often that not, he's a despicable excuse for a human being! Riding in here from the faraway mountains with every intention of taking Dorie away. And as if he has a perfect right to! And that backwoods ruffian in deerskins is instructing *us* as to trails and creaky wagon wheels and where we should and shouldn't stay. Who put *him* in charge?"

"Rachel," her mother tried to hush her.

Chagrined that her voice had climbed so as to be heard beneath the wagon, if not halfway across the camp, Rachel lay back down again, wincing as her injury made contact with the floor. Pillowing her head again, she added in a whisper, "Some bargain *he'd* be! He doesn't even shave on a regular basis. Who'd ever give a man a second look when he doesn't take the trouble to scratch the whiskers off his face every day or so?"

Her tirade had dwindled to an inaudible muttering. Her mother's hand came in contact with her damp, matted hair. Combing fingers gently through it, Clara said softly, "A man's worth rests on who he is, on his unique personality, on the abilities God has given him and what he's done with them, not on his appearance or his occupation.

"Your father, for example. Do you consider it witless of me to have fallen in love with a sea captain? A man who spent months from home, involved with a job that he loved?"

Rachel was forced to admit, "Our way would have been far more pleasant if he'd been a regular husband and father, don't you think?"

For a long moment, Clara considered the question. She finally replied, "When our marriage was young, yes, I yearned for that. I was jealous of the sea, of his ship, of his crew. I waited and fretted and stewed for him to be home and then when he finally was, I was so out of sorts with his having been away for so long, that I made both of us unhappy.

"But eventually, God spoke to my heart, pointing out my foolishness, and I learned that until I accepted your father for who he was, job and all, there would be a constant cloud over me.

"In a similar way, Rachel, I think you're going to have to accept Adam Hawk on his own terms, or there'll never be any peace between you."

Into the silence that followed, Rachel injected the spirited words, "When it comes to Adam Hawk, peace is the farthest thing from my mind. Anyway, he'll be with us for a few more days at the most, then we'll see the last of him."

"Maybe," her mother conceded. "But so often things have a way of turning out as we least expected."

Long after her mother had fallen asleep, Rachel lay awake, mulling over her words. Why would Mama suspect her involvement with Adam Hawk was more than what it appeared? Now that Dorie had agreed to go with him, the man considered Rachel nothing but a nuisance. Even if she were mindless enough to be vaguely attracted to him, he certainly gave no indication of harboring any warm feelings for her. In fact, she thought he might be the sort of man who had little use for women. After all, when a man could cook his own meals, sew his own buckskins, and make a home of a horse and saddle, what would he need with a woman?

When Rachel awoke the next morning, her first fear was that she'd slept much too late—the light of dawn and the stir of the camp warned her she'd hadn't any time to lose! Why hadn't someone called to her? Stiff, head still a little sore, she rose quickly and pulled her clothes on over her fresh petticoat. The tag end of the makeshift bandage Adam had tied around her head was hanging in her eyes. Wondering now over the severity of the wound, she gingerly unwound the strip that had once been a tie on Dorie's faded dress. She winced as the piece of fabric against the dried blood came off with the tie. Probing the wound with her fingers, she encountered the goose egg surrounding it, and bruised skin, tender to the touch.

For want of a mirror, Rachel went down on her knees beside her mother's pallet. "Mama?" she called softly. "We'll be going without breakfast if I don't hurry. But look at my face, and tell me—do I look like a war casualty? Should I put on a fresh bandage, or . . ." Her words trailed off as, for the first time, she noticed the unnatural stillness of her mother's form beneath the blankets.

"Mama?" she whispered a prayer, a plea. Battling a rising cry of alarm at her mother's lack of response, she somehow found the courage to tunnel a hand beneath the covers to search for warmth, a heartbeat, a pulse.

Her hands trembled. In the pale streak of dawn, she stared death in the face. The serenity etched upon the beloved frail features was not a serenity shared by Rachel. As if from a great distance, she heard her own cry of agony pierce the calm of the stirring camp.

chapter 9

SHE'D STOOD TRANSFIXED as the dirt covering the hastily-constructed coffin became a dark mound. An hour had passed since the job had been completed, and still she stood by her mother's graveside, head bowed, gloved-hands clasped.

The breeze teased the rich fabric of her dress, filling the skirts and upper sleeves. The crown of her fashionable bonnet was high, sloping upward, only partially concealing the lump and the bruise at her temple. Dry-eyed, she was a picture of contrast, a trail-weary, battered reed, bowed but not shattered, out of place in her fine Boston clothes, yet with a quiet dignity that rendered the others, though kind and anxious to help her, helpless.

Francis, red-eyed and shaken, had tried to usher her away from the grave, but she'd wordlessly stood her ground. Reverend Clark, seeing the morning pass and feeling the heavy responsibility of getting the travelers on the road to take advantage of a sunshine blue-sky day, had tried as well, and met with failure. Some in the group were growing restless, while others merely took advantage of the delay, greasing wheels, patching canvas, or splashing out a few dirty garments in the creek.

Adam continued tinkering with his gun as those around him made preparations to pull out. They weren't really insensitive to Rachel's loss; on the frontier, sensitivity was a luxury few could afford. At the same time, he couldn't stamp out the memory of a day long ago when he'd stood by as *his* mother was buried. For days afterward, he'd run into the woods to cry, not much caring about the dangers, not much caring whether he lived or died. 'Course, he'd been much younger, not even as old as little Dorie. But a good mother was a hard thing to lose, no matter how young or old a body was. So when Julia Ferguson and Reverend Clark took Dorie aside, in preparation to send the child to do a job none of the rest of them cared to tackle, he ambled over to intervene.

Predictably, Samuel objected to pulling out without Rachel, panting and puffing, managing to imply the impropriety of Adam's offer to wait her out and return her to the group when she was ready. But Francis, more noble-minded, thanked him and accepted while Reverend Clark hustled off with obvious relief, to get his party underway.

When they'd gone, Adam added a log to one fire left burning, and made a rare pot of coffee. That done, he ambled down to the creek to catch a fish or two.

Rachel was aware of the departure of the group, knew in one functioning corner of her brain that nothing could be accomplished by standing here, refusing to take part in a world that marched on. Yet, she made no move to follow. She was glad they'd gone. Glad to be alone.

Lifting dry eyes, she glanced in the direction of the creek to see a familiar horse grazing alongside Sada. Adam's gelding. So that was why they'd gone without urging her to leave her mother's grave. They'd left *him* in charge.

Her head hurt, and she felt brittle, stiff, achingly sore both from the long ride on Sada and her battle in the creek. Was it callous, irreverent, unloving of her to notice her own private discomfort when Mama . . . Dragging in a deep breath, she slid her hands down the smooth blue-green brocade with the dainty rosettes Mama had so painstakingly worked into the bodice and the cuffs. *I'm wearing it, Mama, like you asked. Can you see me? Do you know I'm here beside you?*

The waves of grief she'd been holding off crashed against her heart without warning as the unspoken words formed in her head. She didn't hear the birds, smell the fragrance of spring, feel the warming rays of the sun. Mama was gone, buried along a muddy track in a grave soon to be left behind, never visited by loved ones or decked in flowers or salted with tears. A shuddering sob broke loose, followed by another. She fell to her knees, buried her head in her hands, and cried until every tear was spent.

Adam caught and cooked the fish without disturbing her, keeping his back to her so as not to intrude on her privacy. What would become of Rachel now that her mother was gone? The shared opinion of Reverend Clark and Francis seemed to be that she ought to get her a husband right away—preferably before nightfall.

These folks had some right curious views. Seemed to think it'd be improper for her to continue traveling as a part of the Pierce family, sleeping in their wagon, fixing their meals, washing their clothes, and the like. Her mother being dead, no legal ties bound her to the Pierce men, and they were anxious no scandal shadow their name or hers. Sure enough, she'd be a temptation for Samuel.

Still and the same, seemed kind of unfeeling to rush her into a wedding. Hunting knife in hand, he pushed to his feet and reached for the scraggly-rooted bush he'd found washed up on the bank. Hunkering down beside her, he cleared his throat. "Found this caught in some reeds along the creek bank. Thought maybe you'd want to plant it b'fore we eat a bite and move on."

Her eyes were dark pools of grief, the skin beneath them puffy and damp with her tears. Her chin trembled as she stretched out a gloved hand and touched the single green sprig on the rosebush that looked otherwise dead, and nodded agreement.

Using the blade of his knife, he dug a shallow hole. She took off her gloves, pressed the roots into the hole and covered them with the dank rich earth. Rising then, she stepped back and brushed her hands.

"Mama'd like that," she said brokenly.

He looked away from her sad dark eyes, scooped his hat off his head and murmured, "My pa was a circuit preacher. Reckon I remember a thing or two, if you'd like it finished off proper."

"Would you?"

The gratitude in her voice outweighed the surprise. He bowed his head and, turning his hat in his hand, rumbled a benediction that seemed fitting to what he knew of the character of Clara Pierce. " 'The name of Lord is a strong tower; the righteous runneth into it, and is safe.' "

"Amen," she whispered, and with one lingering look at the sprig of life amidst the rose thorns, let him lead her toward the fire and the meal he'd prepared.

It seemed finished. She felt as if she could go on, felt almost in a hurry to do so. She ate the fish and drank the last of the coffee he'd prepared, little knowing it was the last he had, a small portion he'd saved for a special occasion.

Events were rushing at her again, flaws and snags making rough the way before her. Galesburg had little appeal without Mama. And she wouldn't marry Samuel! No one could make her. If they didn't want her in their party any longer, fine. Somehow or another, she'd make her way alone. No, not truly alone. The Lord was with her; she felt his presence in this dark hour.

Hurriedly wiping the tin plates and cups, she glanced over to where Adam was throwing a saddle across Sada's back. "Where'd you get the saddle?" she asked, pulling her gloves on again.

"Ferguson loaned it. Nice folks, the Fergusons."

In mute agreement, Rachel stood by as he kicked out what remained of their fire, repacked his saddlebags, and prepared to leave. Glancing back at her, he seemed belatedly to realize he might have helped her into the saddle.

"No, go on," Rachel said hurriedly, knowing her climb into the saddle in these full skirts was going to be less than graceful. He urged his horse ahead, leaving her to her own devices. After three attempts, she made it, but every muscle in her body screamed a protest. Somehow the physical pain drowned out some of her mental anguish, and she plodded along, legs too short for the stirrups, elegant skirts billowing in the capricious breeze. Adding to her discomfort was the tight pinch of the front-laced corset, an undergarment she'd found herself making less and less use of lately. It was for Mama, wanting to look her best, that she'd laced into it today.

Adam paused once during the first hour, turned and asked, "Making it all right?" but in no other way intruded upon her thoughts. In early afternoon, when they came to a stream, Rachel grew stiff with foreboding. But the waters lapped peacefully, no more than six inches up their horses' legs. When it had been crossed, Adam asked her if she'd like to climb down and rest a spell.

Aching muscles applauded the idea. Rachel half-climbed, half-tumbled out of the saddle. Disconcerted at her lack of grace, she limped painfully to a tall oak and braced herself against it. Adam led the horses down to drink, and when he returned, offered her a tin cup filled with water. Hands settling around it, she drank deeply, then glanced up to find him scrutinizing her.

"Quite a knock you took from that bucket," he commented. "Gonna leave its mark, I reckon. Wouldn't hurt to clean it up a bit. Still hurt, does it?"

The jagged cut and the bump, surrounded by an ugly bruise, hurt no worse than any other part of her body. But if it looked to him as if it needed cleaning, then it must be a sorry sight indeed. Rachel stirred herself to make allowance for her appearance. "I didn't have a mirror or my wits about me, either. Perhaps Julia'll have a look at it for me this evening."

"No call to bother her; I'm an old hand at this thing myself. You'll have to get the bonnet out of my way, and come up with a bit of clean cloth."

Rachel gingerly eased down on a nearby boulder, and untied the wide strings beneath her chin. Taking a clean handkerchief from her pocket, she set her teeth for the inevitable pain. Yet his hands, so tough and brown and sure, were surprisingly gentle as he dampened the hanky and cleaned her wound.

Feeling awkward with the silence, as well as his ministering touch, Rachel murmured, "A trapper has to be his own physician, I suppose."

"Most of the time," he said, frowning over a bit of dried blood that clung stubbornly to the wound, "I had a good teacher, though—my pappy. Folks expected more'n a good fire-and-brimstone sermon out of him; good part of the time, he was their ears and eyes to an outside world. Might have to yank a tooth, set a leg, and preach a funeral all in one day. And then set up all hours of the night, settling a feud or passing along news of an Indian raid, politics, or the price skins were bringing up the road a piece."

"He sounds like a good man," Rachel murmured, her view of Adam shaded a little differently as she acknowledged there was more to him than the tough and capable man's man that was so evident on the surface.

"He was. Learned a lot from him." Changing the subject, he withdrew a small flask from his saddlebag and advised, "Better brace yourself. This'll sting a mite, but it'll clean it out good and you won't be likely to have trouble later on."

It did sting. Mightily. Rachel bit her lip and sucked in a deep breath to keep from yelping. But once the burning stopped, her thoughts turned, for he stood before her, careful how he replaced the bonnet so as not to chafe the wound. He tied the ribbons, too, and in so doing, held her steady gaze.

Struck by the blueness of his eyes, the tiny suncreases fanning outward from them, she thought once more how well he blended into these wilderness surroundings. He seemed a natural part of the trees, the skies, the hills, plains, and cold clear streams. He took on the nature of the wilderness itself. So why did she suddenly feel drawn to him? What had the wilderness dealt her but discomfort and hardship and pain? Uncomfortable with the silence that hung between them, she lowered her lashes, and made a project of pulling on the silk gloves that were as out of place as the rest of her attire.

"Any thought to what you'll do now?"

In this place, stripped of the pretensions and proprieties that had governed her first in Boston and later, as a part of Francis's family, she lowered her pride and admitted, "No idea whatsoever."

Sliding a hand along Sada's shoulder, then stooping to raise the stirrups on her saddle, he commented, "Young Samuel'd be dependable. A girl could do worse by herself."

In a sudden spurt of indignation, she came to her feet. A spasm of pain shot through her, sharpening her tongue as she closed the distance between them. "I'm not marrying Samuel Pierce or anyone else!"

Circling Sada to fix the stirrup on the other side, he glanced over the top of the saddle and commented, "No need to get so riled; it was just a thought that came to me."

"Thought, nothing! You've been eavesdropping. You must have the ears of a mule!" she sputtered, face heating up at the humiliating memory of Samuel's proposal, phrased not in words of love, but words of necessity. *"Father and Reverend Clark think that under the circumstances . . ." Bah! Pooh on them all. On Adam Hawk, too.* Emboldened, half hoping to shock, she said without giving it the least serious thought, "I don't need a man to take care of me; I can take care of myself. I'll open a shop somewhere, designing and stitching fine dresses."

"Won't find much of a market for fine dresses around here," he said mildly, and with an arc of his hand, indicated the emptiness, the absurdity of her proclamation.

Flushing, but unwilling to admit defeat, she said rashly, "Chicago, then. I understand it's booming. How far are we from there?"

He squinted, gazing through the trees that skirted the stream toward the narrow trail wiggling on across a green horizon. "If you got on this horse and rode hard for a day and a half, reckon you'd be there. But I wouldn't recommend it. It's a rough-and-tumble town, overrun with land speculators, lakefront riffraff, bawling livestock, and meatpackers. No place for a lady on her own." Meeting her eye across the saddle again, he amended, "Unless you've got kin there."

"No," she said, and swallowed another large dose of pride, enabling her to ask, "What would you do if you were I?"

A ghost of a smile curved his chapped lips. "Ma'am, that'd take a tall stretch of the imagination. Come on around here, and I'll help you up."

She circled to the left side of the horse, so intent on finding a solution to her dilemma, she was slow to notice he'd cupped his hands and was waiting to give her a foot up. "If not Chicago, then where?" she asked. "There must be a civilized town somewhere in this great wilderness where the service of a seamstress would be appreciated."

Dropping his hands, he slanted his hat and considered. "Might be a few places farther south. Hundred, hundred and fifty miles, maybe."

"That far? What's becoming of all these people who are supposedly flocking into the western states? I thought settlements were springing up like spring flowers. Francis and Reverend Clark claimed the population in Illinois—"

"It's exploding, all right," he agreed. "But it's simple settlements, struggling folks who do for themselves. A lot of these folks still wear homespun. They aren't used to the idea of mill fabrics, let alone the notion of hiring a seamstress. It'd seem a sinful waste to them."

He was right, of course. She would have realized it for herself if she wasn't so distraught. Chewing her lip, she let out a sound of discouragement.

"You could always go back to New York," he said, breaking into her troubled thoughts.

"No," she murmured. "That wouldn't do."

"Boston, then," he said, and cupped his hands again. She slipped her foot in, grabbed the saddle horn and accepted the boost into the saddle, belatedly trying to modestly deal with an overabundance of skirt and petticoat that somehow failed to cover her shoetops.

He tugged at her foot. "Try those stirrups. Better, aren't they?"

Attention diverted, she assured him they were fine, then returned to mulling over the possibility of going home to Boston. She could reestablish her trade; no doubt of that. But a return trip would be costly. And she had many a reservation about traveling alone.

Mounting his gelding, Adam lead the way back to the path, ducking beneath a low branch that scraped at his hat. Following suit, Rachel observed that the trees, in just a matter of days, had leafed out. Spring had arrived. The men in the party were anxious to get to Galesburg where they could till their fields and plant their crops. But what did Galesburg have to offer her? Yes, the thought of Boston was far more inviting. But the great distance!

Pausing on the trail to let her draw abreast of him, Adam shot her a thoughtful glance. "Could just go on to Galesburg as planned. I'll be takin' Dorie soon. Maybe Julia Ferguson'll make room for you in her wagon."

"I couldn't ask; they're already overcrowded," Rachel told him. "They brought everything they could possibly pack because they couldn't afford shipping freight."

He fell silent and set a steady pace that covered the curving trail, took them around mudholes, and brought them to within sight of the group by late afternoon.

While still a good distance behind the wagons, Rachel pulled Sada up short and engineered another clumsy dismount. Without questioning her reasons, Adam swung off his horse, too. Reins loosely in hand, he fell in step with her.

Her legs were so stiff and sore, she wondered if they were permanently misshapen; her back and shoulders were in no better shape. Shrugging out the kinks, she hobbled along, knowing the wagons would have to stop before she'd be able to catch up with them.

"You know, if Galesburg doesn't suit, you wouldn't have to stay," Adam said. "You could book passage on a riverboat down to New Orleans and from there sail on around to Boston. Be a sight easier than backtracking across the country."

Her dark eyes were thoughtful. "It's something to consider, I suppose. Thank you, Mr. Hawk. For today, for . . . everything."

After a time, he said hesitantly, "If you're short of funds, and of a mind to go back to Boston, I've got enough to cover your passage."

As he'd feared, his offer came as an affront to her pride. Her chin came up, and her expression, shadowed though it was by the wide brim of her bonnet, was unmistakably determined. "It's kind of you to offer, but I couldn't possibly accept. You've already gone the extra mile where I'm concerned. And I, in return, haven't been terribly gracious, or considerate of your feelings. I apologize, Mr. Hawk."

"For what? Seein' what you see—a backwoodsman who mixes better with trappers and traders and Indians than he does with ladies and civilized folk?"

"I think you're mocking me. Either that, or you're doing yourself an injustice." Her lashes fluttered up as she turned, the better to read his intent.

"My having an itinerant preacher for a pappy impresses you, does it?"

She paused and looked him square in the eye. "It's you I find impressive."

Cautiously, he asked, "You do?"

Again, she swung around to face him. "Yes, Mr. Hawk, I do. I had no right to look askance at you. You are equipped and capable of taking care of yourself. You depend on no one but your own keen wits. That must be a powerful feeling. You have no idea how horrible it is to suddenly have to face your own helplessness, like an overnight charity case, dependent on the kindness of others. At this very moment, I'd like nothing better than to trade places with you. The first thing I'd do is climb on that horse, turn my back on Francis, Reverend Clark, and Samuel, and ride away!"

"Those are kind of strong words, don't you think? You'd earn your keep, cookin' and washin' and patchin' and—"

"I don't want to be 'kept'!" Her dark eyes seethed with resentment and frustration. "I don't like to cook, I don't like to wash, I'm not even too partial to patching, if you want to know the truth of it."

"Well, pardon my sayin' so, but that doesn't leave more'n a couple of possibilities, and of those that remain, there's one or two I wouldn't put my tongue to."

"That's just the rub of it," she said, words undergirded with a passion against injustice. "Look at you! Endless possibilities! You could be a preacher or a teacher or a logger. You could sail ships or forge trails or plow ground. You could be a soldier or a cobbler or a doctor. What choice do *I* have? I have to provide for myself and all I know how to do is design fine dresses and stitch a seam! But if I go on to Galesburg with them, I'm not marrying anybody and I'm not apologizing for burnt mush, either!"

chapter 10

Rachel knew that Francis was suffering too and wished she could offer words of comfort. But her own grief was too fresh, too devastating. She felt no resentment, harbored no black grudge, though it did occur to her that her mother's life might have been prolonged had Francis not so whole-heartedly plunged her into emigrating to Galesburg. It had been her mother's choice to support Francis's decision, to encourage and believe in him. To bear hard feelings toward him now would be to dishonor her mother.

Yet her respect wouldn't stretch to allowing her to be coerced into marriage. Her determination on that point strengthened as she cooked supper, Samuel hovering so near she could scarce add a log to her cooking fire without tripping over him. Her nerves were as raw as her saddlesore bottom. After supper, she tried to slip off to get water.

"Here, Rachel, let me," Samuel offered, taking the bucket and falling in step with her. "Devotions will begin soon, and I want a word with you before I speak with Reverend Clark. Have you given any more thought to what I said earlier?"

She blew out a weary sigh. "I appreciate the sacrifice you're willing to make, Samuel, but I don't think losing my mother is reason enough to get married." Tears filled her eyes, but she blinked them back.

He paused a moment, catching her arm. "Rachel, it's no sacrifice.

I love you; you must know that. I'd be honored if you'd be my wife."

His sudden humility caused her to gentle her words of refusal. "I love you too, Samuel, but it's the love a sister has for a brother, the same love I feel for Philip. You deserve better than that."

"It would come if you'd give it a chance," he said, the sound of pleading shading his voice. "And Rachel, what alternative to marriage is there for you? You are a woman of high character. How can you continue to travel with us, and once at Galesburg, live with us, without fearing damage to your reputation?"

Tired, sore of spirit, and suddenly impatient, she shrugged his hand off her arm and resumed walking. "Perhaps I can't, Samuel. Although, as long as my conscience is clear, I'm not sure what it is I'm supposed to fear."

"I have the greatest respect for your clear conscience," he began, a sudden chill entering his voice. "Especially after your having spent the entire day in the company of Adam Hawk. But as for this sudden independence of yours, it's utter nonsense! Father and Reverend Clark have your best interests at heart in trying to make arrangements for your future."

Not about to let his insinuating remark about Adam pass, she said pointedly, "Adam Hawk was a gentleman and a comfort to me today. As for being independent, that's a far cry from the truth. I'm more frustrated than you can imagine at having to depend on others—"

"Rachel," he interrupted impatiently, "God designed women to be cared for by men. Stop struggling against his will. Let me take care of you."

As if he knows God's perfect will. She jerked the bucket out of his hand, saying, "Go on to devotions, Samuel. I'll get my own water."

He turned back toward the camp, his bearing rigid as a stony cliff. Rachel let out a sigh. She hadn't meant to hurt him. But his taking care of her was a two-sided coin; on her side, years and years of taking care of *him*—cooking, cleaning, gardening, rearing children. No! She wouldn't, and they couldn't make her.

Later, as she warmed water for bathing, Adam ambled over to stand near her fire. Glancing at him, she said, "Sit, if you'd like."

He broke off a flimsy green branch from a low-hanging maple, then sat near the fire, stripping the leaves and twigs from it. "Nice evening," he commented, catching her eye.

She arched an eyebrow. Idle conversation? Hardly his style. She studied him from beneath a thick fringe of lashes as he stretched long legs toward the fire and stirred the glowing embers with his stick. The sap oozed out of the green maple, sizzling and popping in the heat. The faint smell of burnt sugar blended with the pleasant odor of woodsmoke.

Adam pushed his hat back, held the stick up, and considered the glowing orange tip. Flickering flames etched patterns upon his face—clean-shaven for a change. Even so, the scar was no less noticeable. Musing that it characterized rather than detracted from his appearance, she wondered how he'd gotten it. What manner of life had he lived to be so molded and marked by it?

Adam caught her gaze and held it as he snapped the thin stick and fed it to the flames. "Been thinking about what you said earlier," he spoke abruptly, his southern drawl pleasant upon her ears. "About my being able to take care of myself. Isn't entirely true. Among other things, my pappy taught me a wise man knows his limitations; a strong man, his weaknesses. Man who won't take God's help is both weak and a fool to my way of thinkin'."

Something inside Rachel coiled tight. Surely he wasn't going to admonish her too, tell her she ought to look upon Samuel's offer of marriage as God's way of helping provide for her. If he did, she'd . . . well, she'd see to it he didn't. Guiding the conversation the way she wanted it to go, she asked, "Is a trapper's life a hard life, Mr. Hawk?"

His gaze was reflective as he watched the bright flames. "It's got its dangers. Lonely too. But trapping gets in a man's blood. The beauty, the vastness, the freedom. I've had some close scrapes. A man doesn't trap beaver in Blackfoot country without a good scare or two along the way."

She shivered and drew her shawl close. "I wouldn't make much of a trapper. Risking my life for a few beaver pelts, even for *a lot* of beaver pelts, is unthinkable."

"It isn't always so dangerous. The Blackfeet are an exception. The British fur companies keep 'em stirred up against the American trappers, encourage 'em to kill off their competition." He tapped his stick against a stone and sent up a shower of sparks. "Arikara people aren't always so friendly, either. But the rest of the tribes can be got along with, if a man's fair in his dealings."

"I think you're understating the dangers," she said. "Stories of the hostiles often make the eastern papers. That's one thing to be said in favor of Galesburg," she reflected almost against her will. "There's no danger from Indians."

"You're right there. Most all the Indians've been driven out of Illinois. If Jackson had had his way about it, he'd have driven all the Indian nations clear across the continent and out into the western ocean. 'Removal', he calls it. Don't reckon the eastern papers pick up much on the government's methods of Indian removal."

"You don't blame settlers for being afraid of the Indian threat, surely."

"Folks fear what they don't understand. Indians suffer poor treatment for it, that's for sure," he said, his voice threaded with regret.

Even in her limited knowledge of trappers and traders, she was aware the men who chose those occupations had a close affinity with some of the tribes. Some wintered with them, even took Indian wives. Perhaps somewhere an Indian woman awaited his return. Abruptly, she changed the subject. "Dorie mentioned Independence as your destination."

"We're stopping off there. Going to meet up with some other folks before traveling on."

"On *West?* Do you mean to say you're going beyond Independence? But that's Indian Territory, isn't it?" Rachel voiced her alarm.

"Yes, ma'am. That's what I've been workin' my way into tellin' you." He shifted his hat, the better to avoid her gaze. "I'm afraid I haven't been straightforward with you, and seein' how you've struck up such a friendship with Dorie, I'm wondering if I don't owe you more'n half the truth."

He paused as if measuring both his words and her reaction. Bracing herself for what was to come, she urged, "Go on."

"Dorie's grandfather, Tall Horse, is an old Oto war chief. No longer active as such, but—"

"You can't be serious! You surely wouldn't take a child into Indian Territory."

"Rachel, the plains are opening up. A lot of children'll soon be going west. Anyway, he's her *grandfather*. No harm'll come to her."

Rachel drew an astonished breath. Why, he was serious! As she grappled with her shock, the water in the kettle began to boil. "I don't know how you can consider doing such a thing. You know the dangers better than most!"

"It's not as risky as you think. There's always a few in St. Louis willing to travel west. In Independence, if not sooner, we'll join up with the supply caravan that will rendezvous on Green River. It's heavily armed. The Indians won't attack it. Not unless seriously provoked. Their men want to trade hides for knives and hatchets, fishhooks and traps and such. And their women want the buttons and combs, needles and jewelry the traders bring. So if it's trouble with hostiles you fear, then—"

"You can't take her to live with Indians! She is used to white customs, white people, white ways," Rachel argued vehemently. "She'd be lost! Who could she turn to?"

"Tall Horse is her grandfather. He wants to see her. He has a right. She's Indian, too, Rachel. Her mother—"

"Is dead," Rachel said coldly.

He rose to tower over her, some stark emotion chasing across his dark features, then masked by steely determination. A muscle rippled along his jawline.

Rachel met his black look without flinching. "Her grandfather is wrong to want her back. He can't protect her from disease or hardship or ridicule over her white blood."

"She wouldn't be alone," he said finally. "I'd be there."

"Small comfort!" Rachel cried. "What do you know about a little girl's needs? How it feels to be motherless, fatherless—"

"She isn't fatherless," he said in a dangerously soft voice.

"Oh?" Rachel came to her feet. "Just what sort of a father does she have, then? Where was he when her people were dying of smallpox? Why didn't he ever pick her up from the Murphys as she expected? Where was he when she was taken by some Frenchman and ridden halfway across the country to be abandoned at a mission school? *Where was this father of hers then, tell me?*" she demanded.

In one sudden lunge, he closed the distance between them, then stopped short, one hand bunching into a fist, the other shooting out as if to forcibly stem her flow of words.

Heart in her throat, she retracted a step, and in so doing, tripped over a root. The hand she'd feared meant her harm caught, steadied, then let her go. The haunted look that had alarmed her drained from his face, leaving the placid determination she'd come to recognize as part and parcel of him.

"In the morning, I'm leaving with her. I thought I owed it to you to make things clearer, hoped you'd see she's going to be well taken care of. I can see I was wrong."

He turned and strode away, his demeanor that of a man slow to forgive. Rachel let out a ragged breath. How soon they'd leaped from harmony to warfare. And she wasn't yet sure what was at the bottom of their quarrel. Dorie's father? Dorie's grandfather? Or simply vastly different views of what was best for Dorie? She watched him go and wondered at her regret.

Adam flung out his blankets, jerked off his hat and boots and lay down with his feet toward the fire. Her question had been a fair one. He'd flogged himself with it time and again. How differently things might have been if he'd stayed in Tall Horse's village that fall instead of wandering up the Missouri setting traps.

Not that he could have saved her if he'd been in the village that winter. If only he'd stayed around awhile, instead of taking off for the wilderness like a wounded animal! Someone might have remembered the Frenchman's taking Dorie, leaving word for Adam that he'd leave her with the Murphys in St. Louis, the same old couple who'd raised Shining Meadow from the age of twelve, when she'd been stolen by the Pawnee and traded for a Kentucky rifle.

Instead, he'd followed the Missouri into Mandan Country, continuing his trapping, rendezvousing on the Green River in July, returning to the Missouri to trap in the fall, wintering with the Mandans. He'd lived angrily, bitterly, recklessly, until the whisper of God suggested he deal with his losses, give up his guilt. Early teachings were not lost or forgotten.

He'd begun, in his wanderings, to keep an eye peeled for the Frenchman. Jean-Claude had once saved his life, and though Adam often didn't approve of his dealings with the Indians, he counted him as a friend. He hadn't actively looked for him, just kept an ear to the ground. Evidence of his comings and goings were plentiful among the tribes. Whiskey was flowing free. Uneasy over what he saw as a lack of judgment on Jean-Claude's part, Adam was sickened by the weakness liquor wrought upon a proud and noble people. Those among the tribal leaders who valued his opinion listened when he told them whiskey was a poor trade for skins and hides.

One dusty July, he ran into Jean-Claude at the Green River rendezvous. He'd greeted the French trader with a hearty clap on the back. But Jean-Claude's countenance had been sullen beneath the brim of his blue wolf-tail cap. He accused Adam of making trouble for him among the Plains tribes, told him to stick to his trappings and leave the trading to him.

In looking back, Adam saw that he could have apologized, could have smoothed things over, cleared the air. If he had, Jean-Claude would have no doubt told him about Dorie. Instead, he'd stuck by his guns and told the trader it was plain foolhardy to keep the Indians red-hot with whiskey. Even more foolish to, at the same time, supply them with guns.

The Frenchman cursed the day he'd saved Adam from the Blackfeet and vowed revenge if Adam didn't keep his trap shut.

Little realizing the card the wily trader held, Adam had shrugged off his threat as liquor talking. Drunkenness, in fact, proved to be the little man's undoing. In sharing a keg with some other trappers and traders at last summer's rendezvous, Jean-Claude had bragged about the fine trick he'd played on Adam Hawk.

One of the trappers, not quite as liquored up as the rest, remembered the tale. Some months passed before he ran into Adam, but when he did, he told him all that Jean-Claude had said. In stunned disbelief, Adam listened to the news that Dorie was alive, had spent three years with the Murphys, then had been taken by Jean-Claude to a mission school in the East.

Adam had started East, stopping first in Tall Horse's village to tell him the news. The old chief, in poor health, found the promise of seeing his small granddaughter again, when he'd thought all his descendants lost by way of the sickness that'd claimed so many of their number, reason to go on living. He'd secured a promise from Adam—the promise he'd return with Tall Horse's granddaughter.

All the time Adam had hunted for Dorie, he'd never stopped to think she wouldn't know him. The reunion wasn't what he'd hoped for. He'd been a stranger to her. He'd come to the conclusion it'd be best to wait until they were alone, on their way to see Tall Horse, before he told her the whole story.

As for the Frenchman, if their paths crossed, that drunken weasel'd best be set to peel his coat and square his jaw. He didn't reckon he'd be completely free of the grudge he was bearing until he'd banged up his knuckles pounding the deception out of the man who'd taken the good deed he'd done and turned it into an act of revenge.

chapter 11

RACHEL STEPPED OUT OF THE WAGON to dispose of her wash water just as devotions were ending. Tumultuous thoughts quieted a moment as she listened to the words of *Am I a Soldier of the Cross?* drift on the night air:

> Are there no foes for me to face?
> Must I not stem the flood?
> Is this vile world a friend to grace,
> To help me on to God?
>
> Sure I must fight if I would reign;
> Increase my courage, Lord!
> I'll bear the toil, endure the pain,
> Supported by thy word.

Mama's favorite song! Spirit bruised by the thought of the lonely grave, the single bit of green on the rosebush, she blinked back tears, and climbed back into the wagon.

She prayed for comfort, prayed for guidance, prayed for Francis, Philip, and Samuel, too. Sorry for her impatience with Samuel, she prayed for forgiveness as well. Too often she used impatience and anger as a tool, a shield to protect her from some weightier emotion, this time, grief.

Was that why she'd quarrelled with Adam, so brazenly opposing his plan to return Dorie to her grandfather? No, sound reason was behind her opposition. He'd said he'd be there with her, to which she'd rudely insinuated he wouldn't be much use to the child. Unfair, perhaps. He did seem dependable—to supply her physical needs. But what of her emotional needs? What of the trauma caused by being uprooted from one way of life and thrust into another, one that would be completely foreign? Could Adam help her there? And how long would he stay before deciding she was settled, that he could go about his own business once again?

The more she turned it over in her mind, the more deeply troubled Rachel became. A plan began to come together. She wouldn't go to Galesburg. She'd go with Adam Hawk and Dorie, and if it took every breath in her body, she'd talk Adam out of this notion of turning Dorie over to her grandfather. She lit a lantern and began preparations.

Some time later, a boot thudded against the floor of the wagon. Philip whispered, "Rachel? When're you going to put out the lantern?"

"I didn't know it was bothering you."

"It isn't. Just saw a crack of light through the floorboards and wondered what you were up to," came Philip's hushed reply.

"I'm making a riding skirt. Go to sleep, Philip; I promise I'll put out the light in a shake."

She shrugged the kinks out of her shoulders, bit off the thread, and inspected her handiwork. The skirt, a black worsted poplin, had been reworked; she'd used a pair of drawers to estimate where the crotch belonged, then boldly snipped and stitched until she had a makeshift riding skirt, the folds of which parted for more comfort and modesty in the saddle.

Hoping George Ferguson would be willing to trade his saddle for some things she'd no longer be needing, Rachel made a bedroll for herself and tucked into it a few necessities for the trail as well as a keepsake of Mama. She made some fabric straps to secure the bedroll to the saddle, then put out the lantern and with a great yawn, fell into a troubled sleep.

Up before daylight, Rachel bolstered her courage by much prayer and the repeating of the lines of Mama's favorite song, "'Increase my courage, Lord. I'll bear the toil, endure the pain, supported by Thy word.' "

Even then, it came as a hard blow to learn Adam and Dorie had already left. Not to be deterred, she did her trading with George while a red-eyed Julia looked on with straight-lipped curiosity.

Feeling pressed for time, Rachel drew her aside and confided her plans.

Julia's troubled look grew as she listened. Her eyes filled with tears. "It isn't easy for me to let her go, but I don't have any choice. There's more to it than meets the eye, Rachel."

"I know. Adam told me his plans last evening. An Indian village! That's no place for Dorie. You understand, don't you, why I have to talk him out of it?"

Confusion added to the worry lines that drew Julia's mouth down. "Rachel, you know, don't you, that he's her father? He told you, didn't he?"

Her father! For a moment, the impact of Julia's words stopped her cold. "He told you that?"

Julia nodded. "He asked us not to mention it to Dorie, said he'd like to tell her in his own way and explain why it'd taken him so long to find her."

He couldn't be Dorie's father! Wouldn't he have told her? Dorie's mother was a missionary to the Indians, he'd told her. That could only mean that the child's father was Indian. Rachel said cheerfully, "I don't know what to believe, Julia. But I'll find out. I've prayed about it and I'm going."

Face full of misgivings, Julia asked, "What about Francis and Philip? What about Samuel?"

"I can't marry Samuel, if that's what you mean. And if I don't, staying with them is going to make everyone uncomfortable. It's best if I go, Julia."

"But you don't even know if you can catch up with Mr. Hawk. And if you do, you don't know that he'll allow you to travel with them," Julia argued gently. Eyes full of concern, she touched Rachel's arm. "Your grief is so new, I don't think you're really thinking this through. Stay with us, Rachel. The Lord will take care of Dorie. We have to believe that."

Her mother had said much the same thing. With a painful breath, Rachel murmured, "I've made up my mind, Julia. Don't make it any harder for me."

With obvious difficulty, Julia bit back more arguments and gave Rachel a parting hug. Tearfully, she whispered, "God go with you, then. And Rachel? Get me word if you can. Let me know Dorie's all right."

Francis and Samuel were occupied with the stock, giving Rachel the opportunity to catch Philip alone. Taking him aside, she told him she was off to St. Louis to open a dress shop, kissed him good-by and left him gaping after her, his expression a blend of youthful admiration and envy.

Though Rachel's head felt much better than it had the previous day, the rest of her body was tender as a pincushion! She adjusted herself to the western saddle, and once out of sight of the creek where Samuel and Francis were watering the stock, urged Sada into a ground-eating gallop. Francis had always been kind to her; it seemed shabby to be making an explanation-free escape. But Adam Hawk wasn't letting shabby actions slow him, was he? She tossed her head. He'd made off with Dorie without allowing time for good-bys. In her case, they weren't needed. With a couple of hours of hard riding, she'd overtake them, find out the truth, and go on from there.

Ahead of her, Adam continued along the trail, but it was hard to ignore instincts that'd become fine-tuned from years of living by his wits. The path had been running parallel to the south bank of the Kankakee. But soon they would leave the river and cut deeper south. Dismounting, Adam led his horse back to Dorie.

"Reckon you're gettin' hungry. We've covered a good piece. Climb down, get you a drink, and rest a spell."

As she obeyed, he opened his saddlebag and drew out a skin pouch containing pemmican—an Indian concoction, buffalo dried in thin strips, pounded into powder, flavored with wild berries, and held together with grease. He wasn't particularly fond of the stuff, but it was nourishing and efficient in warding off hunger.

After Dorie'd satisfied her thirst, he offered the pouch to her. "Eat a bit, then lead the horse down to drink. If I'm not back by then, stretch out and take a nap."

Accepting his instructions without question, she settled under a tree and opened the pouch. His promise to return her to the Fergusons if she couldn't be happy any other way hovered like a worrisome fly.

The sound of a lone rider drew nearer. Adam peered around the tree to see it was Rachel Whitaker.

Though her horse was plodding along easily enough, it looked as if she'd been run hard earlier. Rachel didn't appear too fresh, either; her chin was tucked down, and the same fashionable bonnet she'd worn the previous day shadowed drooping eyelids. She was wearing some sort of split skirt, and held the reins loosely, looking for all the world as if she had dozed off.

The absence of motion jerked Rachel back to reality. Rather shamefacedly, she rubbed her eyes. How could she have fallen asleep? Her first thoughts ground to a halt as she saw Adam Hawk planted on the trail. He was holding Sada's head, an irritated glint narrowing his blue eyes.

Rachel straightened and rested her hands on the saddlehorn. "Good day, Mr. Hawk. I'm glad I've caught up with you." She struggled for composure. "Where's Dorie?"

"Up ahead, having a bite to eat," he said, not appearing a bit more gracious or inclined to patience. "Where are *you* going?"

"I've decided not to go to Galesburg, but to St. Louis instead—to see about opening a dress shop."

"You're traveling alone?"

She flicked a bit of trail dust off her skirt. "I was hoping you'd let me ride along with you and Dorie. You *are* going that way?"

"Yes, but you're not. Not with me, at least."

Mind racing, outdistancing intimidation, she gave a small shrug. "I suppose I'll have to go alone, then. It's a public road, isn't it? No law against my following you, is there?"

He snatched the reins from her hand and turned Sada back down the path. "You go right back the way you came. If you aren't aiming to go to Galesburg, that's your choice. But you aren't tagging at my heels."

She started to swing down out of the saddle, but he rumbled, "Stay put and do what I say. I got no time to nursemaid you all the way to St. Louis, and even if I did, I wouldn't. You're trouble."

She attempted again to step out of the saddle. "I'll do my part; I'll carry water and cook and help look after Dorie. You won't have to put yourself out for me at all, I promise."

He caught her right leg in a steely grip, preventing her dismounting, and when her color rose at the impropriety of his actions, hardened his jaw and demanded, "Does Francis Pierce know where you are?"

Wise enough to make no further attempt to climb down, Rachel slapped his hand off her leg and replied, "I suppose by now he does. I told both Philip and Julia."

"I'm beholden to you for that," he said with a trace of sarcasm. "Reckon I can expect a handful of indignant farmers and that jealous pup of a stepbrother of yours to come racin' along anytime, suspicious of my intentions."

That thought had never occurred to her, but now that he'd stated it, its likelihood seemed alarmingly real. Nonetheless, she stood her ground, saying, "And if they do, I don't see that it'll be such an inconvenience to you. I'll simply explain my decision and that'll be that."

Rubbing one hand across a day's growth of whiskers, he glanced across the Kankakee, then jerked his attention back to her. "I oughta whisk you out of that saddle and give you an almighty whippin', that's what I ought to do! You're causin' me no end of trouble, wasting my time, taxin' my temper. If you weren't a lady—"

"If I weren't a lady, there'd be no problem, now would there, Mr. Hawk?" she retorted with a trumped-up show of courage. "If I were a child, in awe of your trail savvy, we could get along splendidly. Or if I were a man, you might welcome my company. We could sit around the campfire at night and swap tales. But because I'm a lady, you're shaking your head at me and looking stubborn, unwilling to listen to a word I say!"

"You are what you are," he answered, "and words won't change it. If it's a dress shop you want, then go on to Chicago with the rest of Clark's party, and book passage back east by lake and canal. It's more sensible and safer too than tryin' to settle yourself in some frontier town where you haven't got a friend to your name. Now you retrace your steps and let Pierce work out the details for you—he'll do it gladly enough."

Lest the threatening wave of defeat crash over her, she set herself against it and searched for a tool by which to gain a verbal victory. Going straight to the heart of the matter, she peered into his upturned face. "Julia told me you're Dorie's father. Is that true?"

A whole series of emotions chased across his face—surprise, defensiveness, unexpected vulnerability—before he swept his hat off his head and combed lean brown fingers through his hair.

"Tried to tell you so last night," he said quietly. "Thought maybe if you understood the whole of it, you wouldn't be so set against my taking her."

"Why did you tell me her mother was a missionary? You aren't the first white man to marry an Indian girl—nor to lose track of your child, I imagine," she added.

Hers was an ill-advised comment. Eyes gleaming, he gripped her around the waist, jerked her out of the saddle, and oblivious to her yelp of indignation, set her out of his way. With outspoken protest, she looked on as he stripped Sada of saddle and bridle, dumping them on the path alongside her bedroll.

With cold detachment, he said, "I should have known you weren't really interested in going to St. Louis. Your purpose in followin' me is just to yammer away and try to change my mind. Well, it isn't gonna go your way, not at all. You should have gone while you had the chance."

With that, he grabbed a green whip, set it across Sada's flanks and put her to galloping back down the road. Wheeling around to face

Rachel again, he tossed the stick aside and gave one last piece of advice.

"If I were you, I'd high-tail it back to the post road. With some luck, you might catch your horse before she regroups with Clark's party. Without it—well, don't lose spirit. Once on the post road, you can't go wrong. Pierce and his boys'll catch up with you eventually."

With a cold, self-congratulatory smile, he tipped his hat, turned, and strode away.

Watching him go, shaking, fuming, sputtering mad, Rachel fought the bitter taste of tears. She straightened the blouse he'd nearly yanked out of her skirt, jerking her out of the saddle, and caught her lip to keep a sob from escaping. The indignity of it all aside, it was an overwhelming defeat! He was gone; Dorie was gone; her horse was gone! She was out here in the middle of nowhere—alone! Self-pity rising to choke her with tears, she stroked her tender behind and rued the day Adam Hawk had ridden into their camp.

Rachel lugged her belongings off the path. Inside the bedroll was a small parcel of dried jerked beef. Little though it was and tough as well, she was grateful and bowed her head to give thanks. Suppose Adam was wrong? Suppose Francis didn't come after her? She'd be left stranded out here! Maybe she should take Adam's advice and hike back to the post road.

But how was she to carry the cumbersome load Sada had carried so effortlessly? Discouraged and a little afraid, Rachel's anger cooled. Closing her eyes, she confessed her headstrong tendency for impulsive action and pleaded the Lord's forgiveness as well as his directing hand. "I don't know which way to turn, Lord. Do I leave my things here and walk back? I can't continue on without Sada. Give me a sign, Lord. Please?"

Eventually, she opened her eyes and moved her tongue across her lips. The beef jerky sat like an unfriendly lump on her stomach. Drawn by the gentle lapping of the Kankakee, she rose and ambled down the south bank of the river to drink her fill before starting back to the road.

A soft welcoming nicker sent her pulse soaring. She whirled around and gave a glad cry. "Sada! You came back!" Sada stamped a hoof and waited as Rachel drew near.

Rachel approached the horse with gentle words. God had given swift heed to her prayers. Could he intend for her to follow Adam and Dorie, unwanted though she was? Only a few steps remained in closing the distance to Sada. Rachel paused, and with the wisdom of hindsight, decided to be specific with her prayer.

Fervently, she said, "Lord, if I can't catch Sada, I'll turn back, find Francis and the boys. But if you allow me, if you *help* me to catch her, I'm going to saddle her and ride after Adam and Dorie. So Lord, like Gideon of old, I'm laying out the fleece. If you think I should return to Francis and the boys, don't let me catch this horse."

Having prayed, she quieted her pounding heart and walked right up to Sada. Sada rubbed her face against her, all but inviting her to slip fingers through her leather halter.

Though Rachel took the return of the horse as the Lord's blessing, she wondered, if she was to follow undetected, how she could accomplish her original mission—talking Adam out of taking Dorie into Indian Territory. And what if Francis or Samuel *did* come riding after her? How would she convince them she knew her own mind?

Questions aside, Rachel was firm in her resolve. The Lord had led her this far: he wouldn't abandon her now. She rode on, the words to "Am I A Soldier of the Cross?" playing over and over through her mind.

Eventually, the trail narrowed and angled away from the Kankakee River, through thick stands of forest. Rachel rode up a small hill, shaded her eyes and gazed west, but saw no sign of Adam and Dorie. Back down the hill, she rode on until she came to a clearing. Evidence of a fall burnoff was nearly lost to the robe of spring. Green, thick-bladed grasses, bright-faced wild flowers and an orange butterfly made a playground for a frisking ground squirrel.

Rachel turned her face to the sun that burned in a cloud-splotched sky, relishing the warming rays. They had to be just ahead somewhere. There were too many trees to see them, that was all. At peace with her decision, she continued riding until she came to a fork in the path.

Time after time, she dismounted throughout the long afternoon to check hoofprints, each time becoming increasingly uneasy over the reception she was likely to receive. She'd join them at dark, she decided. Who would be so callous as to turn out a helpless, hungry city-bred girl!

Ahead of her on the trail, Adam made an early camp along a tree-skirted stream. He fashioned a shelter by slanting branches and brush against the huge trunk of a fallen tree near the snarly root section, then installed Dorie, along with their belongings, inside. After watering the horses, he hobbled them where they could graze.

"We're going to get wet, Mr. Hawk," Dorie said softly.

"No more'n damp; I built her snug." said Adam, bent on calming her fears.

She was quiet a moment, then confided, "I'm a little afraid. The thunder, the lightning. We're in a fix."

Gruffly he murmured, "Aw, I've been in lot worse fixes than this. This is just a sprinkle of rain, won't hurt a thing."

Seeming unconvinced, she tunneled deeper into her bedroll as the next jagged finger of lightning raced across the night sky. With an awkward hand, he patted the lump she made in the covers, but she gave no sign of being consoled.

"Would you like to hear a story? A story about a couple of fellas caught in a snowstorm in the mountains?" he asked, settling on the first account that sprang to mind. Leaving out the gruesome beginning, his capture by the Blackfoot braves, leaping past the events of his escape, he began the story with the gray skies, the whistling wind, the sudden pelting of icy snow.

"Were you on foot?" she interrupted, proving her attentiveness.

"No. I had a horse. My companion did, too. But they were growing weary, we'd covered a lot of hard ground, and had a bad feeling we were bein' followed by some unfriendly types."

"Indians?" she asked with interest.

"Blackfeet. They hate trappers worse'n a cat hates water. There's a story about that, too. Maybe you'd like to hear it."

"Maybe," she said. "But finish this story first."

"The snow turned blinding, and it was piling up fast. We hadn't had anything to eat in a spell and neither had the horses. They were worn out, straining against the wind. Darkness fell, but we were afraid if we stopped, those fellas would catch us. So we kept movin' until my companion's horse dropped dead in the snow."

"Did you eat the horse?" she asked, seeming to find nothing shocking about the thought.

He hadn't planned to tell her that part. But since she'd asked, he admitted, "Enough to keep us alive."

"Were the Blackfeet still after you?"

"We thought so. We heard them hootin', but later we realized they were lost, just like us. They had been tippin' the jug, and like I said, it was a blindin' snowstorm. In morning light, we saw what'd happened. They'd known they were near their camp, and they'd kept up their hootin' until those in camp heard them and directed them in."

"So you'd slept right next to their camp?"

"Only for a few hours," he said. "We climbed on the horse we had left and made fast tracks."

"Until you came to a friendly village, and then you stayed with them until the storm passed," she said.

It was an obvious conclusion, he supposed. But something about her intonation made him uneasy. "You heard this story before?" he asked.

"Yes. The Frenchman told me." she said. "Do you know the Frenchman, Jean-Claude?"

"I know him," he said coldly.

She was quiet for so long a time, he thought she slept. The drumming of the rain calmed the tension in him. The thunder rumbled, but softer, more distant. The lightning was no more.

"Mr. Hawk?" she intruded softly into his thoughts. "You'd tell me if you were my father, wouldn't you?"

chapter 12

A MILE OR SO FURTHER DOWN THE ROAD, Rachel was having a miserable night of it. With the fall of dusk, she'd realized there were no longer fresh tracks for her to follow. Somewhere, she'd taken a wrong turn. Either that, or she'd ridden past their camp without spotting them. And that seemed unlikely.

Thinking it foolish to ride on, she'd been about to turn back when a stand of trees in the distance caught her eye. Was there a chance of finding shelter? Over the past mile, she'd noticed a tilled field and evidence of livestock. Perhaps she would find a family who'd take her in for the night.

Rain-scented winds chilled her beneath her garments as she urged Sada on. Her heart was soon cheered by the profile of a cabin within the near woods. With her rush of relief came plans for the morning—she'd set out at sunrise and backtrack to the last small stream she'd crossed, for that was where she'd last seen their tracks.

As Rachel drew nearer to the ramshackle cabin, she saw the door was covered only by a stiff and weather-stained animal skin tacked in place at the top, and stopping short of the bottom portion of the opening by at least three feet. What she could see of the inside of the cabin didn't look promising. Surely no one would live in such a hovel!

Dismounting, catching Sada's reins in her hand, she called out timidly, "Hello? Anyone home?"

The only answer was the mocking laughter of the wind sweeping through big gaps in the chink between logs. Taking a reluctant step toward the door, she called out again and again was met with no reply.

Pushing the animal skin aside, she stepped into the dim interior, took one look, and backed out to draw a breath of clean air. The dirt floor was hardly visible beneath the animal droppings, which were relatively fresh, judging by their foul smell. She circled to the back of the cabin, but found nothing other than the crumbled heap of a stick and mud daub chimney.

"Dear Lord," she murmured. "Just look, would you? What now?" Drawing a steadying breath, she searched for a glimpse of a homestead, but found none. Beyond the scattering of trees, the thick lush grass rolled gently on. Evidence of livestock assured her of a homestead somewhere. But could she find it before the rains came? As she hesitated, the skies opened, first with a gentle sprinkle, then a thunder-rumbling, lightning-licking downpour.

Rushing around to the front again, she caught her breath and plunged inside, pulling Sada along after her. It was no better at second glance. A partially rotted loft sent puncheon planks splintering down from the ceiling. Bird litter whitewashed the log walls; nests, scattered and torn, strung down from overhead; all manner of debris had blown in to mingle with the animal dung on the floor. The cabin's only virtue was that it was reasonably dry.

Gingerly circling the crude enclosure, Rachel came upon a bunk built into the wall. Just a slab supported by log wedges, it was at least up out of the dung. She coughed as she dusted off the worst of the filth, then turned to unsaddling Sada.

Using the saddle blanket, she gave the horse a thorough rubdown, all the while crooning encouragement and words of praise. "Such a good girl, and here I am, not a thing to feed you. Hardly seems right, does it, old girl? Plenty of grass out there, though. Once the rain slackens, you can eat your fill."

Exhaustion dragging at her heels, she smoothed the saddle blanket out on the bunk, shifted the saddle to one end and spread out her bedroll. In the fading light, the sight of the brocade dress she'd rolled into it brought fresh tears to her eyes. She fingered the intricate rosettes, sorrow flooding her heart. Mama! her heart cried. If you could see me now!

Carefully she folded the dress and put it beneath the saddle, out of harm's way. Hungry, with sore muscles throbbing, bottom feeling like one big bruise, she leaned against the wall, drew her knees to her chest, and in that huddled position, wrapped a blanket around her shoulders. Too edgy to lie down, fearful of rodents and snakes, and vermin, she listened to the storm and prayed. Her eyes grew heavy. Night noises receded and oblivion drifted in.

A guttural sound awakened her. Sound? Sounds! The cabin was alive with them. Grunts and snorts and quarrelsome squeals. She'd been invaded by hogs while she slept!

It was degrading enough to have to seek refuge in a hovel where the very air reeked of the foul smell of hogs! She would *not* share quarters! Rachel stood on the bunk, raised herself on tiptoe, and felt around for the broken plank she'd earlier noticed hanging down from the loft. Getting a grip on it, she gave a mighty yank. It came so easily, she nearly toppled off the bunk into the milling hogs.

One big fellow scraped a horny tusk against the bunk, emitting a contentious grunt. Rachel leaped back, flattening herself against the log wall. Brave words belied by a trembling voice, she ordered, "Out, I say! Go, before I make hamhocks out of you!" She swung down with the plank and landed a warning blow on the back of the nearest hog.

He gave an enraged squeal, then an ugly snarling series of grunts. Instead of retreating as Rachel had been confident he would, he backed off a step, then rammed toward her, his tusk just grazing her shoe.

Too late, she realized her error. These hogs were half wild! Not like those Francis had raised at all. And here she stood, trapped against the wall, the door too far to make a hasty exit.

"Dear Lord!" she prayed, and swallowed a sob.

She raised the plank again, this time sparing nothing. The second blow held him off a moment longer than the first, but he was anything but defeated. Rachel knew with a quaking heart, she'd better make the next blow count. Pulse throbbing, cold fear in her veins, she tightened her grip on the plank, lifted, lifted, lifted, then brought it down with a strength she'd never have guessed she possessed.

It was later than his usual waking hour, but Adam wasn't regretting the time they'd lost. The race to catch up with his past was over. Years ago when he'd married Shining Meadow and returned her to her people, Tall Horse had accepted him as a son. He felt a deep loyalty and affection for the old man. For his part, he could stay. But the decision hinged on Dorie's reaction to a lifestyle and a culture she'd long since forgotten.

He nudged her into wakefulness. She emerged from the cocoon of her blankets and sat up. Her hair was tangled, her eyes heavy with sleep. She bid him a solemn, "Good morning, Papa." Then she ducked her head and rushed on to complain, "My blankets are wet. It didn't stay so dry in here."

"Ground's damp. Shake 'em out and hang 'em where the sun'll do its work. I'll take care of the horses."

Sada was with his horses. In all the catching up, Rachel'd slipped his mind. He glanced around, expecting to find her huddled somewhere, shivering wet. But a hasty search yielded no sign of her.

"You, you! You'n up thar! You the one beat the Indiana stuffin' outta my ma's hawgs? Come down from there b'fore I yank ye down on the end of this stick, don't think I won't."

Rachel opened both eyes, squinted against the sunlight flooding through wide gaps in the roof, and turned onto her stomach. Below, in the middle of all the hog muck, was a short, brawny, irate young man. Head slanted back, close-spaced eyes half-hidden by an oily, untidy tangle of hair, he declared, "By cracky, yer female!"

Rachel sat up, careful not to tumble through the gaps of missing boards. Her pulse quickened. What did he want of her? Catching sight of the stick in his hand, she winced and rubbed a sore neck muscle. It was none other than the plank she'd used to do battle. Splintered and broken, it was a vivid reminder of the horrors of the previous night. Shuddering, she murmured, "If you'd please step outside, I'll gather my things together and be out of your way."

"Not so fast as all that, you won't!" Indignation widened his eyes. "Not if you's the one what walloped Ma's hawgs. She's plenty lathered up about it, don't think she ain't. They limped home all bloodied up, one of 'em missin' his snout and another with an almighty gash 'cross his shoulder."

"Sir, your hogs nearly ate me alive," Rachel countered, as indignant as he. "I had a right to defend myself, didn't I? Why, if I hadn't taken a chance on this rickety loft holding my weight, you wouldn't be talking to me right now!"

He shifted his weight and hitched his homespun britches. A shyness gentled his glance. He dug a toe in the muck and lowered his eyes. "I'd be the poorer 'un fer that, sure 'nuf. But all the same, Ma sent me to get the brute that bloodied her hawgs. So I'd be obliged if ye'd come along peaceful like and explain it to 'er."

All things considered, it didn't seem such an unreasonable request. Ascending the loft in a prudent and hasty retreat had been no easy accomplishment. She hadn't been troubled by modesty or decorum. Descending with the young man below was a different matter.

She swept a hand through her hair. "If you'd be kind enough to carry my saddle there out and see if you can locate my horse, I've no objection to explaining the dilemma I found myself in to your mother."

He nodded and crossed to the bunk, the littered floor sucking at his boots. Rachel watched as he shouldered the saddle, then glanced in curiosity at the dress she'd tucked beneath it.

Remembering the clean drawers and chemise wrapped within the dress, she said hurriedly, "Don't trouble yourself with that, I'll get the rest of my things and be right out."

Lord, let her be an understanding motherly sort, she prayed as she dropped her bedroll to the bunk below, then cautiously felt her way down. *The type who'll soften into forgiveness, perhaps even offer me a bite of breakfast before sending me on my way.* Her growling stomach voting in favor of that idea, Rachel hastily combed her fingers through her hair. With the corner of one rough blanket, she scrubbed at her face, then completed her pitiful effort at making herself more presentable by tucking in her blouse and tying on her bonnet, which was a bit bent and sadder looking than it had been a day ago.

It was early enough, with a morning chill in the air, but the sun beamed down from a cloudless blue sky. She drew in a deep, clean breath as she stepped out of the cabin and let it out slowly. "I'm ready to go, sir."

"Don't see no sign of yer horse, ma'am," he said, gawking at her, now that she was out in the light where he could better make out her features.

As she met his gaze with a level look of her own, he averted his eyes and hooked a thumb through his suspenders. Impatient to make her explanations, plead a bite of food, and be on her way, Rachel said in exasperation, "I suppose she's wandered off."

"Would you try whistling for her, sir? She's well trained, though a bit inclined to pranks. A whistle usually brings her."

The stocky young farmer obliged by splitting the morning air with a series of shrill whistles that made the birds sit up and take notice. But no sign of a galloping horse rewarded them.

"Could be yer horse got to feelin' thirsty. We could check out the pond back of our barn, seein' how it's right on our way. That's our place, kinder nestled in amongst some low hills."

"I see," she murmured upon spotting a dim drift of smoke.

"Whatcha doin' way out here alone?" he asked, setting out, heaving the saddle over his shoulder with disconcerting ease.

"I'm not alone, not exactly," Rachel said, arranging her words with care as she fell in step with him. "There's some folks who started out a bit ahead of me, and I'm trying to catch up with them—I should manage to do that some time today. That is, if I'm not delayed too long," she added with a swift sidelong glance.

"You got a purty way of puttin' yer words. You a schoolmarm, are ye?" he continued his questioning with an open curiosity that would have been considered unforgivably rude back in Boston.

"No, a seamstress. I plan to open a dress shop in St. Louis."

He regarded her with a puzzled glance. "Pardon my sayin' so, ma'am, but I don't hardly think you'd find much of a market fer that in St. Louie. I drove me some cattle down that way a coupla years back. Never in my life saw so many rough sorts. Injuns and hunters and trappers—all decked out in buckskins. Hardly tell the white 'uns from the redskins. And not a one of 'em wearin' a dress."

He guffawed at his own poor joke, then wiped the spittle from his mouth. "'Course I didn't see the whole works. Weren't no sightseeing tour, just tryin' to git a fair price fer my beef. They's shrewd as a crooked pence down thata way, don't think they ain't. Feller's gotta keep one hand on his pocketbook and t'other on his pistol when he's doin' business across the Big Muddy."

Warming up to his subject, he rambled on without noticing Rachel was having a hard time keeping up with him. They cut across a pasture, then skirted around the earth and stone ridge to pass through a second pasture where cattle grazed.

Listening to him talk, Rachel decided she had nothing to fear from him. He was no doubt a hardworking, talkative fellow, glad of a bit of unexpected company. And, if he sprinkled a liberal number of repetitive "don't thinks" throughout his sentences, well, who was she to notice?

The pond and the homestead soon came into view. But no Sada!

"Aw, don't fret none, we'll find 'er," he brushed aside her concern. "Horses is peculiar creatures—you don't corral 'em, they wander off. She won't git fur, though, I'll see to that."

Unconsoled, Rachel felt a childish urge to burst into tears. He paused and shifted the saddle to his other shoulder as he waited for her.

"Come along, ye hear? Ma's tolerable poor 'bout bein' kept waitin'. Reckon she's spotted us headin' her way." He cackled to himself and added, "I'll calculate she's a mite surprised at what I'm bringin' in. None of us reckoned on it bein' a female what bunged up our hawgs. You must pack a tall wallop," he added with a hint of respect.

Warmth rose to Rachel's cheeks as she followed on reluctant feet. Looking ahead to the double cabin separated by a dog-trot, she felt a surge of misgivings. "I explained how it was, sir," she murmured. "Your mother'll understand, won't she?"

"Ma? Ma understands jest whatever she's of a mind to, that's all. She kin be a rough customer, don't think—"

"—she can't," Rachel finished with him.

"Ma! Lookee 'ere what I found in the squatter's cabin beyond the ridge. Here's yer brute—ain't she a mean-lookin' critter?" He laughed and swept a hand through stringy hair.

Eyes slow to adjust to the dim fire-lit room, Rachel hovered in the opening. Her nerves leapt at the sound of a creaking rocker. Ponderous feet shuffled across the floor, supporting the bulk of a mammoth old woman.

"You be the one what walloped the snouts off my hawgs?" she demanded.

Alarmed by the fiery intonation of her words, Rachel swiftly backed out the door and nearly tripped over her saddle. Catching her balance, she forced herself to meet the woman's glare. Eyes nearly lost to folds of flesh bored into her like sharp needle pricks. Her shoulders, from which hung an ill-fitted tent-sized dress, were wider than most men's and her fleshy fists were balled up.

Rachel swallowed hard and framed a formal apology. "Madam, I'm truly sorry. I assure you I didn't mean your animals any harm. I simply didn't want to *sleep* with them, or be devoured by them. If I was too zealous, then perhaps I can make retribution somehow," she drew to a timid close.

Arms akimbo, the old woman narrowed her eyes and looked her up and down while despair thundered through Rachel's body. Eyes shooting sparks, the old woman rounded, "And jest how'd you like it if'n *I* clipped off *yer* snout? Or bloodied up yer shoulder? Whadda ye reckon that'd make *you* worth?"

"Ma'am—," Rachel protested weakly, only to have the woman cut her short, commanding, "You jest haul yerself in here and set while I make up my mind what to do with the likes of ye! And don't be slow about it neither, my boys'll vouch fer my short wick!"

Rachel crept over the threshold. The woman prodded her in the back with a fat hand as she inched her way across the cabin toward a crude table and bench. Once seated, Rachel darted a glance around the cramped cabin interior and picked out two more men hunkered down in a shadowy corner hear the hearth. They gawked at her, though neither uttered a sound. *O Lord,* she began a frenzied petition for deliverance.

The old woman wedged herself into a carved rocker, wheezing as if the short walk from the door had rendered her breathless. Breathless she might be, but the flame in her eye was as bright as the coals on the hearth!

"Jest what sort o' retribution you got in mind, Missy? Don't look to me like you got much to retribute *with,* by the cat-dragged shape of ye."

Pride prickling, Rachel bit her lip and remained silent before her accuser, eyes downcast. Littered cornbread crumbs and a dried hunk of fat contributed to the slovenly look of the place. The puncheon board had shrunk, giving a glimpse of muddied ground beneath the floor. A damp musky stench rose from it to sour the air, and sluggish flies crawled about on the unswept floor.

"I don't have much," Rachel murmured after much hesitation. "Perhaps I could do some mending for you?"

"Mending, ye say?" The old woman sounded outraged, and behind her, Rachel heard the young man who'd brought her here snicker.

"Them's valuable hawgs you damaged. Our livelihood! I kin do my own mending, thank ye. What else can you do?"

At a total loss now, Rachel shrugged and sat with head ducked. Out of the corner of her eye, she watched one man move out of the shadows, and flinched when he paused only a foot from her.

Taller than her original captor, he cocked his head to one side, considering. "She ain't got much meat on her. Don't reckon she'd be much good fer plowin' ner plantin', Ma."

Behind her, another voice chimed in. "I found her, Ma. If anyone gits some help with chorin', it ought by rights be me."

"Hesh, both of ye!" the old woman scolded. "I'm thinkin'." She fixed her black eyes on Rachel and stroked a hairy chin. "There's more churnin' and cardin' and spinnin' than one body can do around here. Not to mention cookin' and fire-tendin' and a host of other chores. Don't suppose you know anything about any of them sorts of things."

"She's got a horse, Ma, only it's run off. Reckon me an' the boys could round it up. What do ye say to that?"

With one stern glance, the old woman motioned him to silence. Rachel bit back the objection that leaped to her lips. A decided craftiness entered into the young man's voice at the mention of her horse. Only ill could come of it. They surely wouldn't make her pay for the damage she'd done with Sada! Sada was worth one hundred dollars, perhaps more!

"You, scat!" the old woman said with a wave of her hand in Rachel's direction. "Light out there on the dog-trot and don't move a muscle. Me and my boys'll thresh this out."

Rachel skittered out the door on trembling limbs. Wondering what her chances of escaping on foot might be, she perched on the dog-trot, and wished she'd been bold enough to pull the door shut behind her. Yawned open as it was, they had a clear view of her. That old woman was just riled up enough to twist off *her* nose if she tried to run off. Defeat a heavy burden, she propped her arms on her knees and buried her face between them, fervently praying for divine intervention. Her chances of ever joining Adam and Dorie grew dimmer with each passing moment. Sada was gone, and if she by some miracle did show up, she would no doubt become the spoils of war—*their* spoils. She was hungry, tired, dirty. Hot tears pressed against her eyelids.

Inside, the family muster got underway. "She ain't no bargain, it's clear," Rachel heard the woman say. "Cain't cook ner card ner spin. But she's learnable, I reckon.

"Tyler, you found her; you know it was Providence dropped her in our laps, so listen at me! Your own flesh and blood wouldn't lead you astray."

Oh, no! Not the same Providence *she* answered to! Rachel clenched her eyes shut tight to hold back her tears. Her Lord wouldn't forsake her, abandon her to the mercies of these . . . these frontier clods!

"Lord, help me," she prayed with renewed fervor, the very thought of sharing a home with that battleship of a woman too full of horrors to consider.

A stealthy drop in the woman's voice made Rachel prick up her ears in time to hear her cajole, "We keep her, an' we'll get what she owns in the bargain, providin' we can find that hoss. Wouldn't mind makin' me a purty shawl outta that dress, even if'n it ain't my color," she added.

Making herself as small and discreet as possible, Rachel kept her head down, her shoulders drooping, and scooted along the edge of the dog-trot, inching nearer and nearer to the wall that would throw a temporary blind between them. Just when she was about to rise and break into a run, the old woman sounded out:

"Jest don't get in sech an all-fired hurry, I told you ta stay put!"

She marched out on the dog-trot, her sons reluctantly stringing along after her. Breathing wheezily, she reached out a meaty hand and hauled Rachel up to stand on the dog-trot beside her. "We're done threshing it out, though I haf to say in all fairness, it's only right you should have your pick. These boys need marryin'. Which one do you want?"

"I can't! I don't want to! I won't!" Rachel insisted, her voice rising with her hysteria.

Looking affronted, the old woman tooted her mouth out like a horn and squinted through those folds of flesh. "No call to be so high and mighty about it. Even a man set in his ways kin be worked around, if a gal knows her stuff. So what do you say?"

"I *say* I won't!" Rachel cried again, then gathered just enough composure to be a bit more diplomatic. Nodding toward the three men, she added, "Not that they aren't all fine young men; I'm sure they are. It's just that . . . that . . ."

Tyler, the stocky one, distracted her by elbowing the brother nearest him and saying, "Rider comin', see there?"

"Don't look like anybody I know," said the old woman, shading her eyes.

No longer the center of attention, Rachel looked back over her shoulder and went limp with relief. God indeed was on his throne! A league of angels couldn't have looked any sweeter than Adam Hawk riding toward the cabin with that careless grace of his, that now-familiar hat shadowing an unshaven face, those out-of-mode buckskins molded to his long legs.

". . . that I'm married, that's why!" she finished triumphantly. "And that's my husband coming now."

The old woman pinned her with a suspicious glance. "Don't recall you sayin' nothing before 'bout havin' a man. What do ye call him by?"

"Adam Hawk—he's the son of a Kentucky preacher, a righteous man, fair in his dealings and he'll settle this matter straightaway, you'll see."

Adam reined in his horse, swept Rachel with a glance which revealed neither surprise nor curiosity, and nodded to the others. The old woman propped her hands on massive hips and invited, "Step down, stranger, and rest a spell. What be yer name?"

Adam swung out of the saddle and caught his horse's reins. "Adam Hawk."

"Where ye headed?"

"St. Louis, then on west from there," Adam replied, taking the inquisition right in stride.

The old woman jabbed the air with a pudgy finger. "This woman yer wife?"

Feet quicker than her brain, Rachel came down off the dog-trot and flew to him, arms outstretched. "Adam, Adam, *dear,* I've been so terrified. What happened to you? Where have you been?" With that impassioned speech, she threw her arms around his neck and hissed hoarsely, "You've got to get me out of here! These people are lunatics, raving mad lunatics! Play along, and I'll do anything you say, go back to Francis, marry Samuel, *anything!*"

Startled, he tried to set her away from him, but she pleaded, "Please, Adam? *Please?*"

His gaze swept her face, while behind them the old woman demanded in a shrill voice, "What aire you two whisperin' about? I say! Is this gal yer wife or ain't she?"

In lieu of an answer, Adam drew Rachel close, lowered his mouth to hers and kissed her with all the fervor of a worried-frantic, now-relieved husband.

chapter

13

"YOU AIN'T DOUBTIN' MY WORD as to the damages, aire ye?" the old woman asked, when again the subject at hand turned to the hogs.

"No, just thought I'd take a look-see myself, that's all," Adam said.

"Go on and take him, if yer a mind to," the old woman said to Tyler. "I'll stay here and keep an eye on this gal so's she don't cause us no more grief."

Unnerved by the woman's savage staring, Rachel turned her attention to Adam's horse. Where had they spent the night? And where was Dorie?

The three men soon returned. Rachel listened as Adam bartered away her saddle as compensation for the damage she'd done to the porkers. Considering the alternatives earlier suggested, she decided she was getting off lightly, and tried not to fret over the loss.

"Ready to go?" Adam turned to her.

Rachel's heart skipped a beat as she brushed past the sour old woman and went inside to roll her belongings back into the bedroll. Her hands were shaking a bit, and in her haste, she didn't do too neat a job of it.

Already in the saddle, Adam reached for her bedroll, then gave her a hand up. It took her a second, after her awkward climb, to balance and settle herself behind his saddle.

"Ready?" He handed the bedroll back to her. She wedged it

between them, glad of the barrier, for his very nearness was a reminder of the shameful way he'd kissed her just a short time ago. Face hot at the equally shameful way she'd invited it, Rachel called back, "Ready."

"Did you mean what you said back there?" he intruded into her thoughts as they left the homestead behind them and struck across the dew-kissed grass.

Rachel struggled with her strong-willed tendencies and said in a wooden voice, "You mean, that I'd return to Francis and the boys? Yes, if you hold me to it, I'll go back."

"And what about Samuel?" he asked at length. "You gonna marry him?"

Rachel let go of his shirt altogether. "No, you can't hold me to that; that was desperation talking. Just before you arrived, that lunatic of a woman offered me . . . suggested I . . . wanted me to . . ."

"Marry one of her boys?" he helped her out.

His voice held the sound of a smile. Rachel prickled like a porcupine. "There's nothing in that to amuse you, surely! I was horrified she'd suggest it with such . . . off-handedness."

"The farther west you go, the fewer the women," he said, as if the old woman's suggestion wasn't at all outrageous, but quite normal.

Mind working fast, Rachel returned swiftly, "Then a girl can afford to be choosy, can't she!"

He didn't bother to reply.

She asked, as they crested the ridge, "Where's Dorie?"

"Back at camp. Told her I was going huntin', just didn't say for what."

Anything but amused, Rachel forced herself to ask, "How'd you happen to come looking for me?"

"Sada was grazing with our horses when I went to get them this morning."

A wave of relief flowed over her. "Then she's not lost."

"Why didn't you do what I said? Why didn't you walk back to the post road and wait for Reverend Clark's party?"

"I was thinking about it. I really was," she insisted, at his noise of disbelief. "I took the matter up with the Lord and laid out the fleece, so to speak. I said, 'Lord, if you intend me to return to Francis, then don't let me catch Sada.' "

"Then you caught her, and decided He'd spoken." He gave his head a shake, the rim of his hat nearly brushing her forehead. "Like my Pappy used to say, 'Lord gets blamed for a lot of things He didn't have a thing to do with.' "

Ignoring what she didn't want to hear, Rachel said, "You never did tell me how you knew to come looking for me."

"When your horse turned up without you, I knew you had to be around somewhere close. Spotted that squatter's cabin, and figured it was the sort of choice you'd make. Inside, I found Sada's bridle and a bit of ribbon off your bonnet. The ground was soft, so it was no trick tracking you."

He pulled up in front of the squatter's cabin and went in to retrieve Sada's bridle. As he came back out with it, he paused in stepping over a broken plank. To her mortification, he picked the bloody thing up and all but waved it under her nose.

"Can't say as I blame that old woman for bein' a bit riled. And you, such a soft-looking lady."

Aware he was baiting her, Rachel lifted her chin and stared straight ahead. No matter how hard she tried, she couldn't keep the tears from filling her eyes. Bone-weary from the trauma of the night and previous day, all of her spirit had fled. She sniffed and wiped the back of her hand across her eyes. "It was self-defense. I have no doubt those creatures are demon-possessed. They'd have torn me to shreds and trampled me beneath their filthy hoofs!" Voice accusing, she added, "I suppose that would have pleased you."

"West is no place for you," he continued as if she hadn't spoken.

Shortly, she said, "Don't trouble yourself about it; you'll soon have me off your hands."

He said nothing further as they ambled along, but he'd succeeded in stirring up old memories. Her father had offered her mother a life in civilized society. It hadn't been enough; her mother had wanted more. Rachel had wanted more, too. They'd wanted *him,* but it was the one thing he never gave them.

When it came to accepting a husband, she didn't want one who'd promise to coddle her the rest of her life. In the West a woman was more than a woman, more than a wife. She was nearly as indispensable as water, fuel, and shelter. Yes, a woman in the West had to have more starch to her backbone than most Beacon Hill girls had to their mountains of petticoats!

The fact that she didn't want to rejoin Clark's group had become perfectly clear to Adam. But St. Louis was no place for her—her Eastern breeding stuck out like a mashed thumb. How glad Dorie would be to see her, though! And how disgruntled with him they'd both be when he put Rachel Whitaker on her horse and turned her back to retrace yesterday's path.

As they drew near the campsite, they saw that Dorie had put out the fire, packed the saddlebags, rolled the bedrolls far more neatly than the one wedged between Adam and Rachel.

At Rachel's greeting, Dorie whirled around and flew to her, her face empty of surprise but alight with joy. "I knew Papa'd find you!" she cried. "But I prayed all the same, prayed no harm had come to you."

Smiling, hugging the child hard, Rachel replied, "How'd you know he'd gone after me?"

"Because Sada was with our horses. He tried to tell me he was going hunting, but he didn't take his gun, so I knew . . ." Dorie paused and looked beyond Rachel, meeting Adam's gaze. "Thank you, Papa," she said softly. "Thank you for finding her."

"Dorie, show her how to roll a bedroll right, then let's get moving. We've lost enough time for one day."

The brooch, the clean drawers and chemise fell out of the roll in a heap. An ivory-handled hairbrush tumbled out on top. Fixing her with a stern glance, he said, "If you're comin' with us, you've got a lot to learn. This isn't Boston; you don't need a fancy dress or jewels. What you need is food and the means to prepare it. You haven't packed anything useful except your blankets."

"I had jerky," she said, hardly able to believe he intended to let her accompany them.

"Another thing," he went on, "you got to learn to respect other folks' property. You don't sleep over uninvited, you don't beat folks' livestock, and you don't turn your horse loose at night unless she's hobbled."

Turning away, he threw Dorie's saddle on Sada and lengthened the stirrups. He heard them behind him whispering as they tidied up the bedroll. Let 'em whisper, he thought, and packed his own horse.

When they'd finished with the bedroll, he fixed it behind Sada's saddle and directed Rachel to climb on. He swung into his own saddle then and motioned for Dorie to climb up in front of him. She shot him a sidelong glance.

"I can ride bareback."

"No need to. We'll reach Danville by tomorrow night. Until then, you're small enough, and we can sit two to a saddle."

"I'll ride with Miss Rachel, then," she said, and before he could reply, scrambled up behind Rachel.

With a flash of irritation, Adam shrugged and set out ahead of them, leading the roan. It occurred to him that Rachel Whitaker held in her soft, white hand the power to separate him from his daughter with an emotional aloofness that could prove as painful as the physical separation of the past five years.

And that made her his adversary.

chapter 14

CURIOUS THOUGH SHE WAS OVER ADAM'S change of heart, Rachel wasn't one to question the warm smile of good fortune.

They crossed the Iroquois River at midday. The wound on her head a fresh reminder of the hazards of such a crossing, she nearly panicked at the very thought. But Adam had the situation well in hand. He put her on his horse, directed her to let the animal pick his own way, then crossed ahead of her, Dorie in the saddle with him. The roan swam after them, and Rachel, not to be left behind, urged Adam's horse into the cold water. She hung onto the saddlehorn for dear life and prayed the whole way.

Though the crossing was made without incident, it drained what remained of her strength. In exchanging horses with Adam, she leaned weakly against Sada's wet flanks and tried to find the strength to pull herself into the saddle.

Adam's eyes narrowed as he watched her make a feeble attempt to get aboard. "When'd you last eat?"

She lowered her gaze. "Yesterday morning. Or was it noon? I don't recall."

He ordered, "Sit down. You're going to have to eat something."

"I don't want to be a bother. I can wait," she claimed.

"You faint or sicken, you'll be more than a bother," he said. Turning away to unfasten a saddlebag, he added, "Reckon Dorie's hungry, too."

He gave them the pemmican. Rachel nearly gagged on the first bite, but forced a bit more down, drank deeply from the river, then climbed back on Sada. Tired though she was, the food revived her to a degree.

They surprised a covey of quail late in the afternoon, and Rachel perked up some at the thought of a hot meal. Further on, Adam made camp. He cleaned the birds while Rachel and Dorie gathered firewood. Rachel couldn't remember when food had tasted any better.

Darkness fell before they'd finished eating, bringing with it a nip in the air. Adam built up the fire, then rolled out his blankets. Picking a spot well to the other side of the fire, Rachel followed suit. She took off her shoes and poor drooping bonnet and lay down, too exhausted to worry about wolves or snakes or any other such unfriendly critters.

Far from tired, Dorie seemed to be enjoying the expedition. When she got no encouragement from Rachel, she struck up a conversation with her father. Rachel fell asleep to the sound of Adam spinning a tale for his daughter—something about how the Blackfoot Indians came to hate all trappers.

The next morning, Rachel awoke to find Dorie snuggled up next to her. Adam was hunkered down near the fire cooking fish.

That was the delicious smell that'd awakened her! Extracting herself from the blankets in a ladylike manner was no easy chore. She awakened Dorie in the process. Suggesting they both go to the nearby pond to wash up, she reached for her shoes.

Bending over, hair curtaining her face, she pulled on one shoe and was sleepily struggling with the other when it dawned on her something was already *in* the shoe, something scrunched down in the toe, something that moved! She flung it off with a cry and hopped back as a little gray field mouse darted out of the shoe, circled it once in confusion, then dashed for the cover of taller grass.

"A mouse!" Dorie fell back on the blankets, giggling in delight.

Trying to collect her composure, Rachel murmured, "It startled me," and wished she hadn't been quite so zealous in casting the shoe away from her, for it'd landed very near to the spot where Adam was crouched down turning the fish, and remaining aloof.

Her big toe peeked out of a hole in her stocking. She drew her foot up to hide in the folds of her riding skirt and, standing on the other foot, timidly motioned toward the shoe, saying, "Would you . . ."

He reached over, picked it up and tossed it in her direction. "It's a good idea to shake 'em out b'fore you go pokin' your foot in 'em."

"So I see," Rachel murmured, and pulled on her shoe with as much dignity as she could muster.

Once she and Dorie had washed up, she braided Dorie's hair, then brushed her own, heartsick over the reflection the surface of the pond threw back at her. The wound on her head had scabbed over, contributing to her rough, hapless appearance. She despised feeling clammy and wrinkled!

Turning, she found Dorie's blue eyes on her—innocent eyes, *trusting* eyes. Her conscience burned as the child said softly, "I'm glad you came along, Miss Rachel. I'd be so lonesome without you."

Suddenly, all the discomfort, the trials, the mishaps she'd endured were a burden light enough to bear. "I'm glad, too," she said, and with a hug, urged her back to the fire, breakfast, and Adam.

"Eat all you can," he said. "We won't be noonin' today. Should reach Danville this evening."

The day proved to be another long, difficult one. Rachel lost count of the creeks they crossed. The roads were muddy and treacherous, so much so, it slowed their progress. Adam took to prairie and open fields for a time. They passed an occasional homestead, rode through a small settlement and stepped down off their horses long enough to let them drink.

Though Adam was patient and considerate of Dorie, he had little to say to Rachel, and what was said was in a distant voice. *So what?* Rachel asked herself. Yet the leaden sensation in her persisted as the day wore on and he managed to exclude her in his explanations to Dorie about the mill and the salt works in Danville, which contributed to the importance of the town.

The shadows were lengthening as they rode through heavy timber and forded two winding ribbons of water to reach Danville.

Modest by Eastern standards, frontierlike in appearance with its many log homes, Danville was nevertheless a center of civilization, which Rachel had begun to fear they'd long since left behind. She noticed as they picked their way along muddy streets, occasional plank-sided houses interspersed with cabins, a church, and the public land office. A courthouse near the public square was built, as were a fair sprinkling of business establishments, of timbers and plank siding.

Adam tipped his hat back and nodded to a flame-haired boy sitting on the steps of a dry-goods store. "We're lookin' for a place to spend the night. Could you direct us, son?"

The boy kept a firm arm around his wiggling pet. "Thar's three to choose from—J. W. Vance's hotel out at the salt works. Not so fancy as the Pennsylvania House on Vermilion Street, but they serve fair vittles that'll cost you half a cent less, and from time to time, a good fight breaks out, owin' to the fact some of the fellers from the salt works get to drinkin' and a braggin'. The McCormack House—Mr. McCormack's bent on makin' it the best hotel in town. And Mistress Priscilla don't 'low no brawling ner swearin'. Jest works fer Mr. McCormack, but she snaps out orders till she'd confuse a body into thinkin' she owns the place and half of Danville as well."

The McCormack House soon came into view—a two-story frame building, the full-length veranda of which served as a second-story balcony. The building, the balcony fence, and the supporting columns were all neatly whitewashed, and the windows were of glass, lending the establishment a prosperous air.

Adam tied his horse to the hitching post and the roan as well. Dorie, who'd ridden with Rachel the better part of the afternoon, scrambled down, and taking the reins from Rachel, followed her father's example. Seeming as eager as Rachel to be a part of civilization again, she was right on Adam's heels as he let himself in the front door of the building.

Rachel paused outside to read the posted notice: "No drinking, no brawling, no swearing."

Below that warning, the rates were posted. Rachel thought of her penniless state. Could she somehow earn her room and board for the night?

The door swung open and Adam, up a step, met her on eye level. "What's keepin' you?" he asked bluntly.

Her lashes swept down to conceal the humiliation she was feeling. She murmured, "Will they let me earn my keep? I'm not so . . . flush."

He was silent a moment. Glancing back over his shoulder, he stepped out beside her and closed the door behind him. "Payin's no problem. Better warn you, though, that woman in there'd starch a baby's breechcloth, she's that proper. That story you told the hog farmers about us being married—want to repeat it?"

She tightened her mouth and gave her head a toss to hide her embarrassment. "If the occasion arises, you have my permission to mislead the woman. For my part, I won't lie to her."

He pushed the door open. Across the room a woman turned from adding a log to a glowing fire. Cheeks flushed, she rose ramrod-straight, smoothed down her stiff white apron and pin-pointed them with a stern gray glance.

"Mr. Hawk, that scar on your face? Are you inclined to fisticuffs, Indian wrestling, or eye-gouging?"

His response was calm and soft-spoken. "No ma'am. Not without cause."

"Then see to it you find no cause while under the roof of the McCormack House."

"I'll abide by the rules, ma'am. Be obliged if you'd tell me where to get some supplies."

"Dry-goods store down the street. Before you head in that direction, take your horses around back to the stable. You'll find a boy there who'll care for them."

As Adam turned to go, Mistress Priscilla called after him, "If no more lodgers come, you and your family will have the room to your left at the top of the stairs to yourselves."

A jolt of alarm went through Rachel. She whirled around to face

Adam, words of objection forming in her throat. His warning look kept them there.

Behind her, Mistress Priscilla continued. "It's the women's room, though, so if we have more business, you'll be expected to remove yourself to the bachelor's room across the hall, Mr. Hawk."

"It'll suit," Adam said.

"Polly, fill the pitcher in the women's room so Mrs. Hawk can freshen up," Mistress Priscilla drummed out an order and, like a nervous cat, the serving girl twitched and leaped to obey.

Adam filled the front door long enough to deposit their meager belongings in a heap on the floor. Rachel started after them, but Mistress Priscilla ordered, "Leave them for Polly; she'll see to them."

Subdued by her own humble circumstances more than the woman's domineering manner, Rachel obeyed and started for the stairs. She'd no more than placed her foot on the first one when Mistress Priscilla had her last word.

"One more thing, Mrs. Hawk. Mr. McCormack runs a clean establishment. You'll take off your outer garments before getting in bed, please. And don't miss supper. Punctuality is expected. We begin serving at sundown."

Rachel met her level gaze, disliking the condescending flick of her gray eyes as they passed over her trail-dusty skirt and blouse. In the past, she'd occasionally encountered that same look from the eyes of a Beacon Hill matron. Lifting her chin, she replied, "If you'll excuse me, I'll change for supper."

The nerve of the woman! Running her eyes over her as if she were a wharf rat or something that had crawled out of a hole!

New England pride affronted to no end, she jerked off her bonnet and peered at her reflection in the small piece of glass hung over a dry sink.

The serving girl knocked softly, and at her response, entered with a sniff and a shuffle. Rachel stood to one side as she deposited a pitcher of water on the dry sink alongside the soap, towel, and face cloth.

"One pitcher won't be enough," she said, then softened her tone when the girl tensed and sniffed again. "Could you return in a bit to refill it?"

The girl hung her head. "Mistress Priscilla don't like extry work."

"Nor does she like trail-dusty lodgers," Rachel returned, though not unkindly. "In fact, I don't doubt she'd turn up her nose at a white-robed angel."

A ghost of a smile touched the girl's pale mouth.

From the bottom of the stairs, a clipped voice rang out, "Polly? No dawdling! The stage from Vincennes is due in within the hour. Hurry along."

Polly skittered out, dabbing her eyes on her apron skirt as she went. Unsure how long her solitude would last, Rachel stripped off her skirt and blouse, poured water into the utilitarian wash bowl and gave herself a much-needed scrubbing.

She was in the process of rubbing the rose-scented soap into her hair when Polly returned with her belongings. Eyes clamped shut, head bowed over the wash bowl, nimble fingers kneading her hair and scalp, she paid little heed to Polly's puttering sounds behind her. Though she'd been stingy with the water, there wasn't enough left to rinse the soap from her hair. Wringing the water from her hair, she groped around for the muslin towel, blotted her eyes, then wrapped it around her hair.

"Needs emptyin'," Polly pronounced and took the wash bowl as well as the pitcher. By the time she returned with fresh water, Rachel had changed into her fresh undergarments.

Rachel thanked her and finished rinsing her hair, squeezed the water from it, and dressed in her brocade before splashing her blouse and riding skirt around in what remained of the water. Doubting they'd be dry by morning, she nonetheless carried them out to the balcony off the central hallway and draped them over the lattice-work fencing to catch the fading rays of the sun.

The evening breeze was cool as it teased a path through her damp hair. She returned to her room for her hairbrush, then came back to the balcony, hoping to brush her hair dry before the supper hour was announced.

From her vantage point, she saw the stage come in with a rumble and a flourish. Three men and an elderly woman—her salvation from sharing a room with Adam Hawk!—alighted.

Good smells were wafting up from the kitchen. Her stomach began to scratch and whine. She braided her still-damp hair in a single thick plait, and listened for the dinner bell as sleepy shadows stole over the street.

Adam and Dorie were coming up the stairs as she headed for her room. Her spirits lifted at the sound of their voices. She stood in the gray corridor, waiting for them with a smile. "How was the shopping expedition?"

"Laid in some supplies. Don't reckon you'll have to force down any more pemmican," he said, his tone faintly mocking.

Rachel murmured, "Did I complain?"

"Not your mouth—just your face." His smile was faint, but it was there. "Afraid we couldn't scare up another saddle though. So we bought you a consolation gift. Go on, show her, Dorie."

Dorie flung open the door to their room, dropped the parcel on the bed, and untied the string. She turned back to Rachel, a bright green ribbon in her hand. Eyes bright with anticipation, she asked, "Do you like it?"

It was just a simple satin ribbon. No reason for her to be so strangely touched. Except that they'd remembered her, included her, selected this particular ribbon from among who knew how many other colors.

"It's beautiful! I love it!" she exclaimed sincerely, and promptly tied it in her hair, securing the thick plait.

"You like it better than red?" Dorie quizzed.

"Infinitely better!" Rachel gave her a hug, then laughed when Dorie shrugged.

"Guess you were right, Papa. How did you know she'd like green best?"

To Rachel's surprise, he looked embarrassed. Muttering a few unintelligible words, he backed out of the room and disappeared down the stairs.

At dinner, Rachel was wedged between the elderly woman who'd come in on the stage, thereby ensuring Adam's banishment to the bachelor's room, and Adam, with Dorie on his far side. Since little conversation flowed, Rachel was left to her own devices, and began worrying about the problem of a saddle. An idea began to form.

Polly was the seed of it. She flitted in and out of the kitchen like a frightened waif. Each time she passed Rachel, her gaze lingered upon the luxurious brocade dress.

Unlike the East where people lingered at the table following a meal, Westerners gulped their food and fled. When Rachel remained behind, Polly came along to inquire, "Didn't you get enough to eat? I'm a-feared the pot's wiped clean."

"I've eaten more than enough, thank you, Polly. It was quite delicious, too." She paused, selecting her words with care. "Polly, I've been thinking about you. I'm in need of a saddle. Would you be interested in trading for this dress?"

Polly's eyes widened as Rachel spread her skirts. "You'd trade that dress for an old saddle? My brother's got an old saddle. It ain't much, but I reckon he'd part with it if I promised to do his washin' for a month of Sundays."

Rachel thrust out her hand and the deal was shaken upon. With a feeling of accomplishment, she went looking for Adam. He was on the balcony, looking out over the town spread below.

If he was impressed by her initiative, he was careful not to let it show. Still a little touchy about the ribbon, perhaps. Strange man.

She started away, then turned back when he called her name. He leaned his back to the railing and studied her face. "Don't suppose you'd like to sell me your horse when we get to St. Louis."

It struck her as an odd request. St. Louis should have horses aplenty. A slow smile crept to her lips. "If you're afraid that, left with a horse, I'd follow you on across the plains, rest easy, Mr. Hawk. I have no such adventuresome intentions."

He turned silent again, giving credence to her suspicion. A touch of mischief stirred in her soul. She said lightly, "And if I did, the small matter of being without my horse wouldn't delay me for long.

Not to boast, but I'm fairly inventive when the occasion demands it."

Mockingly he tipped his hat to her, and rumbled, "So I've noticed. And it's landed you in more than a bit of trouble."

A bit miffed, she quickly recovered. After all, he'd been the one who'd bailed her out of more than one predicament. And there was the ribbon to soften his words, too. She fingered it lightly and smiled. "I'll tell you what, Mr. Hawk. I'm in your debt and will remain so until we reach St. Louis. In payment, I'll *give* you Sada. Fair enough?"

"No," he said evenly. "I'll pay you, or she'll remain yours, and finding a place to board her will be your headache."

Despite her efforts to be gracious, he was getting under her skin. Bidding him a less than warm good evening, she gathered her damp clothes off the railing and slipped off to her room where the old woman was snoring and poor Dorie was huddled against the wall with her fingers stopping her ears.

Rachel draped her dress across a chair, her damp skirt and blouse from the wash stand, then blew out the candle. Once in bed, she found herself wide awake. But she lay very still, so as not to disturb either Dorie or the old squeeze-box. By and by Dorie curled into her arms and the tension left her. Gently, she kissed the child's brow and closed her eyes.

chapter 15

BEFORE DAWN came an annoyingly persistent rapping of knuckles upon the door. Rachel scrambled to her feet and padded to the door.

"Yes, what is it?" she called in a sleepy voice.

"It's Polly, ma'am. I've stowed the saddle in the stables."

Rachel pushed the hair out of her eyes and opened the door. While the girl twitched from one anxious foot to the other, Rachel gathered up the dress, and after a moment's hesitation, contributed her bonnet as well. "It goes with the dress. A bit ragged for the past few day's wear, but some new ribbons and such should put it to rights."

The girl's eyes filled with tears. Clumsily trying to hide them, she stammered, "God bless you, yer kindness makes it harder." Dropping her gaze from Rachel's face, she murmured, "Miss Priscilla's waitin' to see you downstairs. Was a young man asleep on the doorstep when she came to start the breakfast fixin'. Say's he be yer brother."

"Samuel," Rachel muttered, and the girl slid her a curious look.

"Jest repeatin' what he said, so don't take no offense."

"Go on," Rachel urged, bracing herself for the worst.

"Says you and Mr. Hawk ain't married," Polly pushed out in a rush. "Got Miss Priscilla riled up somethin' awful. She's one fer keepin' a proper establishment. Don't like no tomfoolery goin' on under her nose. Already tore a piece off Mr. Hawk's hide and ordered him out. Said to wake up you and the girl. Wants the pair of you gone, too."

Rachel closed the door and yanked on clothes still damp from yesterday's washing. She jerked the brush through her hair and arranged the new ribbon to secure it at the nape of her neck.

Using the candle Polly'd left behind to light the candle on the wash stand, she called softly to Dorie. At the child's sleepy reply, she said, "Get dressed and come downstairs. We're getting an early start."

Less afraid of Miss Priscilla than she was of the damage Samuel had done to her plans to continue with Adam and Dorie, she set her chin and marched into the kitchen.

Mistress Priscilla swung away from the iron stove. Her eyes glowed from a stormy countenance. Prodding the air with a finger, she let go with a rush of clipped words: "What you are, madam, is between you and your God. This much, I know. You intentionally deceived me. You mock the institution of marriage and set a black example for little Polly. Quite smitten, she was, with your fancy dress and your pretty manners. The devil wears many disguises." So saying, she pointed her pinched nose toward the door and ordered, "I want you out!"

Rachel's chin climbed, her back grew poker straight, her gaze fiery, but steady. Haughtily, she said, "I assume Samuel's gone?"

"What he has done is none of my affair."

"And Mr. Hawk?"

The woman sniffed. "Out in the stable."

Rachel smoothed her riding skirt. "I'll join him there. You'll be kind enough to give Dorie a bite of breakfast before sending her out?"

Fresh waves of indignation set that woman's tongue to clattering again. Eyes narrowing, she declared, "No business rearing a child, neither one of you. What possible chance does that little girl have? What will she ever know about right and wrong? A half-breed spawned in sin."

A great wave of fury swept through Rachel. Hands trembling, she replied, "And you, my dear woman, are a half-wit!" She marched out the back door, the rage within boiling and unsettling her stomach.

It was Samuel's misfortune to step out of the shadows just as she neared the stable door. She screeched to a halt and eyed him coldly. "If it has escaped your attention, Samuel Pierce, I am a full-grown woman, accountable before God and man for my own actions. I neither want nor appreciate your grim feeling of responsibility toward me. Now if you please, ride back to your father with this message: I'm traveling on to St. Louis where I plan to open a shop much like the one back in Boston. I'd appreciate it if he'd send my trunks. I will write, informing him of my safe arrival. The letter should beat him to Galesburg, but upon receiving it, I want him to consider his duty to me fulfilled." She ground to a halt and drew a deep breath, the heat of her anger flushing her face and carrying her words on the still, predawn air.

Samuel moved into her path, preventing her bursting into the stable. "You're clearly overwrought, Rachel. I don't know what that man has done to you, but whatever it is, you're not to blame. 'Twas in the depths of your grief that you chose rashly to follow the likes of him. Your thoughts were muddled and you went in innocence. And as far as I'm concerned, if you return with me now, your reputation is firmly intact."

"How large-minded of you, Samuel!"

He gripped her arm, his voice changing. "Don't take that tone with me, Rachel. I'm your brother, and I'm trying to remove you as gracefully as I can from a damaging situation."

Snatching her arm back out of his reach, she replied, "You are no more my brother than is Adam Hawk, and if the truth were known, I doubt that your thoughts toward me are as noble as his. He has not, nor will he, take advantage of me. It is *I* who've taken advantage of *him*."

"You don't know what you're saying!"

"That's right, Samuel. I've taken advantage of his knowledge of the land, of his experience in traveling, of his ability to deal with every unforeseen circumstance. And I intend to do so until I reach St. Louis."

"Please, Rachel, use your head!" Samuel gave one last try. "If you're bent on going to St. Louis, then buy a ticket on the stage. It'll be a more comfortable trip, more speedy, too. And you'll be safe."

"Nonsense. I'm perfectly safe with Adam Hawk," Rachel stood her ground. "I trust him, I like him, and I adore his little daughter. Their company is undemanding and comforting, too."

Samuel drew himself up into a straight, slight line, his whole being distressed to the limit. His voice an ominous hiss, he declared, "If your mother could see what's become of you, she'd turn over in her grave."

All the rage left her. She slumped against the stable door, far more wounded by his parting words than the doubt he'd cast upon her character. As he mounted his horse and rode off without a backward glance, she felt the last of her earthly ties being crisply severed. She wouldn't see Samuel again—or Francis or Philip. And somehow, she felt she had willfully failed them; abandoned them; selfishly, purposely set them aside to pursue . . . what?

She covered her face with her hands, aware of a dull ache where tears should be. Her head was beginning to hurt, and the chill of the air was creeping in. "Dear God," she prayed. Nothing further would come.

The smell of the stables wafted toward her as Adam swung open the door and led out their horses. The glance he gave her was none too approving. She flushed at the knowledge he'd overheard every word. Tears—repentance or self-pity?—stung her eyes. Unmoved by them, he motioned for her to take her horse.

"Not too late to catch up with him," he pointed out.

She shook her head. "Even if I wanted it to, it wouldn't work."

He pushed his hat back and looked east. The shade of night was edging away. "He made a good point. You could take the stage. Much easier trip."

He knew she didn't have any money. Too proud to voice it again, she murmured, "I'll go on with you and Dorie, if you're still willing."

He scratched a stubbled chin. "Don't know why you're makin' it so hard on yourself."

Avoiding his gaze, she swung up unassisted. "Let's say I like your company. You're capable. Unthreatening. I feel safe."

"That much, you are," he said, and ambled off to meet Dorie as she bumped out the back door, rubbing her eyes.

The day of travel passed, quiet and uneventful, and the next, much the same. Rachel did her best to be useful, fetching wood, carrying water, fixing whatever game Adam skillfully claimed for meals. The cinch on her saddle broke in late afternoon of the third day. Though several hours of daylight remained, Adam elected to make camp.

After they'd eaten and Rachel sat cleaning the fire-blackened skillet, Adam put his capable hands to fixing the cinch.

Frowning at the makeshift job, he said, "Might get you to St. Louis. Should reach the Mississippi tomorrow, if the good weather holds together better'n this saddle of yours."

Mildly affronted, Rachel made her defense saying, "I traded sight unseen."

"Seldom puts you on the winning side of the fence," he observed.

Slapping at a thirsty mosquito, she eyed the repaired saddle as Adam cast it aside, and spared her lovely brocade dress a wistful thought. Her earthly possessions had dwindled down to a precious few—Mama's brooch, the hairbrush, the clothes on her back.

Dorie settled next to Adam and began unbraiding her hair, a huge yawn overtaking her. Adam watched her, his hands idle.

Covertly studying the man, Rachel thought she detected a yearning in the depths of his fine blue eyes, a shyness toward his own child. It hurt her in some queer way that reached back into her own childhood. Why didn't he hug the child and meet the need within Dorie and himself? Exasperation entangled with unexpected tenderness, she found her hairbrush and pitched it to him.

His gaze, now on her, was questioning. She gestured toward Dorie, saying, "Give her a hand. She's nearly asleep."

The shadows were lengthening, but enough light remained for her to make out the awkwardness in the big, rough hands that accomplished so many tasks with such apparent ease. Dorie winced a time or two as he tugged the brush through her hair, but seemed pleased by the attention. When he made short work of the ritual, she fixed her blue eyes upon him and complained he'd fallen short of the customary one hundred strokes.

His slow smile came out. "You can collect those remainin' from Miss Rachel in the mornin'. Time to bed down now; long day ahead of us tomorrow."

The child tarried a while longer, battling with heavy eyelids. Her black hair fanned against the fringe of his buckskins as she leaned against his shoulder and studied his face. "Papa? What made the mark on your face?"

Rachel caught her breath as dark memory stole the serenity from his features. His hand rose to the scarred and unshaven cheek, then fell back to his lap again.

"A coupla unfriendly sorts makin' a point, that's all. Nothin' for you to worry your head over. Go on now, climb into those blankets and get some sleep."

Dorie detoured for a hug and a kiss from Rachel, then settled down with a sigh. Adam tossed a log on the fire and mumbled something about checking the horses. Rachel sat watching night come down. Coffee remained in the pot. Glad he'd been able to restock his supply, she resisted the urge to put it back on the fire. They'd reheat it in the morning. It'd taste like plowed ground by then, but Adam wouldn't notice. It never got too thick or too black for his taste. Or maybe he was just the uncomplaining sort. Not once had he made a negative comment about her cooking, and in all honesty, it wasn't one of her strengths.

Bone-tired, she let her hair loose and drew the brush through it. Then she knew the penalty for giving away her bonnet—the natural side part in her hair had sunburned. The bristles bit into her tender scalp.

Adam reappeared to throw an armload of sticks on the fire. He spared her a glance and commented, "Wishin' for your bonnet back, I'll wager. Sunburn's a mite painful, is it?"

"I'll survive it, I suppose," she said, and continued her brushing.

"A little bear grease'd put you to rights."

Her glance was skeptical. "If that's the same foul-smelling concoction pasting that pemmican together, I'll decline, thank you all the same."

His chuckle was amicable. "Good thing St. Louis is your jumpin' off place. Further west a body goes, the more sensitivities give way to common sense."

He was as determined as ever to take Dorie into Indian country, she knew. Did she dare try to bring him to his senses? Somehow, she was reluctant to quarrel with him on this, their last night together. Beneath her blankets, she turned to the Lord in prayer. He knew the paths of the sea, did he not? He'd called the mountains into being and knew the minds of both peasant and king. She could not sway Adam Hawk's plans, but God could, and it was her fervent prayer that he would take the matter under immediate consideration and expedite circumstances that would prevent Adam from following through with his intentions.

Sleep soon overtook her, but once its hard edge wore thin, night noises intruded upon her shallow rest. Twice, she opened her eyes—once, to identify the glittery yellow eyes of a talkative hoot owl; the second, to reassure herself that Dorie, who was a bit of a night-thrasher, hadn't rolled too near the fire. She was in the act of gathering her blankets when Adam cried out. First stunned, then chilled by the wildness in his voice, she clutched the blankets to her and whirled in his direction. He lay motionless. She let out her caught breath, her pulse steadying. But as she moved past him, circling to the other side of the fire, he thrashed with his arms and legs and let go with a scream that curdled her blood. Knowing he'd awaken Dorie if not silenced, Rachel whispered, "Adam! Adam!" and prodded him with her foot.

A great shudder ripped through him, and he jerked free of imagined fetters, snatched his knife, and seized the prodding foot.

Rachel hit the ground, her indignant cry rending the still night air. Still vibrating from the impact of crashing to earth, she felt all the air driven from her lungs as he threw himself upon her. It unfolded within a fraction of a second, yet she saw it clearly, succinctly, like neatly aligned stepping stones—the spill, his hard-muscled body pinning her, the knife, wicked-looking, clutched in his uplifted hand. Too little time, too numb, too terrified, she squeezed her eyes shut, hardly aware of her own scream.

And then she could breathe again. He was off her, backing away, slumping against the solid black trunk of a tree. The trembling spread like a violent rockslide until she was almost physically sick with it. Too shaken to move, she lay staring at unblinking stars, letting the terror diminish.

"You hurt?" he asked, his grim-sounding words intruding upon the electrified silence.

"No, I don't think so." She flexed her limbs and slowly untangled herself from the blankets she'd been carrying.

He sank to the ground, back supported by the same tree. His hand was unsteady as it combed through his hair, and though the air was cool, beads of perspiration moistened his brow. Without warning, anger rushed in to cover less-decisive emotions. He jerked to his feet and pointed an accusing finger. "That wasn't jest plain stupid, it was flirtin' with death. Don't ever *ever* slip up on me like that again!"

Indignation restored a bit of her spirit. She lunged to her feet and glared back at him. "Slip up on you? I didn't slip up on you. You were thrashing around yelling in your sleep and I poked you, that's all. Don't tell me I was supposed to let you scream until you awakened Dorie?"

He gave his head a disbelieving shake, and spoke softly. "I could've killed you."

"It must have been some dream you were having," she ventured awhile later, handing him a steaming cup. "Perhaps it would help to talk about it."

"Talk's what brought it on." As he spoke, he touched his scarred cheek.

Understanding rushed in. "The scar?" she murmured, and he nodded.

Rachel sipped the strong brew and turned her face toward the fire. A breeze sighed through the trees. What kind of life had he lived that his sleep should be as scarred as his face? If she was ever to know, now was the time to ask. He sat down next to her, close enough so that she could have ventured a sympathetic hand on his arm.

Rachel firmed up her grip on her coffee cup and drew a quick breath. Her question floated out airy and uncertain: "Was it hostiles?"

"You could call 'em that. Yep, 'hostiles' describes 'em fair to accurate." He reached for a stick, fingers toying with the limber green end of it. Without warning, words weary and haunted-sounding spilled free.

"It was a Blackfoot raiding party. Caught me trapping in the north country. Set about making me see the error of my ways." He drew a deep breath, and it seemed to shudder on the air as he blew it out slowly. "They draw death out, test a man's courage a hundred and one ways. Cry out, and you earn scorn and a slower death."

Rachel hugged her knees to her chest and buried her face in them as he continued. "There was seven of them. Knocked me around a bit, then built 'em a fire. I did some fast repentin' while they gathered some green sticks and got the ends of them glowing orange. Took turns then, one of 'em poking a stick against my face while the others held me down. My brain kept shouting down the screams, and I never uttered a sound. It's just in my dreams . . ."

She shut off his voice, the horror of his words crawling along her nerve-endings. And how dare he sound strangely prideful! Were all men such stubborn stupid creatures? He'd earned his nightmares, that's what she'd tell him. But Dorie . . . Dorie was a helpless child.

". . . hadn't come along when he did, there'd be nothin' left of me but a pile of bleached bones along the banks of a cold, swift-running stream. But the Frenchman had a gift. He could barter with 'em all, even the Blackfoot," he was saying.

Rachel bit back her calculated cold words and drifted into listening again as he told how Jean-Claude had purchased Adam's freedom with a keg of whiskey; of the storm they'd braved making their escape; of the friendship that had ensued, and finally of their trip to St. Louis where Jean-Claude introduced him to the Murphys and to Shining Meadow, the Oto girl who became his wife.

His voice gentled at the mention of his dead wife, then became shrouded with guilt as he spoke of the smallpox epidemic and his absence from the village at the critical time. She remembered then an earlier quarrel, and in the light of this new understanding, realized the cruelty of the questions she'd hurled at him. *Where had Dorie's father been each time she'd needed him?*

"You were going about the business of supporting your family." She struggled to be fair.

"It was more than that," he said, regret marking his words. "We wouldn't have starved without those winter furs. I knew that. It was the itch to be on the move. That, and the hard feelings of an Oto brave. I figured the way he felt toward me, one of us'd be dead before spring if we both spent the winter in the village. And me bein' a natural-born rambler, it was easy to go." He blew out a sigh. "The comin' back and findin' things the way they were—that was the not-so-easy part. I lit long enough to see the death, the chaos, the grief. Long enough to assume the worst."

He went on to tell her of Jean-Claude's good intentions in taking Dorie to safety, and of the hard feelings that later developed, causing the Frenchman to seek revenge, his target, Adam's most vulnerable spot.

"And should you run into this Frenchman again? And what of the Indian you mentioned? It appears to me nothing but trouble awaits you. Don't go, Adam. Please don't go. Dorie's your child, your responsibility, a responsibility that outweighs any promise you made to her grandfather!"

chapter 16

RACHEL WAS STIFF AND TIRED OF RIDING long before they neared the Illinois bank of the proud Mississippi. The sight of the broad-backed, slow-moving waters failed to relieve her.

On the opposite bank, built on ground that rose to overlook the national waterway was St. Louis—the end of the journey for her. Tomorrow, Adam and Dorie would continue without her, crossing the plains into the very heart of Indian territory. Though the day still held its warmth, she shivered as she studied the other shore.

Even from this distance, it was clear that St. Louis was an up-and-coming city. Impressive structures of brick, stone, and timber lined ribbon streets. Church spires reached skyward and the waterfront, running as far as she could see, was dotted with steamboats, ferryboats, barges, and waterworthy vessels of various description.

The sun curtsied in the west, bleeding pink and glorious. Rachel turned her attention to her own side of the river. A convolution of wagons and carts, livestock and people crowded toward the river where the ferries docked. Campfires dotted the public grounds like fireflies at twilight. The sight and the sound, the smell of the river was familiar, but with the black water beyond them, Rachel felt the vulnerability of these restless, hopeful people.

What was she doing here? Why had she come? In a moment of youthful honesty, she admitted that more than concern for Dorie had induced her to stick to the pair of them like a bit of lace to a cuff.

"You got a plan of your own, or are you comin' with us?"

"Aren't we crossing?" she asked.

He pointed out the length of the line waiting to cross the river. "No point in waiting—we wouldn't get a turn before mornin' anyway. Come on. I know some folks in Cahokia who'll put us up for the night."

It was dark by the time they reached Cahokia. Adam's friend was French; a retired trapper, Pierre Benét was now engaged in the business of operating a billiard hall that linked onto his home.

Pierre embraced Adam with an affectionate warmth, then ushered them into his lamplit, slant-roofed cottage. The cottage was built of stone; additions jutted off at odd angles, giving it a hodgepodge personality, but the furnishings were elegant, and looked to have come from Pierre's home country. Gay curtains hung at the windows and soft-hued woven rugs covered the floor. The settee was grandly carved, the cushions worked in intricate needlework and sweetly inviting. Pierre intercepted her glance, made a sweeping bow and begged them all to sit while he went for his wife.

Not so tired as to forget common courtesy, Rachel remonstrated, "Don't trouble her if she's retired for the evening."

"No, no. She's in the summer kitchen fussing over the stove. Perhaps a sparrow told her we'd have company tonight." A white smile split his sun-weathered face. He clapped Adam on the back. "Adam Hawk come to our house is an occasion. We'll make a party. Sing, dance, play a small game of billiards, perhaps?"

He bowed again and disappeared through a door at the rear of the house.

Rachel sank onto the settee with a weary sigh. Dorie leaned against her and was soon dozing. By and by their host reappeared with his wife at his side. A plump round-faced woman in a satin gown, Ann-Marie Benét smiled and extended a hand. Adam bowed and brought it to his lips, saying, "It's good to see you again, Ann-Marie. It's been quite a spell. Pierre's treatin' you well, is he?"

Unaccustomed to this courtly side, Rachel listened to his polite inquiries after her family. The dark-lashed, big-eyed Ann-Marie accounted for four daughters, all of whom had married and left home since Adam's last visit.

Pierre wrapped an arm around his wife. "Our daughters are beauties, it is true. But not a one is as lovely as their mother whose eyes will rain like the dew if our friend Adam Hawk comes with bad news of her brother. If you have seen Jean-Claude, tell us, Adam. It has been too many years since we've heard from him."

"And then, only a brief message from Madame Murphy in St. Louis," Ann-Marie spoke up, her voice soft with concern. "She told us it was your wish that Jean-Claude take the little one to the East where she could be taught the social graces of the 'Bostons'. This is the same child?"

When Adam nodded, she implored, "Then you *have* seen Jean-Claude?"

"Haven't seen Jean-Claude in some time," Adam spoke at last. "But I hear tell of his dealings." His hard tone settled the mystery.

So this visit to a village some miles out of their way held a purpose other than a night's lodging. He was looking for news of Jean-Claude, but Ann-Marie obviously had nothing to tell.

Pierre had changed into a silk blouse and a gold-buttoned blue satin jacket. He took charge of smoothing away the awkward moment.

Ann-Marie was a superb cook and a gracious hostess. No more mention was made of her brother over the meal of gumbo, spit-roasted turkey, bread, and pastries.

Pierre challenged Adam to a billiard game and led him away. Without the cheery support of her husband, some of the gaiety fled from Ann-Marie's face. Her gaze direct, she murmured, "Monsieur Hawk has been in *les montagnes luissants*—the Shining Mountains—too long. When it comes to sharing word of his friend, my brother, he turns shy as a mink."

Rachel grew uncomfortably warm. She dared not tell the woman anything vital. She said, "You're most kind, inviting us into your home and providing such a fine meal."

But her hostess was not so easily put off. Her voice a plea, she murmured, "We're friends, *oui?*"

Rachel's hand tightened around the crumpled napkin in her lap. "I hope so, yes. But as for news of your brother, I can't help you. Adam Hawk doesn't confide in me."

Ann-Marie's sigh was troubled. "It was on a trip home to St. Louis that Jean-Claude brought Monsieur Hawk into our lives. Those were happy days, before the devils of drink raged within Jean-Claude." She laced her plump fingers together and rested her hands on the lace tablecloth.

"It is a hard thing to understand that my brother should be controlled by drink. Now the 'Bostons' . . ." She waved her hand in an expansive manner that led Rachel to believe the term included all Americans and the English as well. ". . . they are known for their insatiable appetite for drink, and the distress it causes. But the French? They are not a people to be so ruled. I confess it steals my joy to think of my brother so possessed."

Rachel was too sorry for the woman to resent her implication that the French, in this matter, were superior to all others. She turned her attention to Dorie who was reaching for yet another pastry.

"You'd better not; you'll be sick," she warned, and gentled her admonition by squeezing the child's sticky hand. "It's a chore just keeping your eyes open, isn't it?"

Once again the perfect hostess, Ann-Marie slid her chair back and stretched out a hand to Dorie. "Come, little one, we'll see you off to bed. Mademoiselle, perhaps you would like to freshen up. Pierre will play the fiddle soon and others will come."

As they traveled a corridor into yet another portion of the stone house, Ann-Marie held her lamp steady. She opened the door to a room modest in size, but appealing in its fine furnishings and cheery colors. Another lamp was lit.

The Indian girl brought warm water, and Ann-Marie left Rachel to the task of preparing Dorie for bed. The girl had no more than slipped beneath the covers when her eyelids closed. Rachel kissed her cheek, then turned to her own toilet.

From another part of the house came the warming notes of the fiddle and the hum of distant voices. Her shoulders drooped as she considered her dusty clothes.

A knock sounded at the door. At her invitation, Adam stepped in. "What's keepin' you? You won't want to miss all the jollification. No one loves fun more than the French."

His boyish grin did little toward bolstering her courage. She turned her back on him, saying, "It's been a long day, all I want to do is go to bed."

She turned to see him frown. When that did nothing to change her mind, he cajoled her, saying, "You're past due for a good time. Come on, Rachel. This is the end of the journey for you. Don't you want to celebrate?"

She blinked to keep tears from filling her eyes. A part of her was crying out for an evening of fun. But the way that she looked, the uncertainty she felt over the days that lay ahead . . . Pleading now, she burst out, "They're like French royalty, decked out in their finery. Would you look at us? I've seen better-dressed stable boys!"

"Before we have a knock-down and drag-out over this, let me say I've been a-watchin' Pierre's front door and there's not been a gal yet waltz through any prettier'n you. So stop bein' so all-fired vain and let's go."

Before Rachel could answer one way or the other, Ann-Marie knocked and stepped in. If finding Adam in the room surprised her, her manner was impeccably polite.

"It is a better party than I'd hoped for," she said. "And you, Mademoiselle, are so weary. I hope that something bright and cheerful will drive the fatigue from your bones. My only regret is, I have nothing finer to offer you."

So saying, she spread a blue calico dress on the bed, and placed a neat pile of undergarments beside it.

Rachel murmured, "You're most kind."

Ann-Marie shook the folds from the blue dress. "It belonged to my youngest, Mimi. The shoes as well. She married a river pilot and now lives in New Orleans. Such fine gowns she describes in her letters!"

She held the dress up to Rachel and eyed her consideringly. "It needs a sash, I think. And a fresh ribbon for your hair."

Ignoring Rachel's feeble protests, she sailed out, leaving Rachel to strip to the skin and wash before donning the clean clothes.

The dress was not a perfect fit, nor nearly as grand as some she'd known in the past, but she was grateful for the clean, fresh scent of it. She was slipping into the silver-buckled shoes when Ann-Marie returned.

Not until Rachel had tied on the red sash and fixed the ribbon in her loose hair did her hostess nod approval. Her gaze was both mischievous and shrewd. She said, "Monsieur Hawk will lose his heart, if he hasn't already. He's your *amant, oui?*"

"*Amant?*" Rachel echoed, her face growing warm.

"Your sweetheart?"

"No, no, you misunderstand."

"But you'd like to belong to him?" Ann-Marie's smile was knowing.

Rachel fussed with the sash and avoided the older woman's gaze. "That'd be foolish. You can't belong to a wanderer. We're traveling together, that's all. The reasons are . . . complicated."

Watching Rachel in the thick mirror, Ann-Marie perched on the bed and pursed her lips. "You are wise, Mademoiselle. Wanderers are difficult as lovers. Trappers, men of the waters, men of the mountains and plains. They answer to a different voice. They are lured by the cry of the wilderness wind, by the rivers and the vast blue sky. I know. When my Pierre was young, he was a coming-and-going man. My heart was often anxious for him."

"But now—" Rachel stopped herself, but too late. Having so neatly trapped her, Ann-Marie smiled sagely. She held a hand to her ear.

"Hear the singing? The dancing? It's that of coming-and-going men and those who belong to them. Most of the wandering ones have left for the long journey and the rendezvous on Green River. There are a few late ones, ones who resist the changes of time. The West changes, too. Still the parties are for those who must be parted. Much laughter and happy memories to store away for the long months of separation."

If those from the village traveled into Indian territory, why was Ann-Marie without word of her brother? So thinking, Rachel blurted the question.

Ann-Marie's small red mouth turned down. "They are my neighbors, my friends. If he were dead, they would feel it kinder to tell me than to leave me wondering. But if it is simply news that would make me feel shame, they keep quiet. I thought Monsieur Hawk would be more frank."

Rachel had no words to comfort. But her hostess didn't seem to expect any. She led the way to the door, saying, "We are missing the party. And you, most of all, should not. It is a small time to know joy without fear of tomorrow. You and your *amant* should learn that."

"He isn't . . ."

Ann-Marie trickled laughter. "Affairs of honor are settled on Bloody Island. But affairs of the heart? Many have been settled with fiddle and dance."

Perhaps, but not so with Adam, Rachel thought later. The door that separated the parlor from the billiard room stood open, and through it, she caught glimpses of him, engrossed in a game. She turned away with a sniff. Had he coaxed her out here simply to ignore her? Perhaps she'd read too much into his insistence she attend the party. The furnishings had been pushed against the wall, the piece of rich, worn carpet rolled back. Bright faces, laughing couples, and solitary dancers darted to and fro, filling the room with noise and warmth and merriment. But Rachel felt removed. Tomorrow was a few hours away and all that lay ahead was loneliness and uncertainty.

What a pitiful thing she was, standing here, unspoken hopes clutched in a fist she didn't dare open! She straightened her spine, drew a ragged breath and looked around to find a young Frenchman watching her, a speculative twinkle in his eye.

Before she could look away, he was bowing and reaching for her hand. "I'm afraid I'm not much of a dancer," she said.

But he brushed aside her excuse and grinned a broad white grin. "Oh, but *I* am," he said. "And an excellent teacher as well. You will learn swiftly, and all the others will sigh and be envious over what a beautiful couple we make."

Rachel couldn't help laughing at his outrageous bravado. She allowed him to lead her through the steps, unaware Adam's preoccupation with his billiard game had suddenly wavered.

"She is a pretty one, is she not?"

Adam surfaced from his churlish reverie to find Ann-Marie watching him, her expression coy, but her eyes uncomfortably knowing.

"She's that, all right," he said, and shifted his weight.

"And light on her feet, too." A small smile crept to the round red lips. "I don't believe she'd tramp upon your toes, should you dare to be her next partner."

Adam responded with a sheepish smile of his own.

"Have you quarreled?" Ann-Marie caught him by surprise.

"No more so than usual," he mumbled, and added, "We don't see eye to eye on loyalty or the honor of a man's word, among other things." Even as he spoke, his attention strayed to Rachel.

Ann-Marie smiled a tolerant smile, but her eyes were deeply troubled. "I wasn't speaking of the girl. It is my brother, Jean-Claude, I question you about—have you quarreled with him?"

Adam chose his words carefully. "Don't reckon I'd worry you with it if we had."

"It is why you've come to my house, is it not? You seek word of Jean-Claude," she persisted.

Looking away from her, he murmured, "He took something precious from me. I've got it back. I want him to know that, in the end, he didn't beat me."

"That's important to you, is it?" The sternness of her voice commanded his full attention. Eyes flashing, she was no longer soft and feminine, but fierce and formidable. "You men with your pride! Your foolish games. Precious things are paraded beneath your nose every day. How slow you are to see them!"

He gaped, slow to comprehend her ire. She shook her head. "You, Adam Hawk! You will lose her. So busy are you in your man's world, redeeming honor, proving loyalty, valor! You will leave her behind and a more deserving man will have her. It was the same with Jean-Claude. More than one village girl set her cap for him, but for him, it was the wandering way. A boy in a man's body, never quite grown up. And now, what of him? Does he have children to honor him? A wife to grow old with him? No, only a sister to fear what will become of him."

Before he could turn away, she murmured, "If I see Jean-Claude, I will pass along your message. If you should see him first, will you give him a message for me?"

At his nod, she swallowed hard, fresh tears brimming. "Tell him his sister still loves him, still prays for his safety each day. Tell him that, Adam Hawk, before there is any blood spilled. And then, if your pride yet pleads satisfaction, remember the hospitality you have always received under this roof."

Adam slipped out the door and leaned against a whitewashed veranda pillar. The night poured down on him, the fresh air cooling his face. He sensed her presence before he heard her soft step. Turning, he found Rachel watching him. "Wear out your dancin' slippers, did you?" he asked, his tone betraying a touchiness he had no right to feel.

Overlooking his tone, she sat down beside him and smoothed her skirts. "Only my feet. What about you?"

"Lookin' for a little rest from all that gaiety. A little fresh air, a little peace."

He draped his arms over his knees and let his hands dangle loose. She stirred beside him and murmured, "If I'm bothering you—"

"No," he said too quickly.

As if discerning his thoughts, she looked at him. Her smile was tinged with sadness, as were her words. "Tomorrow, you and Dorie will go. I'll be on my own. Truly on my own."

He hardened himself against the doubts, the uncertainty in her voice, for to weaken now—it was unthinkable. "And so you're making one final argument?"

She leaned forward and rubbed at the dainty-toed slipper that peeked from beneath her skirt. Her hair drifted forward and curtained her features. "No. No more arguments, Adam. I wanted to say good-by tonight. Alone. Tomorrow might not afford an opportunity to thank you for letting me tag along—for offering me comfort—for making me feel safe in some less-than-favorable circumstances. I'll never forget your kindness."

"I've gotta admit, I was wrong about you from the start," he said, surprising himself as much as her. But once into it, he plunged ahead. "You aren't shallow or vain or self-centered, not like I thought."

"Adam!" she protested, her indignation so real, he laughed in spite of the tightness in his chest.

"That isn't the worst of it. Also thought could be you had some plan to make things hard for me by bringin' Dorie around to your way of thinkin'. About going to see Tall Horse, I mean. Thought you might do your level best to drive a wedge between us."

"I would never do that," she cried, and clutched at his hand, then awkwardly released it. No longer looking at him, she murmured, "A little girl needs her father. It would be terribly wicked to damage that bond. Take care of her, Adam. Let her know every day that you love her. Don't stand back on saying it or showing it. I'm going to give her my hairbrush, and you make good use of it. She adores you, you know."

"One hundred strokes," he promised, and stretched to his full height. When she rose beside him, he brought her hand to his lips and kissed it. Her hand, slipping free of his, fanned out across his scarred cheek, stroking it ever so gently. Her eyes glistened with sudden moisture as she leaned nearer, his name on her lips.

chapter 17

On a deep steady intake of breath he drew nearer, the reserve melted from his eyes, indecision giving way to vulnerability. Her heart turned over with renewed hope, and her dread of tomorrows faded. He *did* care for her, he did indeed. With that knowledge, she could endure much, even a long separation. But words came of their own volition, in direct conflict with her thoughts: "Adam, don't go," she whispered.

His reaching hands fell back. Caution flowed in as he murmured a gentle reprimand: "Thought you weren't going to argue."

Behind them, the door swung open. Lamplight and laughter and heavy-booted men streamed out onto the veranda. Instinctively, Rachel stepped away from Adam and turned to face the intrusion.

The twinkling gaze of Louis-Baptiste Duralde and that of his two smiling friends, ran between them. Rachel's cheeks grew warm, but the men took no notice; lighting up their pipes, they fell to making plans to accompany Adam in the morning.

She stole into the cottage and away to her room, feeling as if she'd been lifted to the heights of heaven, then unceremoniously dropped. All her apprehensions slipped back into comfortable seats, and she spent the night twisting and turning and tossing about. But morning came, all too soon.

Louis-Baptiste and his friends accompanied them on the crossing. Dressed in the garments Ann-Marie had given her, Rachel huddled on the deck with Dorie, sharing warmth against the early morning breeze.

A jumble of farm wagons, carts, livestock, and people crowded the heavy-laden ferry as they pushed away from the Illinois shore. The sun was growing bright, but the waters were a choppy, unfriendly mud-green. Movement seemed tediously slow. Louis-Baptiste and his companions indulged in an impromptu and somewhat rocky card game. Standing near, but vaguely aloof, Adam pointed out Bloody Island and the widening channel between it and the Illinois shore where the waters lashed and foamed and ate away at the land.

Weary of chasing down wind-swept cards, Louis-Baptiste soon joined them. He shook his head and said of Bloody Island, "It is where those too dignified for knuckles and knives defend their honor. The blood of many a fool has stained the sandy soil. And for what? A slight? A word spoken in anger? The hint of scandal?" He gave his cocked head a wry shake and shrugged slim shoulders. But his eyes mirrored the amusement with which he accepted a futile waste he didn't try to understand.

"Curious thing is, some of those gentlemen who've been so all-fired quick to aim pistols later shake hands and end up the best of friends," Adam chimed in. "That is, if their aim's off the mark and they live long enough to let their tempers cool."

Rachel gave the strip of land a closer look. Nothing about it hinted at the gore and death it had witnessed. Louis-Baptiste pointed out a crew of men working along the western shore of the Island.

"The new port at St. Louis is threatened already by the changing current of the Mississippi. Riverboats have grounded on the sandbar that grows from Duncan Island." With a stubby finger, he pointed out a large island further south along the Missouri shore. "It has become a two-hundred-acre monstrosity. Cottonwood and sycamore flourish among the sand and flood-wood. The sandbar creeps along, and if not stopped, will soon meet up with Bloody Island. Even now, no steamboats dock below Market Street."

"The men have been hired to build underwater dikes from the Illinois shore to Bloody Island and on down along the west shore of the Island," Adam explained the work crew. "Unchecked, the waters would continue to rush between Bloody Island and the Illinois shore, widening the channel there. As the current on the eastern side of the island increases, the current on the western side decreases. Eventually, there'd be no channel on the west side of the island and Illinois would have the port instead of Missouri."

As they drew nearer the burgeoning city of St. Louis, Rachel saw what a disaster that would be to the commercial trade. The levee was a beehive of unrest. Steamboats, ranging from the very elegant to unpainted, river-worn hard-cases, shared the docks with industrious ferry boats. Each carried its own precious cargo. A constant bustle of loading and unloading, a constant swaying sea of colorful motion went on.

The ferry slowed for the landing in full view of the city market. Overwhelmed by the noise and confusion, Dorie took Rachel's arm as Adam and the men lead the horses off the ferry and onto the swarming dock.

Giving Dorie a moment to adjust to the madness, Rachel waited until the traffic of those disembarking had cleared. She and Dorie were the last ones off the ferry.

On the shore, black roustabouts sang and called to one another over the cry of the steamboat whistles. The sun glistened off their muscled bodies as they heaved bales of cotton and hemp and moved wooden crates and barrels into heavy tandem-driven drays. The heavily traveled area was ankle-deep in mud. Horses and mules shied in fright as cursing drivers fought for control, lashing whips and steering away from the wharves, up the hill and through narrow streets.

Dorie pressed closer, her blue eyes large. "Where's Papa?"

Rachel climbed up on a crate and scanned the waves of moving bodies and faces. "I see them; come on," she said. By the time she reached Adam's side, the Frenchmen were nowhere to be seen. Adam told her they'd parted, with plans to meet in the morning.

Though she said nothing, Rachel clutched at the momentary reprieve and relocated her smile. Unassisted, she mounted Sada for what very well could be her last time, and followed Adam and Dorie along a thin cobblestone street. They passed grand old homes, rich with wrought-iron fences and sweeping lawns and gardens encased in stone walls. But many of the graceful aging homes were giving way to business establishments.

Adam made a few stops, and Rachel browsed through well-stocked shops, staying out of his way except when he asked for advice on new clothes for Dorie. While picking out a ready-made dress for the child, Rachel asked the shopkeeper if he had need of a good seamstress. The man shook his head, but offered the name of a merchant who might make her a job offer. She thanked him, drew a steadying breath and walked out into the sunshine.

Adam and Dorie soon joined her. "I'll need a place to stay," she said, gazing up and down the street. "Perhaps someone can suggest a good boarding house. It would be best, though, to secure the job first, don't you think, Adam?"

He took her elbow and pulled her off the central path of the walk where she'd been impeding foot traffic. "B'fore you go makin' all sorts of plans, I'd like you to meet Katri Murphy. She's getting up in years, and must have more work around her shop than she can keep up with. She'll put you up, too, and be glad for the company, I'll wager. She's that sort."

Thinking it was a rather poor start she was making, letting Adam handle decisions and smooth the way for her, she nonetheless went along, consciously drawing out each moment, postponing the inevitable parting.

Katri Murphy's combination home and shop occupied a lot on Second Street. It was a deep, steep-roofed cottage, not in the best of repair. The proprietor welcomed them with obvious pleasure.

Though not French by birth, Katri had lived among the French since St. Louis was young. Her tranquil acceptance of life reflected the influence. Short, round, and imperturbable, she appeared to assume that Rachel would stay.

They passed through the shop, where a glass case, stocked with knives, pipes, and Katri's own special blends of tobacco, was in prominence. On through the parlor and into the kitchen, Rachel noted evidence of a leaky roof. The floorboards were a bit warped and the furnishings throughout were rough, yet the atmosphere was one of cheer.

Katri's reunion with Dorie was touching. They fell to chatting like old friends, Dorie exhibiting none of the reserve Rachel had expected. It was as if the Dorie's years of absence fell away and a firm, affectionate bond was strongly intact. When it became clear their presence wouldn't be missed, Adam excused them both, and took Rachel for a walking tour.

The noonday sun was streaming down as they walked along First Street. At Adam's suggestion, they stopped at a pastry shop and ate their fill of light pastries and thick, rich cakes. Then they paused in front of the home of William Clark, the famed explorer, general, and Indian agent for all of the tribes west of the Mississippi. But not until she'd gazed a moment on the gracious two-story brick house occupying a lot running east to the river did Rachel realize Adam intended to introduce her to the owner.

"Adam, do you really think we dare?" she stammered, her Boston upbringing enduring a shock at the audacity of his intention.

He grinned and told her thousands of moccasined feet had found their way to Clark's door. Not at all sure she wanted to be lumped in with such company, Rachel trailed along after him with the greatest of reluctance.

The servant who answered the door told them General Clark was not in, but was expected shortly. He invited them in to wait, and to Rachel's consternation, Adam informed the servant they'd do their waiting in the general's council chambers, if it was all the same to him.

Meekly, mutely, miserably, Rachel, the unwilling intruder, followed Adam and the servant through the well furnished house to a south wing, a great spacious room hung with massive chandeliers and decorated with all manner of curiosities.

When the servant had left them, Adam grinned and swept his arm wide. "General Clark's trophies," he explained. "Quite a collection, don't you think?"

She stared in amazement at feather headdresses, robes etched with crude drawings, beaded moccasins, leggings, and dresses. "What . . . where did he . . . why . . ."

"Many of the things are gifts to Clark by way of his fair and honorable negotiations with a multitude of different tribes. The room itself was built as a place to hold council with the Indians who travel great distances. They come to seek Clark's help in settling disputes or maybe to air an opinion or grievance against a trader or trapper or the white men in general."

He lead her around, identifying cooking utensils, tools, and instruments. She was intrigued with the children's playthings—Indian dolls, games of chance, and deadly looking child-sized bow and arrows. Shields, boldly painted with fierce designs; ceremonial clothes; and ornaments of every description filled every space. She listened with great interest as Adam explained the importance of the snowshoes and cradleboards.

"Can you guess what this is?" Adam asked, leading her past a canoe to a large, round tublike object. Rachel studied the hide stretched over the framework, but didn't venture a guess.

"It's a bull-boat. The women and children use them in crossin' swift waters. Most of the men splash on across on horseback, but occasionally they too'll make a dry crossin' in one."

Returning her questioning gaze, he said, "I thought it might ease your mind a bit if you understood somethin' about these people. Their ways are different; there's no denying that—the way they travel, the foods they eat and how it's fixed, their homes and their worship. But they have a beauty about them, something soul-deep that escapes explainin'. It's tucked away in Dorie, too, jest like your tender spot for little ones is a part of you."

He paused and tapped his worn hat against his leg. "Wish I could protect her from the hardships and the harsher side, but it isn't in my power. She deserves to know her people—who they are and who she is. That's one gift I can give her."

When he fell silent, Rachel struggled to put her doubts aside and yield up understanding, for that was what he was asking of her. That was his purpose in bringing her here, and she was touched by his effort.

"I'll pray for you both everyday," she said finally.

That evening, when Katri and Dorie had gone to bed, Adam joined Rachel on the veranda. He wandered the length of the wood planks and poked at a weak piece of lumber.

Distracted by his fidgeting, Rachel voiced a question she'd been worrying over for a couple of days. "This Indian you mentioned—the Oto who harbored such hard feelings toward you that you thought it unwise to spend the winter in the village—what's become of him?"

He stopped scraping at the piece of rotting wood and turned her way. Voice cautious, he asked, "What makes you ask?"

The chair creaked as she rose and moved toward him. "Faith is my hope, Adam. Too often, my faith has been weak and unstable. But God is strong, and I'm clinging to him. I told you I would pray."

He stirred beside her. "So why do you ask about Hole-in-Chin? Just to give yourself another worry?"

"No, I ask so I can offer what has already become a deep worry over to God. Prayer is the only thing I can do for you. But simply asking God to watch over you and Dorie makes for a limited conversation. I want to know the dangers. I want to be specific in my petitions. If it means praying for this . . ."

"Hole-in-Chin," he again supplied the name.

". . . Hole-in-Chin, then I will."

He moved past her and settled into the chair she'd vacated. Left standing, she leaned against a weather-chapped column and waited him out.

"It's all way in the past," he said at length. "I reckon he's still in the village, but he'd be well-grown by now. Don't suppose he's harboring any harsh feelings. But if you're wantin' to pray a hedge against trouble, then I'll give you the long and the short of it."

"Go on," she murmured.

"He was called by that name for the deep crevice in his chin. Gave his face a delicate look, and in lookin' back, I can see he'd probably been out to prove how rough he was from the first time he'd played war games with the other little boys. But at the time, I was young and full of beans, and I took to the Indian lifestyle right eager. Their feasts and their games and their boastin' were all a part of it, and Hole-in-Chin—well, he had a mouth you heard everywhere. He couldn't have been more'n fifteen, wasn't much of a hunter, lost more'n his share of mock war games and had yet to count coup on an enemy, but you never heard the like of the braggin' and bullyin' that came out of that boy's mouth whenever his elders weren't listening in."

"Count coup?" Rachel cut in. "I don't understand."

"Means to strike an enemy. There's grades of coup—a brave gets more glory for the deeds requiring the most daring. Touching an enemy during battle calls for more valor than killin' him, and from there it goes on down to lesser degrees. Takin' scalps and such as that."

He continued. A small raiding party of Pawnee had slipped into the Oto camp and stolen some ponies. A council was held. Tall Horse, though no longer a reigning war chief, was among those to advise caution. No lives had been lost. Did they risk warfare by retaliation?

So, with a handful of young men out to prove their valor, he and Hole-in-Chin, both of whom disagreed with Tall Horse, had set out after the Pawnee. Three days and nights of tracking brought them to the enemy camp, where a boy not more than eleven was guarding the horses.

Hole-in-Chin, knife drawn, had crept toward the boy and Adam had intervened, snatching the youngster himself. The boy had cried out and instant chaos erupted as the camp came to life.

But the horses were free, and those they didn't manage to steal were scattered, leaving the Pawnee to pursue on foot, or wait until they'd rounded up some mounts. In the midst of the commotion,

Adam'd dragged the boy up on his horse. He'd seen the mad gleam in Hole-in-Chin's eyes and had realized he'd robbed him of his first scalp. He knew if he set the boy down, Hole-in-Chin would kill him.

They'd stopped to rest the horses late in the day. While the others slept, Adam gave the boy pemmican and set him free. A celebration awaited their return. Adam spoke of feasting and dancing and boasting on the part of the men who'd participated in the raid.

Though Hole-in-Chin had received songs of praise for his part in the raid, he hadn't been satisfied with such crumbs. He'd boasted of counting coup on an enemy. Adam knew he hadn't touched the boy and said as much, little realizing what disgrace Hole-in-Chin had brought upon himself in the eyes of the older warriors, for in the matter of boasting of deeds of bravery, absolute accuracy was required if any respect was to be given.

Adam had expected Hole-in-Chin's bitter resentment to mellow in time. But if anything, his fury grew. Maybe it was that very tension that hampered the boy's later efforts to redeem himself in the eyes of his elders. "His arrows swept wide of the mark at the critical moment," Adam said. "The vision he'd sought was cloudy and whatever boasting he did was always received with a degree of doubt."

"And he blamed you for all his troubles?" Rachel asked, when he shifted in the wooden chair and gazed past her into the night.

"Reckon he did. He was like a keg of gunpowder, just beggin' for a spark." He blew out a sigh and shifted his thoughts forward in time. Rising to stand beside her, he said, "Suppose that's all in the past by now, though. He'll have plenty of coup feathers hangin' from his roach, and when he does his braggin', he'll be gettin' the cheering approval he wants."

"You don't expect any trouble from him, then?" Rachel asked, anxious to put this worry behind her. He hesitated a moment too long for her liking.

"I don't figure on him being a problem, but if I'm wrong, then there'll be two of us prayin' on his account."

Rachel gazed across the narrow street where a young French couple took their ease in front of a steep-roofed stone cottage. Soft lantern light cast a friendly glow from a gay-curtained window. Shot through with envy, Rachel wished for the same shared intimacy with Adam, wished *they* were sitting close on a short bench, counting stars, sharing tomorrows. As it was, though he stood but an arm's length away, he had the same reserve that had once made her feel so safe. Had she imagined it, or had that reserve indeed lifted for a few precious moments but a night ago?

"How long will you be gone?" she asked quietly.

"Plan to winter with Tall Horse, then start back in the spring. Told Katri not to look for us much before April."

Nearly a full year. She mounted a show of passive acceptance, thinking again, *How weak my faith! How much room for growth!*

"Once more, you've put me in your debt," she murmured. "Katri wants me to stay and help with the shop. Maybe I'll soon plunge into some sewing. I can't take advantage of her hospitality for long."

His expression grew thoughtful. He tapped his hat against his leg. "It's more than that. You're wonderin', the same as me, if you can be content here. Could be, in a month's time, you'll be itchin' to go back East."

She shook her head, but he paid no heed. A cautious smile drifted across his mouth. "Hope you meant it when you said you were feelin' in my debt. I've got something to tell you and I don't want you gettin' your dander up."

She made light of his wariness, saying, "I'm not feeling too temperamental. Go ahead."

He twisted his hat in his hand, then tossed it toward the chair. It landed with a soft plop, then slid to the floor. "I won't make the mistake of sayin' again that you aren't the adventuresome sort. You proved me wrong there. But St. Louis could be more adventure than you want. It's headed toward refinement—plenty of ground to cover, though. So if you find you're yearnin' for the East, speak up to Katri. I've tucked a little back, and left it with her. There's more'n enough for your passage back home.

"If you decide to stay, then that's fine. But if you should want to go home, I don't want anything trifling standin' in your way."

Like money. She blinked back the tears and said nothing.

Awkwardly he stretched out a hand and squeezed hers. "Don't mind sayin' you made an interestin' traveling companion. Traveled with some who knew a lot more about trails and weather and game, but none were so uncomplainin' nor willin' to learn." He inhaled deeply, then chuckled. "None of 'em smelled half so nice, either. But then, they were trappers and traders and Indians, mostly."

She struggled to return his smile, and managed by one thin thread to hang onto her composure. He still held her hand, but she suffered the sad fatal feeling nothing would come of it. She saw it on his set features and felt it in his impersonal touch.

"I can't ever thank you enough for your kindness. I've depended on you, leaned on you, learned from you. Your being gone . . ." She swallowed hard. "It'll take some getting used to." She pulled the ribbon from her hair and pressed it into his hand. "Take it as a token, a reminder that I'm praying for you." *And waiting for your return.* Only she wasn't free to say it, for he hadn't asked.

It was the same green ribbon he and Dorie had chosen for her in Danville. He considered it a moment, then doubled the shiny strand and made a crease. Using the splintered corner of the column, he sawed along the crease until he held two pieces. He returned one to her, then slipped an end of his piece through a notch in his shirt. While he looked on, she tied the shortened piece into her hair. A fragment of a smile softened his mouth.

"Best get yourself a bonnet. Ribbon's not doin' a thing to protect that sunburned part of yours."

Her eyes filled again and his name trembled on her lips. He opened his arms and she found her haven of comfort as they folded her close, but passion was missing from his embrace. He held her quietly, tenderly, his chin resting on the crown of her head as the hot tears stole down her cheeks.

"We'll be leavin' at first light," he said after a time. And all too soon he was letting her go.

chapter 18

ROLLING OUT OF WESTPORT, MISSOURI, to rendezvous at Green River twelve hundred miles to the West, the caravan of wagons, pack mules, and horses bearing traders, returning trappers, and adventure-seekers had a seven-week journey before them.

Adam, Dorie, and the Frenchmen had linked up with them two days earlier. They'd traded rapid travel for the relative security of a larger group, and were adjusting to the slow pace.

The weather remained sunny and mild as they left Missouri behind. The partially wooded eastern fringe of prairie where the wildflowers were beginning to wither soon gave way to vast unbound plains where swift-growing grass danced beneath the endless blue sky.

A fair-sized hunting party stopped them on their second day out. Recognizing them as Iowa Indians, a Sioux-speaking tribe related to the Otos, Adam left Dorie with Louis-Baptiste and went ahead to meet them.

Tall and regal upon the back of a spotted pony, the leader remained impassive as Adam introduced himself.

With a sweep of his arm, Adam indicated the long caravan at his back. "They are taking supplies and trade goods further west. The Indians will come from their villages, the trappers from the mountain streams to exchange goods for pelts."

The Indian gave no indication of understanding. Gesturing

toward his band, Adam asked, "Do your men have hides they wish to trade?"

The Indian was slow in responding. His bronze chest glistened in the noonday sun. His moccasins were decorated with fine quill work, and the leather wristband he wore as protection against the whip of his bowstring was intricately painted with tiny designs, obvious when the man drew his right hand across his forehead, the unmistakable sign for "white man."

"White men are now crossing the hunting grounds of my people. They shoot the buffalo and put them to flight. The antelope and the deer too hear the great noise of your passing."

"We don't wish to cause your people hardship," Adam said. "If we've taken more than you're willing to give, we'll make amends."

A spark of interest shone from the black eyes. A few men from the caravan joined Adam. The Indian raised his hand to the sky.

"The Great Spirit sent the buffalo to fill the stomachs of my people. The hide is warm when the winds sweep snow across the land. No warmth will come from the buffalo the white man has eaten." Once more, he drew his right hand across his forehead.

Adam returned to his pack horse and untied the straps that held the pack secure within a weatherproof tarp. He took out a blanket and gave it to the Indian, saying, "This too will provide much warmth. Take it, a gift from your friend Adam Hawk."

"The muscle of the buffalo makes thread for our women; the sharpened bones, awls for sewing."

Adam retraced his steps and took a packet of needles and thread from his pack. The mounted braves looked on with interest as he presented his offering to their leader.

"The women of my people are skilled with the needle, too. Take this as a gift for your woman."

Accepting them without comment, the Indian studied the shimmering horizon where sky and earth blended. "The sacred buffalo was sent to the Great Spirit to fill the need of the red man. The bone of the buffalo shoulder makes a digging tool for the women. The stomach is a pouch for carrying water. A bone, when chewed soft, can tell a story." So saying, he showed the designs painted upon his leather wristband.

Deciding to draw arbitration to a close, Adam returned once more to his pack, drew out an offering of tobacco and set it to one side. In full view of the Indians he secured his pack, a sign negotiations were over.

A look of pleasure lighted the Indian's face when Adam gave him the tobacco. Swiftly, he regained his aloof expression, flattened his mouth, and remarked, "The tail of the buffalo drives the fly away."

Adam grinned and spat in the dirt. "You sure you've never been to Kentucky, my friend? There's men there'll sell you a horse, then turn around and try to charge another two bits for his teeth."

"Gray Wolf Kentucky Warrior," the brave boasted, and his band of followers hooted.

Behind Adam, the men began to relax as Gray Wolf once more considered the items he'd received in exchange for the caravan's safe passage across Iowa hunting grounds. Adam had been generous. Next to acts of courage and bravery in suffering, generosity was most respected among many Plains tribes. It accounted for the near-poverty of the most renowned warriors—they gave to the elderly, the widows, and orphans to a degree that put a lot of Christian folk to shame. But no Indian respected a fool; Adam's adding much more to the trade would have marked him as one.

"Your eyes are open to the movements of your brothers, the Otos," Adam said, watching Gray Horse remount. "Do you have word of Tall Horse?"

Gray Wolf was cautious, asking why Adam sought such information. Exercising respect and patience, Adam eventually learned that Tall Horse's people had planted their crops of corn, beans, and squash along the Platte bottomland, then moved further out on the plains for the spring hunt. Their fields had been left in the care of those too old or too weak to be of use on the hunt. Tall Horse was not among them.

"When did they leave?" Adam asked.

"When the bitten moon was delayed."

The last quarter—they'd been on the trail for a week. On further questioning, Gray Wolf confided he thought the Oto band would stay to the south of the Platte, for the Pawnee, rivals to the north, were far more numerous and in a warring mood.

Small in numbers, seminomadic by necessity, the Otos could be hard to find without a general idea what direction they'd taken. Adam thanked Gray Wolf. The band of Indians remounted and rode off. The caravan was once again underway.

As Adam fell back with Louis-Baptiste and Dorie, the Frenchman gently goaded, "Not but a handful of them, my friend. They were bluffing, were they not? If push had come to shove, we'd have passed through without one wee gift changing hands."

"A little good will goes a long way." Adam remained unruffled. "Learn that, and you might hold onto your scalp."

Louis-Baptiste ran a hand through his thick black hair. His voice took on a teasing note. "Miss Rachel be plenty impressed if Louis-Baptiste should return without his top hair. A mark of much valor, would it not be?"

"Or much stupidity," Adam returned mildly.

Louis shot him a wicked sidelong grin. "What? You don't wish to talk about the Boston girl? She is a fine-looking thing, is she not?" When Adam refused to encourage him with a reply, he turned and winked at Dorie. "Louis thinks your papa is sweet on Miss Rachel, but just too contrary to admit it. Am I right?"

Dorie sneaked a look at her father, then ducked her head. She made a grand production out of patting Sada's neck.

Irritatedly, Adam remarked, "Air's getting a mite rank-smelling. Let's ride ahead, Dorie."

When they were alone, Dorie slowed her mount and turned a questioning face his way. "Papa? Were those Indians my people?"

"No, they were Iowa Indians."

She fidgeted with the reins, then admitted, "I was frightened."

"Nothing wrong with that. I wasn't restin' so easy myself," Adam said. "All they wanted, though, was to be reimbursed for the buffalo we've killed."

"Some of the men grumbled. They didn't want to pay," she confided. "Louis-Baptiste didn't."

"They're wrong," Adam said flatly. "When you lived with the Fergusons, did they keep chickens?" She nodded and he went on. "Let's say someone stole a hen from Mrs. Ferguson's chicken house and Mr. Ferguson found out who it was. Wouldn't he be within his rights to demand payment?"

The furrow disappeared from her brow. "Yes, Papa."

"Well, then, there you are," he said, going on to tell her of the information he'd gleaned from Gray Wolf, slipping into the conversation much that would later help her understand the habits and customs of her people and the reasoning behind much of what they did.

It passed the time and served a good purpose to tell her of days when her mother was alive; when they'd lived among the Oto a life based more on living than on getting and gaining. The Otos' reverence for all they found in nature touched a receptive spark within him. Though their religion differed from his, Adam never doubted their depth or sincerity. He'd never met an Indian who didn't believe in the Creator and all that sustained him; never heard an Indian abuse his name.

Adam and Dorie remained with the caravan another two and a half days before angling south to search for Tall Horse. At the hour of their departure, a fuzzy-faced old mountain man hugged Dorie and pressed a bit of stick candy into her hand. Louis-Baptiste joked and wiped a tear from his eye, but it was a much less painful departure than in St. Louis.

They rode hard all afternoon without seeing another living soul. That night, they made a dry camp near a low stream bed. Adam wasn't taking any chances on attracting the attention of a far-ranging Pawnee. The Arapaho, the Cheyenne, and the Kansas, all more powerful than the small Oto tribe, weren't averse to foraying into Oto territory, either. At his instructions, Dorie ate some beef jerky, washed off the trail dust and curled up in her blankets. He hobbled the horses Indian fashion, giving them enough freedom to graze, but without the danger of them wandering too far.

The horses blew dust from their nostrils and chomped greedily at the grass. Insects chorused from secret hiding places, and far off, a wolf howled. Dorie stiffened beside him. He stretched out a hand and rested it upon her blanketed shoulder.

"Nothin' to worry about. Go to sleep."

She was still for a time, but he could feel her wakefulness. As the darkness grew deeper, she whispered, "Papa, do you ever get homesick?"

"Been a long time since I had a place to call home. But I get to thinkin' of the green hills of Kentucky sometimes. Pretty country, Kentucky." He hesitated, then forced himself to ask, "You homesick?"

She emerged from her shell of blankets, nodding her head.

"Fergusons were fine folk," he said.

She propped her head on one elbow. "Not the Fergusons. I meant Miss Rachel. Do you miss her, Papa?"

"Just a mite, maybe," he conceded at last. "But then of course we would. She was more tolerable company than a hard-bitten bunch of bewhiskered traders and mountaineers." Though she said nothing, he could feel her satisfaction, and was a little touchy about it. Gruffly, he ordered, "You go to sleep now, hear?"

It wasn't long before her even breathing let him off the hook. But she'd left him thinking of Rachel. And feeling lonesome.

Adam jerked awake, his heart pounding loud at the realization he'd not only slept, but slept soundly. It was still dark, the predawn air cold and empty of sound. He reached toward Dorie, some of his uneasiness fading at the natural rise and fall of her breathing. His thoughts skipped to the horses.

He could smell the dust, the green of the grass, no hint of smoke from dung or wood fire. The stars were gone from the sky and the earth was unnaturally quiet. What had awakened him? The absence of sound?

He moved to his pack and the saddles. All was as he'd left it. He waited until dawn peeled away the darkness and a pale pink edge cut the horizon. Rising, he shook Dorie and went for the horses. By the time he'd watered them, she'd rolled their bedrolls and was chewing on jerky. He thought of building a fire, cooking something just for her sake, but he could not shed the raw-edged unsettled feeling.

It wasn't until he had the horses saddled that he identified its source. The earth held an unnatural motion, the faintest tremor, like the twitch of a muscle. Far from view, buffalo thundered along, shaking the earth in their passing. Unsure of their direction, Adam waited to see if it would grow to a tremble. It did.

"Climb into the saddle," he ordered Dorie. And still he waited. Mounted, ready, but unmoving. No point in riding right into them. As yet, he didn't know from what direction they'd come, or how close.

Dorie's sharp eye spotted the dust first—a mere vapor on the western horizon. "Buffalo move fast, and they don't stop for what gets in their path," he told her, loading his rifle as a precaution before setting off in a southerly direction.

Time hung suspended as they covered ground, occasionally glancing to the west. Adam knew the throb of panic that drove the swift, mammoth creatures. They were well out of harm's way by the time the herd came into view, and though he'd watched the scene unfold countless time, his blood rose and the skin on his arms prickled as they grew from a speck on the horizon. The dust mushroomed, enveloping the creatures, then spitting them out as they came closer, closer until massive shoulders, woolly heads, and flashing hoofs filled the air with sight and sound and awesome motion.

Dwarfed by the size of the herd, nearly lost to the dust and the roar, Indian hunters were in swift pursuit, quivers of arrows on their left, bows poised. Stripped though they were to breechcloth and moccasins, Adam recognized the hunters as Oto. Their hair was closely cropped so as to have only a central ridge across the crown. Intent on the hunt, Adam strained forward in his saddle.

Energy surged through him as a hunter's arrow sang from the

bow. From his position, it looked like a perfect shot. A buffalo crumpled on the spot. He heard above the din of pounding hoofs, the shout of exultation: "Yuhoo! Yuhoo!" and could barely refrain from shouting as well.

Drawing ever closer, a second hunter let his arrow fly. The chosen buffalo wobbled, then fell and what remained of the herd veered around and thundered onward while the hunters unsheathed their knives and crouched down beside their respective kills.

Dorie finally found her voice. "Such huge creatures, Papa, and such little arrows." Her eyes were on the Indians.

Despite the lack of attention on the Indians' part, Adam knew they'd been spotted. Moving forward at a leisurely pace, he explained in a reassuring voice, "These are your people, Dorie. We've found 'em."

When they had drawn nearer, Adam called out a greeting in the Oto tongue. The hunter who'd made the later kill had just begun the skinning process. He snapped alert at the sound of Adam's voice. His eyes narrowed as he strung together a few terse words. Recognizing him, Adam felt a small tremor—Hole-in-Chin, looking just as surly, just as turbulent as Adam remembered. Or was it shadows of the past unnerving him? Making him feel as if the years had peeled away to that long ago summer when he'd incurred Hole-in-Chin's wrath.

Voice dripping contempt, Hole-in-Chin acknowledged recognition. "You keep Tall Horse waiting. Adam Hawk cannot be trusted to keep his word. So I told Tall Horse."

Unwilling to risk a confrontation, Adam replied, "That's a big cow you singled out. Good shooting." He gestured toward the arrow protruding from the skull, and if his words rang hollow, Hole-in-Chin appeared not to notice.

"Big mother cow," he boasted and tossed his head toward his companion. "Perhaps it was her calf Little Crow killed."

Hole-in-Chin's mocking laughter didn't trouble the clear-faced young man who crouched ten yards away skinning his kill. The thrill of the hunt still shone in his eyes.

Adam dismounted and greeted Little Crow heartily, then gestured toward Dorie. Though the Oto loved children, the men thought it beneath their dignity to pay them much heed. He didn't acknowledge the child, rather teased, "Hawk is like the sleepy bear. You arrive too late for the hunt."

Adam grinned. "There'll be others." He went on to ask about Little Crow's wife and children, aware of Hole-in-Chin off to one side, his knife in hand.

"My children grow tall and my wife grows round." Little Crow circled his arms and held them out to indicate her girth. "I will take the liver to her and still she will scold. It takes a fat buffalo to feed a fat woman."

His wry gesture indicated he'd been more sensitive to Hole-in-Chin's teasing than he'd let on. It wasn't a calf he'd killed by any means, but neither was it fully grown.

Anxious to search out Tall Horse, Adam remounted. Hole-in-Chin had grown weary of teasing Little Crow, and returned to his huge animal. But he'd no more than made a slice through the thick, matted fur when mayhem broke loose. Without warning, the huge cow clambered to her feet and whirled around, grazing Hole-in-Chin's hand with her right horn. The knife flew from his hand, and landed out of reach. Revived, the wounded buffalo whirled in an angry arc, to destroy the one who'd inflicted pain upon her. With lightning swiftness, she moved while Hole-in-Chin, recovering from the surprise, grabbed her tail as she spun.

"Kill! Kill! Kill!" he screeched.

The monstrous animal whipped around in a dizzying circular path that promised certain death for Hole-in-Chin, should he lose his footing or his grip on her tail.

Adam and Little Crow lost a few precious seconds, trying to take it all in. Adam was the first to recover. He leveled his gun, but it was impossible to hold the beast in his sights. If he missed by a hair . . .

"Shoot!" Hole-in-Chin's shouts grew breathless.

Little Crow drew an arrow back, but did not release it. Adam winged a prayer and squeezed the trigger. Both the buffalo and

Hole-in-Chin hit the earth and lay motionless. Little Crow shot forward and dragged Hole-in-Chin free of the buffalo. He knelt over him, then rocked back on his heels.

"Your shot was true," he called to Adam.

Adam gripped the gun hard. "Is he . . .?"

Little Crow shook his head and laughed. "The buffalo knocked the wind from him. He is not hurt."

"Thank God."

But Little Crow was beginning to enjoy himself. His wiry frame shook with silent mirth. "He is a fast runner, is he not?" he joked. "And what of this shot? Did he mistake the buffalo for a pony he wished to capture?"

Adam watched him jerk the arrow out of the skull of the buffalo. He'd seen Indians make just such a shot when capturing wild horses. It was intended to daze, not kill. But he didn't join in the mockery. Hole-in-Chin was coming around. He would anger all too easily.

A string of dead buffalo pointed the way to the Oto camp, where stood a circle of tepees, the openings all facing the east. Adam recognized Tall Horse's tepee by the war scene painted upon it.

A crier had come ahead to confer with his elders, and it had been decided the kill was plentiful enough to warrant moving the camp to a more central location. The women had turned from cutting long poles and forked sticks for drying racks and were disassembling their homes. Working with a thorough efficiency, they soon had their belongings piled upon horse drags and were ready to move.

In the midst of the activity, Tall Horse did little more than acknowledge Adam and Dorie's arrival. Now, near the front of the band, he gave the signal and the long line began to move.

The hard life the old war chief had led had stooped his shoulders and bowed his legs. His face, once proud and handsome, was now lined by age and scarred by the ravages of smallpox. But he hadn't lost his aura of dignity; he was an imposing sight, astride the piebald pony, his coup feathers trailing from a graying roach.

Bony dogs barked and chased the dust stirred by the horses and drags. Dorie was quiet as they fell into line, retracing their way back to the scene of the kill. The tepees went up, and the women turned to making meat with their men. Raw liver was a great temptation to people who'd wintered on pemmican and small game. Some indulged in premature feasting as they worked. Huge campfires were made in the middle of the circle of tepees. As strips of raw meat began to fill the drying racks, Tall Horse found his way through the flurry of activity to welcome Adam and Dorie. Joy mingled with old sorrows as the old chief lifted his weathered face to the heavens, raised his hands, and acknowledged the great blessing of a daughter restored to her home.

His sister, Break-the-Morning, and her eldest daughter had put Tall Horse's tepee in place, and when they had entered in, he fell into silence, sifting through his thoughts.

Eyes resting upon Dorie's face, he reflected upon summers past, times that would not return. He drew a long breath and began to speak.

"Once many gathered in the lodge of Tall Horse. His daughters, their husbands and children. There was laughter and joy, bickering and sorrow, and always, many stomachs to fill. And yet, Tall Horse knew contentment. Then came the sickness more deadly than the most warlike enemy, sweeping clean the lodge of Tall Horse, just as a wild prairie fire sweeps away the grass in its path."

His eyes, shuttered by loose-fleshed wrinkled lids, reflected painful memories. His hand was unsteady as he placed it upon Dorie's head. His voice was strong and resonant. "You, Little Blue Eyes, have brought hope and renewal to the heart of Tall Horse. He has a daughter once more."

Adam caught Dorie's anxious glance. If she was to understand her grandfather and the ways of the Oto people, it would be through watching, listening, reaching out with innate senses. He couldn't shelter or coddle her.

While he and Tall Horse talked, a great-niece of the old man came in to make a small pit and lay a fire beneath the overhead smoke hole. The girl finished the chore, then stood to one side, sending curious glances in Dorie's direction.

Tall Horse spoke to her. Her response, though spoken in the Oto tongue, was halting. Speaking for her, Tall Horse said, "Spotted Fawn would have Blue Eyes go with her to bring the fire."

Again, Dorie darted Adam a searching glance. He nodded encouragement, and she followed the girl. Watching them go, Tall Horse explained her halting tongue.

"Spotted Fawn and her brother were stolen by the Pawnee seven years ago. Only recently did they return. She speaks the Pawnee tongue and is only beginning to learn the words of her own people. Her brother is older. With him, it is as if he was never away."

He fell silent as the girls returned. When the fire was glowing, he found his calumet in a leather trunk yet to be unpacked. Settling cross-legged before the fire, he offered it to the sky and the earth, then the four quarters. The smoke blended with that of the pit fire and lifted out the smoke hole. The old man passed the pipe to Adam and spoke of his sister.

"Break-the-Morning will teach Blue Eyes all she must learn. It is good that she has come during the hunt when there is much to be done. She will soon learn the ways of her people."

Tall Horse expected Dorie to stay. Resting his hands on his knees, Adam addressed the matter directly, falling into the careful pattern of speech used by the old man. "It is an honor to visit Tall Horse. It is right that Dorie should know of the ancient ways. It is good that she can know her grandfather and hear of the days when he was a war chief of much valor," he said, careful to use her white name. "When the hunt is finished, we'll return with you to the village along the Platte and stay through the harvest and on through the winter. But in April, the Moon of the Red Grass Appearing, we'll be going."

Tall Horse was silent, his mouth grim, offering no words of disagreement. Adam had great respect for Tall Horse, and knew it was right that Dorie should learn of her heritage—but among the Oto, silence didn't necessarily mean compliance.

chapter 19

THE NIGHT WAS ONE OF SINGING and dancing and feasting. Dorie sat close to Adam, her dark head brushing his arm, her face washed in shadow. It must all seem strange to her, the abandon with which they danced, the fervor of their songs, the men's boasting of the hunt and of the brave deeds they'd accomplished, and the cries of approval by which the boasting was greeted. Adam saw that many—but not Hole-in-Chin—had donned their best clothes for the celebration.

Sullen-faced, Hole-in-Chin didn't dance or boast, though the hour was late. Didn't he dare, for fear Gray Wolf would tell of his poor shot that day? Did he, now a man, still fear the scoffing and laughter that would come his way should his peers hear that his arrow had stunned rather than killed his buffalo?

A feeling of loss, of disillusionment settled upon Adam. He rose and led Dorie to Tall Horse's tepee. Wearied by the journey and the anxiety of the day, she was asleep almost instantly. Adam stretched out on the woven mat Break-the-Morning had provided and pulled his blanket over him. The sounds of the celebration continued, the tremolo of women's voices rising and falling in their songs of approval. Thankful though he was that they'd reached their destination safely, he was uneasy over Hole-in-Chin. He shared his thoughts with his Maker, seeking guidance, for the one thing he *didn't* want was contention with one of Dorie's own people.

The days that followed were fraught with activity. Readying the meat was first priority. It was dried, pounded, and mixed with berries, then stored in parfleche trunks, boxes fashioned from large hides and painted with geometrical designs. The women went to work on the staked hides, hacking away the fat and muscle with toothed fleshers. Dorie spent a good deal of time with Break-the-Morning, learning tanning, sewing, and decorative quill work. She and Spotted Fawn became good friends. Their chatter was a mite confusing, for Spotted Fawn's dialect was a strange combination of Pawnee and Oto. Dorie picked up words from both tongues and tossed in a generous sprinkling of English. But it didn't seem to hamper their ability to communicate.

The days grew still and hot, slowing the growth of the prairie grass. Scouts sighted more buffalo and the tribe was on the move again. Adam rode with the men. As the weeks of hunting passed, he saw less and less of Dorie. She spent the long, mosquito-infested evenings playing games with Spotted Fawn and the other children. But one evening, she sought him out and with a timid smile, presented him with a pair of moccasins. Though the quill work was simple and the seams not as tight as they might have been, Adam was lavish with praise.

He poked his feet into the moccasins and took a turn around the campfire. "Perfect fit, Dorie. Perfect! I declare, I don't know when I've put my feet into anything more comfortable. You did a mighty fine job."

"You really like them, Papa?" Her face was anxious as her gaze traveled from the moccasins to his face.

"Like 'em? Reckon I'll wear them until there's nothin' left of 'em." He stopped his pacing and gave her a pat on the head.

To his surprise, she threw her arms around his waist and held on tight. He hugged her, her doeskin dress soft to his calloused hands. When she sniffled into his shirt-front, he stepped back and turned her face up. Tears stood on her black lashes. Adam went cold with remembered promises. Aware of Tall Horse's watchful gaze, he caught her hand and led her across the camp.

They made their way around staked hides and sidestepped the poles by which the flaps that closed the smoke-holes atop each tepee were maneuvered.

Pausing where the horses were corralled, Adam rested a hand on her shoulder and searched for the right words. He'd forgotten there was more to it than relearning a forgotten language and being taught the chores that made up a day. This lifestyle was far different from anything to which she'd been accustomed. She had friendships and kinships in her past, too—remembered times and places and events he'd been no part of. He cleared his throat and made himself say,"B'fore we ever left Reverend Clark's party, I made you a promise, didn't I? I promised if you couldn't be happy with me, I'd let you go back to the Fergusons."

In the gathered darkness, he sensed more than saw her alarm. Her hand grew tense in his and she went very still. "Do you remember?" he prompted.

"I remember."

Nearly afraid to go on, he dropped down, and resting on his heels drew her closer. "Were you cryin' because you aren't happy here? Tell me what you're thinkin', Dorie. I'm no good at guessin' games."

"I get a little lonesome," she said at great length.

"Are you wantin' to go back to the Fergusons?" he made himself ask.

Eyes downcast, she caught her lip between her teeth and refused to meet his gaze. "Is that what you want me to do?"

He pulled her close and rocked her in his arms. "No, 'course I don't. It'd hurt me bad to let you go. Don't you know that?"

"I didn't know," she said finally, her voice barely audible. "You go with the men every day. I thought maybe . . . I try to be good, Papa, and not get underfoot. I don't want you to . . . I've been afraid you might . . ."

"Might what?" he asked when she drifted into silence.

"Might go away again."

All the memories of the past rushed over him, adding to the

weight of her blow. Didn't she understand the purpose of this visit? Didn't she know he was trying to give back to her a rich heritage she wouldn't be able to recapture if he let this opportunity pass? Did she think he was just looking for a place to leave her again?

Humbled, inadequate, accused by those troubled blue eyes, he whispered her name and strengthened his hold on her. "God willing, we won't ever have to be separated again. Not until you're a full-grown lady and go of your own choosing."

"I wouldn't, Papa," she murmured. "I won't ever leave you."

He curled his fingers into her arms and held her back, trying to make out her features in the dusky light. Against his will he thought of Rachel's admonitions and warnings. How little he knew about taking care of a child! A prayer formed in his heart. Softly, he said, "Don't guess I've explained things well to you, have I? I didn't bring you here to leave you. I brought you so you could see your grandfather again and so you could learn the ways of your mother's people. Sometimes, you know, children and grown-ups, too, say things that can hurt a child like you. Do you know what I mean?"

She dropped her gaze, but he'd seen the remembrance of taunting words thrown her way. She knew. Maybe more painfully than he'd ever guess.

He stroked her hair with a gentle hand. "When God made you, Dorie, he made somethin' real special. You got the blood of the red man running in you and no race of people ever reverenced God or his creation more 'n them. And you got the blood of the white man, and they're great ones for accomplishin' things. Trouble is, some folks aren't comfortable with special people like you. Out of fear or misunderstandin' or whatever, they poke fun and say things better off not said."

Her head moved ever so slightly. He pressed on.

"Well, I got to figurin' the best way for you to understand about being special is to know the ways of the red man as well as the white. Both got their good ways and both make mistakes. Now you, you can kind of cipher out for yourself what's good and what's not so good about each of 'em. Then when people say things you'd rather not hear, you won't be afraid of their words. You can smile to yourself, knowin' that you're special, and that sometimes other folks just don't understand."

Seeing she had no answer, Adam rose to his full height and reached for her hand. "I told your grandfather we'd stay until spring. That'll give you a chance to take part in harvest and to sit in on some of the ceremonies. But if you aren't happy here, if you don't want to stay any longer, I'll speak to him again and we'll make other plans."

"Papa?" she broke silence. "If we leave, where will we go? Back to St. Louis?"

"It'd be a startin' place," Adam said. "I could find work there, for sure. Somethin' where I'd be home every evenin' and hear about your day. You could go to school. Mrs. Ferguson told me you were an able student."

Her hand grew more relaxed within his. She looked up to ask, "Would we be with Miss Rachel?"

Adam chewed that one over, then shrugged. "Can't make you any promise there. Miss Rachel'd have a mighty tall say in that, and I wouldn't venture a guess what it'd be. Could even be she's gone back East."

Dorie grew quiet again as they walked back toward Tall Horse's tepee. Just short of their destination, she asked, "If we stay for the winter, would you go off trapping like you used to do, Papa?"

Surprise slowed his feet. "You remember that?"

"Break-the-Morning spoke of it. Sometimes she tells me things I'm too young to remember." She shot him a shy sidelong glance. "She tells me stories about Mama. Sometimes when she talks, I think I remember Mama a bit."

Her voice told him she found the dim memories pleasing. He squeezed her hand. As for the trapping, that way of life was behind him. He had ties now. He wasn't sure what he'd put his hand to once he left the Oto village. Lord willing, he'd find something steady, reliable. His days of risk-taking were over. Or so he thought.

Tall Horse moved along the front of the line as the people journeyed back toward the winter village along the Platte. Summer was gone, the fall hunt finished. They marched through frost-bitten grasses, a remote sun matching wits with a chill breeze. All welcomed the making of camp when evening approached.

Adam turned from tending his horses to hear a scout, then an echo of dogs, raise an alarm. A slump-shouldered, dispirited man rode into the circle of tepees, a dusty pack mule keeping pace.

Adam secured his animals to the picket line, then angled toward the center of camp. Dorie strutted along beside him, her arms full of buffalo chips for the fire. As they drew nearer to the intruder, Dorie's steps slowed. She studied the newcomer closely, then dropped the buffalo chips near the opening of Tall Horse's tepee.

Adam felt an urgent tug at his sleeve. Dorie's eyes had grown large, her face unnaturally pale. Voice hushed, she said, "It's the Frenchman, Papa. The one who took me to the mission school."

Belatedly, Adam recognized Jean-Claude. He braced himself for the rush of bitter emotion, the grim satisfaction over this long-awaited encounter. But Jean-Claude was a mere shadow of the man who'd covered the gamut from friend to bitter enemy. Gone was the cocky stance, the starch from his posture, the lilt of his grin. Bleak misery haunted a countenance once merry with mischief. In keeping with the rest of his features, the pouches beneath his eyes were deeply creviced and unhealthy in color.

Wordlessly Adam moved through the rest of the men to face the Frenchman. Spotting him, Jean-Claude slumped back against his horse and raised a trembling hand as if to ward off a blow. Beads of sweat broke out upon his brow. His mouth sagged open but words were slow to come from the cracked and bleeding lips.

"Hawkeye," he said at last, his voice the grating of pebble upon pebble. He swayed and rubbed his grimy brow, licked his tortured lips. Whining, he said, "You have come for the leetle one. She is not here. I took her to St. Louis, to the Murphys. There was a bad sickness, and I took her to save her. Tell him, Hole-in-Cheen. Tell Hawkeye how Jean-Claude took ze leetle one so she could lif."

Hole-in-Chin glowered at the Frenchman. He shot Adam a glance, offering nothing but sullen hostility.

Jean-Claude was growing more distraught and confused. He pushed himself toward Hole-in-Chin, insisting, "I left word wif you, Hole-in-Chin. You were to tell Hawkeye where I'd taken ze child. Tell him! Shining Meadow is dead. The leetle one gone. Tell him!"

The circle of Indians surrounding Jean-Claude stirred restlessly. Lost in his own private hell, the Frenchman didn't notice as they began to mutter among themselves. Adam heard their whispers of sickness—or was it madness?—but was coldly taking in Jean-Claude's babbling revelation.

Was Jean-Claude speaking the truth? Had he indeed left word for him the day he took Dorie? Slowly, he faced Hole-in-Chin. The knot in his gut curled and ignited. Voice deceptively soft, he asked, "Does the French trader speak the truth? Hole-in-Chin was to deliver a message when I returned to the village to find my wife dead, my child gone?"

Hole-in-Chin met his question with a stony silence. Adam clenched his fists and fought for control. He asked again, "You knew she was alive and in St. Louis? You let me think she was dead? You didn't tell anyone the truth? Not even Tall Horse?"

Hole-in-Chin turned as if to walk away, but Jean-Claude lunged at him, babbling, "You must tell him, or he will theenk Jean-Claude was not a good friend."

Hole-in-Chin seized the little man in powerful hands and flung him back into the circle of Indians. Black eyes flashing violence, Hole-in-Chin pointed an accusing finger at Jean-Claude's crumpled form. "The French trader is sick out of his head. It is his madness that speaks. Fear him. His sickness will spread. Our old people will sicken and die. Our children will die. Once again our numbers will melt like the snow upon the plains."

His foot shot forward to deliver Jean-Claude a vicious kick. With a malice-streaked glare in Adam's direction he strode off. Adam stood fast, aware of the fear and suspicion Hole-in-Chin had cast over the group. The remaining men widened the distance between themselves and the still form of Jean-Claude. Some muttered and shook their heads; others drifted away in silence. Only a handful remained.

Adam could sympathize with the fear showing upon their faces. If their own devastating losses weren't reminder enough, smallpox among the Mandans and Hidatsa had nearly wiped out the neighboring tribes. Adam had heard the morning prayers of the men as they faced the East and lifted their hands to receive a blessing from the Great Spirit, and asking deliverance from the dread diseases of the white man. If they believed Jean-Claude had brought such a sickness into their midst, they'd show no mercy.

At Tall Horse's grave invitation, Adam was among those who sat in the council tepee. He listened carefully to their words. It was in their minds to leave Jean-Claude where he lay, abandon camp with great haste, and outdistance the sickness.

When Tall Horse gave Adam the opportunity to speak, he chose his words with care. Choosing an illustration that would cause the men to think carefully, he said, "The prairie rabbit is a skitterish critter. He bounds at his own shadow and leaps across the grasses, zig-zagging a mindless path away from an imagined enemy. Overhead flies the hawk. While hidden, the rabbit was safe. But now he is exposed to the soaring hawk. The hawk swoops down for the kill."

The most respected men in the camp considered Adam's words silently. Exchanging glances with Tall Horse, he continued. "The Oto must guard their ways that they do not, like the rabbit, scurry away from an unseen enemy into the arms of real danger."

A lesser chief spoke up, saying, "Hole-in-Chin was not wrong when he said the trader's words were crazy. It is sickness that makes the trader talk so."

Adam agreed with a solemn nod. "But I don't believe it's the same sickness that killed many of your number. I know this trader. He trades in whiskey. By the look of him, he's consumed his own wares. He's been left with empty jugs and a sour stomach. In a day or so, he will mend. No one else will catch his sickness."

Every one among them had tested the power of whiskey. Adam continued. "I have seen this among the men of my country. Many times. The hands that tremble. The sweat on the brow. The confused words and aching belly. His body craves drink, but he's got none left to give it."

The discussion continued, Hole-in-Chin's warning cropping up from time to time. But the shadow of doubt that clung to all Hole-in-Chin's words and deeds was in evidence.

"We will not break camp until morning. Our old ones and our young children need rest. You may care for the trader in the tepee of Tall Horse. But he must be kept away from the others in camp. We will see what the morning sun brings. If spots break out upon the trader, he will be left," Tall Horse concluded.

Certain Jean-Claude wasn't suffering from smallpox, Adam agreed. And so it was that he found himself caring for the very man he'd vowed to repay for his act of betrayal.

Dorie and Tall Horse went to the tepee of Break-the-Morning. The medicine man, uncle to Hole-in-Chin, would not see the French trader. He feared him, saying he'd seen a vision of great sickness among the Plains tribes. Nor would he offer medicine. His refusal fanned a rise of panic among the people.

Adam closed the tepee flap and peeled off Jean-Claude's filthy clothes. He bathed the emaciated form, which stirred and moaned in abject misery. Deciding the trader needed food more than a good rest, Adam roused him sufficiently enough to push what he could down his gullet. Pleading nausea, Jean-Claude soon lay back upon the woven mat and whimpered for a drink.

"You're a sorry-looking creature, Jean-Claude. Isn't enough of you to break over my knee. By the look of you, you been drinkin' to the exclusion of eatin'. Now open your mouth, or I'll eat it all myself and let you die the death you're beggin' for."

Focusing bleary eyes, Jean-Claude raised up on one elbow. He swallowed bits of the stewed rabbit and wiped a trembling hand across his mouth. A tear of self-pity trickled down and disappeared into his unkempt beard. "Jean-Claude does not deserve your concern," he said, and closed his eyes.

So the miserable rattle of bones was having an attack of conscience. Sure sign his mind was clearing. Adam was grimly silent.

After a time, Jean-Claude asked in a timid voice, "Why do you not let them kill me?"

"No one's wantin' to kill you," Adam avoided the question. "Not unless they decide you've brought them sickness. Lie back there and concentrate on not breakin' out in a heat rash. If you do, we're both in a heap of trouble."

The Frenchman summoned the strength for a shrug. "You haf already borrowed big trouble, my friend. Your trust of these people is too great. They are changeable, and will turn on you at a whim."

Curious he should preach that particular sermon. Adam tackled his own meal in silence. But Jean-Claude was unwilling to let the matter drop. Food having strengthened him some, his faculties of reasoning were sharpening. He fumbled in his pack and drew out a short clay pipe.

"The one they call Hole-in-Chin is most of all to be watched. It must be that he hates you. *Oui,* that is it. Jean-Claude was foolish enough to trust him once. You are foolish if you trust him now."

"I don't," Adam growled. Even now, in the shelter of Tall Horse's tepee, he could feel the waves of mistrust and foreboding washing over the camp. They would be gathering in clusters, considering the trader and Hole-in-Chin's dire warning.

Jean-Claude filled his pipe, then held it out to Adam. "What did you do to inspire such hatred, my friend?"

"Same thing I did about you—told the truth." Adam lit the pipe and returned it to him.

Jean-Claude smoked in silence, then observed, "The truth is a powerful weapon. Some do not admire it as well as others."

"Man doesn't have to apologize for speaking the truth." Adam said. "Doesn't matter who cottons to it or who doesn't."

"The truth, my friend, can kill you," Jean-Claude warned softly.

"And so can lies," Adam countered.

"It is true Jean-Claude has not given much worry to ze matter of shortcomings. Perhaps this St. Peter fellow is a man's man and will barter. A clean slate for a jug of spirits."

"What of your Maker? What will you say for yourself when you answer to him?"

Jean-Claude pulled at his pipe. The scent of the smoke blended with the strong smell of the food Adam had cooked. Propped on one elbow, glowing bowl of the pipe obscuring the twitch of his mouth, the trader remarked, "Could it be God is not ze grim judge you make him out to be? Might he not haf an understanding heart for a merry Frenchman such as Jean-Claude?"

Adam thought out his reply. "Didn't say he was grim. Reckon he's more understandin' than we have a right to expect. But he's fair, too. Good Book says he's as fair as he is loving."

The shadowy light picked out the Frenchman's smile. "That's better, my friend. It is not a kind thing to whisper frightening warnings to a man as sick as Jean-Claude."

It hadn't been Adam's intention to reassure him. But if he found justice comforting, that was between him and God. Adam fell into a watchful reverie. Across the fire, the trader finished his pipe, then curled up on the mat, tugging the buffalo robe close, then easing out a long sigh.

Adam rolled up in his blankets and listened to the night settle in. As sleep began to steal over him, he relaxed his vigilant guard, giving entrance to the subconscious imps in his mind. They marched forth, parading visions of Rachel. Rachel laughing, Rachel storming, Rachel braiding Dorie's hair. Rachel crying. Rachel astride Sada, the wind in her hair.

At the sound of a horse's soft nicker, he separated dreams from reality. The memories of Rachel fled on swift feet. He held his breath and listened hard. A rider was leaving camp. Was it fear of the smallpox? Would he wake up to find the entire camp gone? He couldn't rest until he'd reassured himself of Dorie's safety. A soundless walk across camp brought him to Break-the-Morning's hide-covered home. He raised the flap to find all within soundly asleep.

It wasn't yet light when Adam awoke, but the Indians were milling around. He listened for the chatter of the women and the children as they prepared for another day of travel, but the chatter didn't come. Hearing a stir outside his tepee, he pulled on his moccasins and hat, then stepped out to meet the ominous quiet. Tall Horse was waiting.

Jarred by his grim look, Adam said, "If it is your wish, have the medicine man look in on the trader. He won't find any eruptions. The man is much better this morning."

Tall Horse's expression remained unchanged. He said, "The medicine man, Crooked Bow, fears the trader. He will not come."

"His fear is without basis," Adam said.

Tall Horse sucked in gaunt cheeks. "Crooked Bow's vision advised that council be sought among a neighboring band of Iowa. Hole-in-Chin rode hard into the night. He returned as the stars slipped away. He brought word from Red Dog's band. They camp a hard ride to the place of the rising sun."

Beyond them, expressions hard-set, a cluster of men—minus Hole-in-Chin—waited in silence. A chill of apprehension chased up Adam's spine.

"What has Hole-in-Chin learned from Red Dog's band?"

"The trader has been among them. He left sickness behind."

Adam felt control slipping from his hand. He challenged, "Why does not Hole-in-Chin tell me this himself?"

"He spent the night on his pony. He rests now before the day's march."

Adam turned and entered the tepee. Jean-Claude was languidly pulling on his dirty clothes. "You been among the Iowa?" Adam asked.

The Frenchman shook his head. "No, Jean-Claude has come from ze west. Ze Cheyenne, they were troublesome. They stole my whiskey, plundered my pack and drove me out of their camp."

Adam scrutinized the little man. Malnourished and itching for a drink he might be, but he plainly wasn't carrying smallpox. Confident of it, Adam returned to Tall Horse, and jerked a thumb toward the tepee. "The Frenchman hasn't been among the Iowa. Hole-in-Chin does not speak the truth."

The circle of men edged closer, a few faces openly hostile, others rimmed in fear. The medicine man separated himself from the group. "The French trader must be removed from our camp, he brings death to our people," he concluded.

Adam threw open the hide flap, saying, "The man isn't sick. See for yourself."

The men hastily backed away. Their dread was as contagious as the disease they feared. Crooked Bow, the medicine man, addressed himself to Tall Horse, his words very sternly spoken. "Hole-in-Chin's warning must be heeded. My vision was clear. The trader carries death. Kill him or have him removed. The decision must be made."

"Reckon it's up to me, then," Adam said finally. "I'll see the Frenchman out of your camp. Send Dorie to gather her things and we'll go."

Tall Horse folded his arms across his chest. He jutted out his lower lip as the cold wind ruffled his roach. "Blue Eyes will not go. She is the daughter of my daughter. This is her home."

Adam wasn't surprised by Tall Horse's words, but had more than half expected this turn of events. Tall Horse had had it in his heart to keep Dorie since the day they'd arrived. Adam had avoided discussion of it, thinking he'd deal with the problem when it arose. The time was now. Yet to raise an almighty stink now would be unwise, for Tall Horse would arm himself for the battle. Better to pretend reluctant acceptance, without appearing too willing to abandon her. So thinking, Adam said, "She has a home with me beyond the great river."

"It is not to be," Tall Horse stood his ground. "Blue Eyes is the last of her mother's clan. There is renewal through her."

"The choice should be hers to make. Call her out here."

Eyes haughty, Tall Horse stepped in his path, lest Adam go for the child himself. "She is a child. Her grandfather will make the choice for her." His deep eyes swept over Adam's face. He added,

"You have been a good son to me. Be rid of the Frenchman. Be sure of your own health, that the sickness is not upon you, and you too will have a home with the people of your dead wife."

Did Tall Horse think he'd suffered too little over the loss of Shining Meadow? He'd suffered much, but healing had come. It'd changed him some, prepared him for a new life away from these plains, these people, the trapped-out streams he'd once haunted. He wouldn't have that second chance yanked out of his hands. "It will be as you say. I'll see the Frenchman to the trading post at Council Bluffs. Then I'll return."

Scrutiny intense, Tall Horse was silent. Adam worried that the wisdom of his years would alert him to treachery. Pushing for the advantage, he said, "I'll speak to Dorie, then I will take the Frenchman away."

At the lift of a hand, Tall Horse had three braves join him in blocking Adam's path. The old man said, "Tall Horse will explain to Blue Eyes. You go now, before the sickness carries on the wind."

Adam hesitated, remembering his recent promise to Dorie. He'd told her they'd remain together as long as it was within his power. "It would mean much if I could tell her good-by," he said quietly, but Tall Horse remained adamant in his refusal. Finally, Adam faced defeat. He withdrew the faded green ribbon from a loop in his shirt and passed it to Tall Horse saying, "It is a gift to Blue Eyes from her father. Tell her I will be back."

Tall Horse lifted his hand in a mute farewell.

At midday, when they paused to eat a handful of parched corn and rest their mounts, Jean-Claude broke Adam's dark silence. Still grieving over the mule he'd been forced to leave behind, he said morosely, "They will eat my fine Henri, I fear. Indians do not know ze value of a good mule."

Adam settled his hat back on his head and consulted the sun. Four hours of daylight left. He quenched his thirst, then looked at the trader. "Might not eat him. Might fear he's got your sickness."

A jovial grin parted the bearded face. "That is not so. Not once has my Henri shared a jug with me. He has no liking for spirits."

They had ridden in silence for some time when the Frenchman released a gusty sigh and regarded him, saying, "Look, my friend. It was good of you to see me safely off. But your heart is heavy for want of your child. Jean-Claude does not need a nurse. Go back to the leetle one."

"Isn't that simple."

"No? What is so difficult?"

Adam repeated Tall Horse's decision to keep the child, then revealed his own plan. "I'm collecting her, and we're going back to St. Louis. Could be I'll need some help."

Jean-Claude's eyebrows jerked upward. "I'm not a well man, more dead than alive. Surely I can be of no use to you," he said, faintly mocking.

"Maybe, maybe not. But you're gonna try."

They rode along in silence again, the breeze roughing the prairie grass, making it whisper. By and by, Jean-Claude asked, "Am I to belief you haf a plan?"

"Nothin' fancy." Adam knew Jean-Claude would be of use only if he could keep him sober. On horseback, they could cover ground in two and a half days that would take the Oto band a week or more to travel. In that amount of time, Jean-Claude should have some strength back. The horses, too, would be well fed and well rested.

Dipping his hat low, he gazed east. "You know the big forest just south of the junction of the Platte and Missouri Rivers? I figure we can camp there for a spell, wait for Tall Horse and his band. When they get within a day's march of their permanent village and settle in for the last night on the trail, I'll slip into Tall Horse's tepee and get Dorie."

The Frenchman's look was full of reproach. "And for that, you need Jean-Claude?"

"I can't be sure Tall Horse isn't expecting just such a plan. Sada's fast over a short distance. She can outrun any Indian pony. But I'm not sure she's got their endurance. I want you waiting somewhere between the Indian camp and the Missouri. On a fresh horse, you can take Dorie on to the river, while I keep an eye to complications. We'll get us a canoe and have it waiting there."

Jean-Claude's eyes took on a new gleam. "A good plan, *mon ami.* In my younger days, I was a voyageur. I haf not forgotten the skill." He flexed arms, the length of which seemed out of proportion to the rest of his scrawny frame. His shoulders weren't as muscular as they'd once been, but by the look of him, he still had the heart and the nerve of a voyageur. Adam was counting on as much. He allowed himself a grim smile.

The tranquility of the pungent autumn forest was a deception. Hunting parties moved within it—Omaha, in their smoke-blackened elk-skin moccasins, and the Iowa as well. Adam used all his skills staying out of their way. Their only contact with the Indians was in trading a few goods for an Omaha canoe—a light, well-crafted vessel that he and Jean-Claude labored to conceal in a bushy stand of willows along the western bank of the cold frothy Missouri.

Ten days passed before Adam spotted the sign for which he'd been watching. Tall Horse and his band signaled by smoke the few who remained in the home village of their impending arrival.

After making certain the canoe was still safe, Adam and Jean-Claude broke camp and made their way through the thick forest. Dusk was falling as they moved out onto the plains, the wind stroking the golden, frost-bitten grasses. When the time came for Adam to ride on alone, he gave last-minute instructions to the Frenchman.

"You lay low, and I'll bring the girl to you before the night is gone."

Jean-Claude clamped an empty pipe in his teeth. "It could be that we will not meet again, *mon ami.*"

Adam replied sternly, "If you don't plan on being here when I return, say so now, Frenchman. I'll know to spare my horse."

An injured tone carried the Frenchman's reply: "Jean-Claude will wait. Until daylight, he will wait. If Hawkeye does not come by daybreak, he will know an Oto arrow has come to rest in the back of his friend."

"Comfortin' thought." Sada was impatient to move on again. Adam stroked her neck, waiting for Jean-Claude to spill what was on his mind.

By and by, the Frenchman broke the ban on a subject they'd both avoided. "Why is it that, when I rode into the Oto camp, you did not snap me like a brittle stick? There are some who would say Jean-Claude gave you cause."

Adam gazed across the black lonely plains. "Appeared to me you'd done yourself enough damage. Not much satisfaction in breakin' a broken man."

A small silence hung between them. The Frenchman bit down on his pipe, his teeth clicking softly against the stem. "Perhaps Jean-Claude is not as broken as you think," he said by and by. "He still knows a few tricks."

"Yeah, well, keep 'em up your sleeve. We might be needin' 'em before morning."

Jean-Claude said, "In St. Louis, if not before, we will settle the bad blood that remains between us."

"Nothin' to settle," Adam said, and meant it. As an afterthought, he added, "Do hanker for your word on one thing, though."

"Perhaps it is within my power to give it."

"If things go amiss, you do what you can to get Dorie to the river. And don't tarry once you're there. Push off for St. Louis."

"And what of you?"

"I know my way," Adam said.

"We are to leaf you?"

"If the two of you are in any danger, yes, go on without me. Don't take chances with her, Jean-Claude. And when you get to St. Louis, take her to Katrina Murphy's shop. There may be a Boston girl there—Rachel Whitaker by name. If I don't make it back I want Rachel to see to Dorie. Will you do what you can?"

"But what of Katrina?" the Frenchman asked.

"A good woman, but she's grown old. If Rachel is gone east, Katrina will know where to find her. I've left funds with her. She knows to see that Dorie is left in Rachel's care. It's the best I can do for her."

"I will do what I can, *mon ami*," said the Frenchman.

"One more thing," Adam added. "While you're in the neighborhood, go see your sister. She's grown lonesome for you."

"A saintly woman, my sister," Jean-Claude murmured, his voice growing wistful. "Yes, I will see her."

"*B'fore* you hit the rum houses."

The Frenchman chuckled. "What a worrisome squaw my friend has grown to be." He waved him off.

Adam turned away, wishing he could shake his premonition of trouble.

chapter 20

IN HER SMALL CABIN ROOM IN ST. LOUIS, Rachel came awake with a start. A light breeze whistled through the eaves, the sound of it overridden by the fierce pounding of her heart.

She jerked upright in her narrow bed, bent her knees, and pulled the covers up close. What had awakened her? Why this state of alarm?

She pushed a handful of hair out of her eyes, and looked around the moonlit room. In a near corner sat two trunks, sent to her from Francis by boat. In the other corner stood her dress form, an unfinished gown upon it. Word of her skill as a dressmaker was spreading. She was thankful for the source of income, for the degree of independence it gave her. But as time passed, she'd grown more and more restless, her concern for Adam and Dorie mounting until it seemed they occupied her every thought.

She bowed her head and prayed for their safety, the fervent words circling over and again, but the anxiety refused to abate.

She slipped from the bed, wrapped a shawl about her shoulders, and moved through the dark cabin, the floor rough and drafty beneath her feet. At a west window, she pushed aside a curtain and looked into the night. The city slept, black, unblinking, familiar after these long, long weeks.

Forcefully turning her thoughts away from the gnawing worry within, she thought of Katri, pleasant and undemanding, working when she felt so inclined, leaving the small, dimly lit shop unattended when she didn't.

While Katri napped on the shady veranda or wandered down to the market, Rachel dusted, chased cobwebs out of forgotten corners, and waited on customers. Katri's clientele ranged from farmers to steamboat pilots, from professional men to soldiers from Jefferson Barracks. A few rough sorts from the riverfront crossed the threshold on occasion, but only long enough to buy their favorite blend of tobacco and eye the display of knives and pipes.

Behind the house, Rachel had discovered the traditional French garden, sadly neglected. Wildflowers grew among patches of weeds. Shrubs and brambles encroached upon untrimmed fruit trees.

Each time Rachel had stepped out the back door, her orderly New England soul had cried out in protest. The day had come when she could tolerate it no longer. She attacked the eyesore with willing hands and a strong back. Katri had watched awhile, then stirred herself to finding an axe, a hoe, and a shovel. From there, her interest had dwindled.

She'd wandered off down the street and returned at twilight with crabs, oysters, and fresh okra. From that day forward, the pattern was established—the garden was Rachel's domain; the kitchen and all it entailed, Katri's. Katri's cooking could not be surpassed. Rachel, learning by trial and error, couldn't have said the same for her gardening. But there was something soothing about the scratch of a hoe against the soil—what did it matter if her vegetables weren't the fattest in town?

A lonely cart rattled down the street, the sound of its passing jerking Rachel out of her reverie. The pony shied as a leaf skated across his path, but took up his steady plod again, headed toward the river. Her thoughts followed, then turned westward, past the manufacturing districts, the lumberyards, the new housing additions. The sky was hung with a bright moon and a myriad of stars canopied that great western expanse where the land leveled out into plains. Somewhere beneath God's quilted sky, was an Indian village, and in it Adam slept, long and lanky, rolled in his blankets; Dorie, her sweet face pillowed on a slim brown arm.

Thinking of them, the heavy burden again weighed her spirit—the burden of waiting, of not knowing, of worry.

But wait, she would. Be it six months or a year, she'd be waiting when they returned. He'd made her no promise, spoken no words of commitment. Perhaps he thought her young and unsure of what she wanted from life. When he returned, he'd see new growth; he'd see she'd learned he wasn't going to become a settled man for her, that if she wanted him, she'd give up what little security life now afforded her and take him as he was. And she would.

But this was the last separation. If his life was in the West, then she'd go west too. Others were going. Wagons waited each day to join up with trains on the long trek to Oregon. Whatever the hardships, she'd face them. She could face almost anything. Except separation. Separation had always been her enemy.

The street was empty again. Loneliness crept in like a cold damp fog. Loneliness and apprehension. She drew the shawl close and bowed her head once more.

chapter 21

In the deep of the night, Adam lifted the hide flap and gained entrance into Tall Horse's tepee. By the dim coals of a low-burning fire, he made out the larger form of Tall Horse. Dorie slept on a rush mat near him, a buffalo robe dwarfing her form.

Adam crouched motionless as precious seconds slipped by. Slowly, slowly, he let go the stale air from his lungs and inched to Dorie's side. He covered her mouth with his hand, but she slept the deep sleep of a worn child and didn't stir. He pulled back the robe, prepared to lift her into his arms, then stopped short. A chill swept up his spine. Tall Horse expected him. He'd tied one end of a rawhide strip to Dorie's wrist; the other end was secured to his own. Heat followed the ice in Adam's veins. Had she slept this way every night since his departure?

Soundlessly, he withdrew his knife from the sheath. The rawhide popped as it lost its tautness to the blade of the knife. The sound provided its own private terror. Though the air was chilly, sweat poured off Adam's brow as he waited for Tall Horse to throw back his robe and raise an alarm. But the old man didn't stir. Adam lifted Dorie in his arms and moved toward the opening. As he crouched down near the hide flap, her lashes parted, revealing sleepy eyes. He didn't have a hand free to cover her mouth, but there was no need. In an instant her wakefulness was as deep as her sleep had been. The relief that flashed in her eyes wrenched at his heart.

Outside the tepee, she slipped from his arms. A mongrel brushed against Adam's leg, sniffed his feet, and wagged a limp tail. Thankful his familiar scent spared certain disaster, Adam motioned Dorie to skirt the outer rim of the camp, for the shortcut through the center was too risky.

The wide sweep around to where Sada and a second horse waited was time-consuming. His nerves leaped at each small sound, but at last, they drew near the horses. He lifted Dorie onto the back of the horse he'd slipped away from the picket line, then stretched out a hand toward Sada. A shadow separated itself from the horse. Senses reeling, Adam forced the trapped air from his lungs. Recognition was swift. Tall Horse held Sada's reins.

He spoke softly, the sound of deep sadness in his voice. "I am an old man. Many winters have I seen with these ancient eyes. It is better to die in battle than to grow feeble, a burden to others. Yet the Great Spirit has lengthened my winters and I must face new sorrow before my bones are parted by the stubborn roots of the prairie grass. I cannot fight you, Adam Hawk. You are young and strong. I am an old man, and short of strength. And so it is that you steal from me what is mine."

Respect for the old man held Adam in place. Dorie broke the silence, saying, "He is my papa; I go willingly. He isn't stealing me."

"Blue Eyes has learned much. But much remains to be taught. Is respect not learned in the white villages? Are they taught only getting and gaining? What of reverence for the Great Spirit and for our mother earth?"

Dorie kept quiet, but Adam dared not tarry any longer. "Whatever our difference, I have valued your friendship," he said to the old man. "I have seen much among your people that deepens my respect for your ways. But I cannot change the blood in my veins. My own people and their ways have meaning, too. I will raise my daughter among them. Maybe in time we will visit again."

"If you flee stealing my daughter, there will never again be a home for you in the Oto village."

"So be it," Adam said.

Tall Horse stretched out his hand and struggled with new words. "Gone are the days when I could ride on the wind and take back what is mine. Many are my winters. I cannot strike you down. So it is that I will send another after you. Beware of him; his hatred runs deep."

"Hole-in-Chin," Adam murmured, knowing it was so.

"He will show you no mercy. He will spill your blood and return to me what is mine."

"He will force my hand," Adam said. "Dishonor lies in killing a man anxious to die."

"Your words are true. It is that which makes Hole-in-Chin a fierce warrior. He seeks death. You are among those who brought him dishonor and shame. To him I will give the gift of taking your life. No other warrior will be sent."

"And what of Dorie?"

"If your valor runs deep, your mind keen, your aim true, she will have her home with you. But if Hole-in-Chin proves more mighty, her home will be with me. I will be both father and grandfather to her."

A winner-take-all stakes. Adam could see a sense of justice in it that would appeal to the Indian reasoning. Thoughts grim, he swung into the saddle.

The old man relinquished the reins and stepped back. Adam turned to the east, but Dorie called back, "Good-by, Grandfather. I'll remember the lessons learned from Break-the-Morning. I won't forget Spotted Fawn. Nor you."

"My daughter."

The mournful sound of Tall Horse's voice haunted Adam even as they sped away, their horses at a full gallop. Setting a course by the North Star, they rode straight east. Adam listened for the sound of a pursuing rider. Fear for Dorie was uppermost in his mind; his one plan was to get her safely into the Frenchman's arms. Then he'd head north toward the Platte and bank on Hole-in-Chin following. As long as the Frenchman was there waiting, Dorie stood a chance of seeing her beloved Rachel again. *Their* beloved Rachel.

Jean-Claude was waiting. Some of the burden lifted from Adam's shoulders at the sight of him. He reined in his horse, leaped to the ground, and transferred Dorie from her horse to the Frenchman's.

Brief with his explanation, he finished, saying, "Get to the river and don't wait. When you reach St. Louis, remember what I said. No rum, Jean-Claude. See Dorie safely into the care of Rachel Whitaker. Lord willing, I'll join her there shortly."

"You have my word, *mon ami.*" An arm around Dorie, the Frenchman urged his mount forward, then paused to ask, "What of my fine Henri?"

Having no wish to tell him Henri hadn't been among the picketed ponies, Adam ignored the question and slapped the Frenchman's horse across the haunches. Dorie struggled to be set free, calling, "Don't go, Papa! Please, stay with me. I'm scared, Papa!"

"You're gonna be fine; I'll see you in St. Louis," he called after them.

With only the wind to witness the mists that sprang to his eyes, Adam watched them go. He spent a few minutes trying to erase any signs of the direction the Frenchman and Dorie had taken. It was a stony, thin-grassed spot. What if by some awful twist of fate, Hole-in-Chin followed Jean-Claude and Dorie east instead of tracking him north to the Platte? But Hole-in-Chin had no interest in Dorie or the Frenchman. He wanted Adam; it was his blood he craved spilling.

Adam dallied a bit longer. By and by, he put his ear to the ground and knew he dared wait no longer. Mounting the horse Dorie had ridden and leading Sada, he set out once again, the North Star his guide. From time to time, he paused to listen. He waited so long one time that every doubt fled his mind. He was being followed. His mind easier on the matter of Dorie's safety, he turned to thoughts of his own escape. He knew the country well, though perhaps not as thoroughly as did Hole-in-Chin. But Lord willing, he'd shake the Oto brave and make his own way to St. Louis.

By and by he mounted Sada and turned the other horse loose. Weary, but nerves tightly strung, he rode to meet the dawn.

A thin ribbon of gray unfurled along the eastern horizon. Adam knew the Platte River couldn't be far. He quickened his pace and surprised a doe from her resting place. He watched her graceful flight.

Among rivers the Platte was a wily deceiver. In places it ran swift and dangerous, making an adventure out of a crossing. In other places it was wide and so shallow its channels lay twisted upon the land like a maiden's braid. But a man could find quicksand beneath its placid strands. "An infernal liar," one trader had termed her. Adam approached the banks as a blood-red sun fired the horizon.

Casting a furtive glance over his shoulder, he dismounted. The river was uncommonly narrow at this point. He scanned it with an experienced eye, knowing it was too shallow for a horse to swim. Doubting the stability of the river bed, he plunged in a hand. Sure enough, the river bottom was the thick miry glue he'd expected. Slow-acting quicksand.

Sada's never been a good crosser. High-strung and skittish, she was. He'd have to keep her moving and gamble on a safe crossing.

Full light was coming fast. He wiped his hand down his dirty buckskins and remounted, then paused a second time. A thin wisp of smoke from the opposite bank caught his eye. He ran his gaze along the opposite shore. Nothing moved but a skimpy line of willows and a tangle of underbrush offered cover for a small party of braves.

He made his decision quickly. There was no readily available place to hide his horse. Hole-in-Chin would see her and be wary, but he didn't have time to waste fretting over something he couldn't change.

After ground-tying her near the river, Adam made a lasso of a rope, then backtracked along the faint trail of his approach. He'd no more than concealed himself in the grass when the sound of a rider coming met his ears. Crouched low, rope ready, he grew tense for the spring.

Perhaps it was a slight movement on his part or an unnatural lean to the grass that alerted Hole-in-Chin. The plodding pony stopped and Hole-in-Chin called out his name, the sound of it curdling upon the Oto tongue.

"Adam Hawk, do you cower in the brush like a rabbit? Show your face," he taunted. "Hole-in-Chin comes bearing a gift."

Cautiously, Adam parted the grass for a glimpse of the Indian. The sight before him turned his blood to ice. A fresh scalp dangled from Hole-in-Chin's waist, and he wasn't alone. Dorie rode with him.

Adam dropped the lasso and rose to reveal himself. For a moment, Dorie sat stunned, her eyes glazed, traces of dried tears upon her dirty face. But then, as if charged with a renewal of spirit, she sprang from the pony without warning. But her feet no more than hit the ground when Hole-in-Chin lashed out with the blunt edge of his spear and knocked her to the ground. He leaped from his pony and stood over her, the point of the spear pressed against her deerskin dress.

Adam's heart, pulse, and blood roared in his ears. A cold sweat covered his brow. Seared with outrage, but afraid to move lest Hole-in-Chin drive the spear through his daughter, he stood motionless. Like the slow drip of a leaden sky, the seconds slipped past. He tossed down his gun and knife.

"Let her go. It's me you want. There is no glory in killing Tall Horse's grandchild. He will have you hunted down like a wild dog."

Madness gleamed in the warrior's black eyes as his gaze flashed from Adam's face to the child at his feet. He goaded, "It is the way of nature. All creatures will fight for their young. Fight for her, Adam Hawk. Defeat me and she is yours."

Adam gave a mute nod, but held back, for the spear was yet poised above the heart of Dorie.

"I will crush your bones," Hole-in-Chin boasted. "I will inflict many wounds and your scalp I will take while you yet live. You, like the French trader, will cry out, no longer the brave white warrior." He plunged the spear into the ground and drew his knife. Stumbling, crawling, running, Dorie scrambled out of his way.

The ice within Adam melted into a raging, ravaging river. He taunted, "Still the boaster, Hole-in-Chin? As a boy and as a man. Come on, then. Inflict your wounds. Fight for a good song to sing around your campfire."

Hole-in-Chin lunged, the blade of his knife flashing, grazing Adam's arm. The streak of pain, the ooze of blood, the shock of it cooled Adam's head. He kicked out, trying to jar the knife from the Indian's hand, but Hole-in-Chin's instincts were keen-edged. Effortlessly, he dodged the attempt and taking advantage of Adam's impeded balance, hooked a foot around Adam's right leg and jerked him to the ground. The wind left his lungs, echoed by the impact of Hole-in-Chin's weight as he flung himself upon him. Seeing the uplifted knife, Adam brought his knee up hard and gained a last-second reprieve. As Hole-in-Chin groaned and fought the wave of dizzying pain, he rolled him off, pinned him to the ground, and beat his hand against the earth, forcing him to release the knife.

The odds were now evened. Hole-in-Chin was quick and strongly built. He kicked out of Adam's hold and sprang to his feet. A fraction of a second slower, Adam was still rising when the Oto dealt a vicious kick to the throat and sent him reeling.

The black, choking sensation blurred his vision. He gasped for air, his brain flashing urgent messages. He couldn't defeat this crazed man, not like this. Fist fighting was his strength. He'd learned it from his father who'd mastered more than his share of rowdies come bent on disrupting his hellfire-and-brimstone camp meetings.

Vision clearing, Adam sprang forward. He led with a right hook and followed with quick, punishing jabs. The Indian backed away and like a dazed buffalo, shook his head. Adam moved swiftly, both fists delivering punches. But the brave shook the cobwebs from his head and proved surprisingly versatile. He connected with a blow to the face that set Adam's ears to ringing. Knowing his life and Dorie's security hung in the balance, he fought on, exchanging punch for punch. The Indian landed a good blow under the chin. Adam's head snapped back; he staggered but stood fast to come back strong, landing a crunching blow to the jaw that sent the Indian sprawling.

Gasping for breath, Adam dropped down and planted a knee in his opponent's chest. Fist cocked, he asked, "Enough?"

Hole-in-Chin struggled to rise, but fell back, collapsing in the mangled grass. Hatred gleamed from his black eyes.

"I spit upon your mercy. Kill me, white man," he panted.

Both fists bunched, Adam could easily have obliged. He thought of the terror Dorie had gone through. He looked upon the bloody scalp lying limp and hideous against the Indian's buckskins. Jean-Claude had died defending his daughter.

Some scant emotion surfaced upon the battered face of the warrior. A slight twitch, a cringing that betrayed fear. Even now as he begged death, he feared it. Adam uncurled his fists and rested back on his heels. The Indian lay motionless.

Grudgingly he said, "It's only a fool who knows no fear. Why hate yourself for something the Great Spirit put within you? You aren't ready to die. Cherish life. Fear the Great Spirit Himself. Be anxious for *his* approval, not that of your people."

"It is white man's talk," the Indian hissed. "Like that of Shining Meadow. Squaw chatter."

The mention of his dead wife and the twinge of emotion that passed on the Indian's swollen face surprised Adam. Had he all this time misunderstood this man's burning hatred? But eighteen when she returned to her village, Shining Meadow was three years older than Hole-in-Chin. Did years really matter, though? Had Hole-in-Chin secretly harbored tender feelings for Shining Meadow?

"Shining Meadow loved her people," Adam said. "That was why she returned to her village. She had a message to share."

"Her Jesus words." Hole-in-Chin seemed to acknowledge it against his will. He turned his face away.

"Great Spirit's Son, that was her message." The memories washed over Adam. At his feet, Hole-in-Chin kept his face turned, features set against him. His eyes were haughty, disbelieving. Adam wanted to walk away, to take Dorie and go, but thoughts of Shining Meadow held him in place. She'd loved her Master and her people. He thought of the intensity with which she'd tried to teach them of

God's Son, and knew that if through her return one soul was saved, she'd have considered her sacrifice worth it. And so it was that he found himself repeating the great truth of God's gift of His Son.

When he fell silent, Dorie pressed up against him, her eyes glassy, her body trembling. At great length, Hole-in-Chin fixed his gaze upon Adam.

"If it is as you say, why did you whites kill this Jesus of yours?"

Adam ignored the scorn that carried his words. "He is your Jesus, too. The Great Spirit sent him for all men."

"White hands killed him."

"Didn't the Great Spirit send the buffalo? The buffalo lays down his life for you."

"It is not the same." The Indian's face remained hard, unyielding.

Adam knew he was right. The buffalo was taken with a reverent and thankful heart. God's Son had fallen into far less merciful hands. Doubting his ability to explain further, Adam said quietly, "Does how he died or the color of the hands that drove the nails and spear change who he was or what he came to do?"

Hole-in-Chin didn't reply. Adam looked into his face and knew he'd failed. The contempt, the hatred, the bitter frustration of defeat remained upon his countenance.

Rising on stiff, sore limbs, Adam wrapped an arm around Dorie. She clung to his hand, her small face pinched and weary. He limped along a few paces, then stopped, picked up his child, and held her close. The tears spilled down her cheeks. Though no words passed between them, he felt the terror leaving her.

chapter 22

AUTUMN HAD LINGERED LONG, favoring St. Louis with unseasonably mild weather. But today's bite to the air warned of approaching winter. Rachel worked pulling the last of the dead plants and spent vines from her garden spot. Limp leaves, their autumn vibrance now faded, cushioned her steps. Gray clouds bullied the blue from the sky and stole the sun's warmth. She rested her back and pushed a lock of stray hair away from her face. Would the rain hold off long enough for her to burn the dead remains of her garden?

She glanced at the sky again, then pitched a few mushy apples onto the pile of debris.

"Why don't you quit for the day? Rain's coming," Katri called from the back door.

Looking in her direction, Rachel saw the old woman cock her nose to the wind. She smelled the coming rain, too. "I'll put my tools away, then come in. I'm ready for a cup of tea, anyway."

The strand of hair was in her eyes again. Rachel loosened the faded green ribbon at the nape of her neck and turned so the wind blew her hair straight back. Catching it all in one hand, she used the ribbon to tie it higher upon her head. Watching her, Katri shifted from foot to foot, then glanced back over her shoulder.

"It'll be more than tea, I'm thinking. We're having a bit of company."

"Company?" Rachel paused in gathering her tools. She surveyed her dirty hands and torn fingernails, her soiled apron and faded work skirt. "Not for a good while, I hope. I'm a mess," she said with a wry grimace.

"You'll be in good company," A wide smile split Katri's face. She stood to one side, clearing the door.

Rachel gaped at the child standing there. Perhaps it was the fringed deerskin dress and the tall, beaded moccasins that confused her, for not until the girl stepped out into the yard did recognition fly through her. Rachel dropped her tools and with a cry of mingled joy and relief, rushed to pull Dorie into her arms.

Tears dimmed her eyes as the child returned the welcoming embrace with a desperate sort of clinging. Struggling for composure, keeping the child close, Rachel cried, "Not in my fondest dreams did I think you'd be home before spring. How *are* you? How was your trip? Just look at you! Look how you've grown!"

Katri looked on, chuckling softly, a gentle light in her faded eyes. She was younger than Shining Meadow and strongly resembled Dorie. And for a moment, finding her on the threshold had shaken her. Katri gave herself a shake. The Lord giveth, the Lord taketh away.

She saw the hope, the eagerness, the vulnerability in Rachel's eyes as she gazed over Dorie's dark head, looking for Adam. "He's coming," she said, to save her the pain of asking. "Around front."

Rachel turned the child loose, and together they reentered the house. There was a tremble in Rachel's hand as she flung off her dirty apron, straightened her skirt and jerked her cloak off the peg. She paused midstride, and turned a panicky face in Katri's direction. Katri smiled and urged, "Go on; he's waiting. He didn't come all this way to see the likes of me."

What had happened to him? How gaunt and haggard he looked! How pale! And that uneven gait. "What's the matter with him?" she cried.

"He was in a fight," Dorie began, and launched into a long account, most of which was overridden by the loud erratic pounding of Rachel's heart.

She curled her hands into fists, the nails biting into her palms. Her heart and her feet were in agreement, willing her to run to him. But long months of separation, doubt and raw, exposed emotions held her in check. Each day since his departure, she'd dreamed of this moment. She'd come through the fire and was ready to meet him on his own ground. But what if it wasn't the same with him? What if he hadn't given her a thought since leaving those long months ago?

Dorie descended one step and called to her father, "Papa? Did you see? She didn't go back to Boston. She's waiting, just like I knew she'd be."

At last Adam turned. His gaze spanned the distance across the yard to the veranda and his womenfolk standing there. A trace of a smile touched his mouth as he leaned against the gate post, but a sad, haunted look shone through it.

"Seems to me the hill's grown steeper while I was away. Or could be I'm not the same man I was when I left. Reckon one of you ladies'd be kind enough to help me the rest of the way?

Both Rachel and Dorie bolted toward him, but Katri caught a handful of fringe and held Dorie back. She murmured, "Let Rachel help him. You're just a little toadstool and weary yourself. Come inside and rest while I lay out the table."

Dorie began to protest, then caught herself and slipped along after Katri, sneaking one small glance back. Rachel reached Adam's side the same moment the door closed behind the child.

Rachel studied his face with anxious eyes, the silence growing between them. He was unshaven, his hair had grown long and fine lines had deepened at the corners of his blue eyes. Growing aware of his counter-scrutiny, she remembered her untamed hair, her soiled hands, and tattered skirt. Inanely, she murmured, "I was working in the garden."

A slow smile tugged at his mouth, once again contradicting the quiet suffering that shadowed his countenance. A sweet ache formed in her throat. Was it physical pain that painted those lines upon his face? She asked, "Is it hurting a great deal?"

"Hmm?"

"Your leg. Does it hurt?"

Leaning upon his crude crutch, he hobbled a step nearer and touched her face with a gentle hand. Something clear and sweet stirred in the depths of his eyes. "Not near so much as finding you gone would have." He traced the firm sweep of her chin with a calloused finger and caught a tear that trickled free of her lashes.

She drew a shaky breath and whispered, "I've missed you, Adam. I've worried and prayed and missed you and thought spring would never come."

"It hasn't. But God willing, it will." The damp autumn air blew between them, but a growing smile battled the pain that lingered in his eyes. He pulled her close and landed a kiss on the side of her head where the silky strands were held back by her half of the faded green ribbon.

She rested her face against the warmth of his shirt front, and heard the rushing of his heart. His chin came to rest on the crown of her head. Content for the moment just to be held, she savored his warmth, his strength, his wholeness, and let go all the thoughts, the worries, the questions.

In time, he laid a hand on the round of her shoulder and began to open before her eyes the emotional wound within him. Chafing her arm, voice grown choppy, he admitted, "I've wanted to be back, counted the hours, but I've dreaded it too. Next day or so, I'll have to go see Ann-Marie. Have to tell her Jean-Claude is dead."

"The Frenchman?" Rachel caught her breath and arched her head back to study his face. A sudden fear rose in her throat. "Adam, you didn't . . ." It was too horrible a question to finish.

His hand tightened on her shoulder. "Nothing like that. The bad blood—it was gone. He died proving his loyalty to me."

Her heart went out to him as he tried to curtain the emotions that found their way to his face. Seeking words that would comfort, she said, "It'll be hard for Ann-Marie, but no harder than constantly wondering, always worrying. And not nearly so hard as if he'd died in dishonor."

"I thought of that," he admitted. "But still, he's dead."

Rachel murmured, "I'm sorry about Jean-Claude, sorry for Ann-Marie, too. But I'd be lying if I said my sorrow was greater than my joy at having you and Dorie home again."

He searched her face, but his words were slow in coming and his eyes gave little away. Heart heavy for him, she let her hands drift up to his strong shoulders, then move inward to lightly caress the tanned column of his neck before linking her fingers behind it. His hair, well down his neck, was thick and coarse in texture, yet comforting beneath her fingertips. A sigh escaped her. His mouth descended to steal it away from her lips. It was an impulsive kiss, with strong undertones of a deeper hunger. Having taken it, he said with a trace of regret, "You're too fine a lady for a man like me; I've always known it. Occurred to me, while I was away you'd figure it out for yourself."

She denied it with a shake of her head. "You're a good man, Adam Hawk. I know no better. I've done some thinking, too. I've been uncompromising. Narrow-minded. Hard-headed and foolish. Your work takes you away, just as my father's did. I resented it with him, and it would be easy for me to resent it with you. But it would also be wrong of me. You are who you are, answering to a voice in the wind. If you ask it of me, I'll follow the same voice, stay by your side."

He tried to interrupt, but she waved his words aside and rushed on, wanting it all said before she lost her courage. "I could say I'd keep the homefires burning, and wait for the winds to change, to call you home again. But waiting isn't one of my virtues; I won't pretend it is. These past months have been a lifetime."

Daring to meet his gaze, she saw a love shining there that stole her breath away. His lips covered hers, no longer impulsive, rather distributing kisses that fired within her an answering passion. Mouth purposeful, seeking, growing more sure with each heightened breath, he stole from her a sweet confession of love as she pressed nearer, less mindful of his injury, hungry to erase the anguish of long separation. The wind wrenched at her cloak, and the clouds released their first droplets of moisture, but she was oblivious to any discomfort, warm and secure within his embrace.

At long last, his lips left hers, his unshaven face rough against her smooth cheek as he kissed the lobe of her ear, the tender line of her jaw, her neck, her white throat.

"I said I wasn't the same man who left last spring and I'm not," he spoke softly against her lips. "I won't be goin' away again, Rachel. Soon as my leg mends, I'll find work here in the city. Find us a house. A school for Dorie."

Fresh tears stinging her eyes, Rachel began to protest that he mustn't sacrifice his way of life, his freedom for her, but he silenced her with a tender kiss.

"Freedom's been costly. Years are gone I can't regain. No point in frettin' over that. But the years that lay ahead, they're a different matter. Seems we're both willin' to work at pleasing one another. We'll make a good marriage. We'll build for the future, lookin' for God to provide the opportunities." He paused a moment and looked deep into her eyes. "Unless I'm takin' too much for granted. You've grown awful quiet. If you've got something needs sayin', best say it."

She saw him brace himself, as if in preparation for new hurt and wondered at his reluctance to expect the best and get it. "I thought I'd already said it all." She hid a smile against the prickly edge of his jaw.

Leaning against her as they started toward the house together, he murmured, "Wouldn't hurt you to say it again."

And so she did, for his ears alone.

ABOUT THE AUTHOR

The author of numerous romances, SUSAN KIRBY says that she's "a romantic at heart" and that she enjoys writing light romance, particularly inspirational novels. Her first Serenade book was the 1985 contemporary romance *Heart Aflame*.

Kirby has also written an award-winning children's book and more than 100 stories and articles for magazines ranging from *Christian Life* to *Farm Wife News*. In addition to writing, she plays the organ for her church, bikes, sews, crochets, gardens, and swims.

She lives with her husband and two sons in Illinois.

A Letter to Our Readers

Dear Reader:

Welcome to Serenade Books—a series designed to bring you beautiful love stories in the world of inspirational romance. They will uplift you, encourage you, and provide hours of wholesome entertainment, so thousands of readers have testified. That we might better contribute to your reading enjoyment, we would appreciate your taking a few minutes to respond to the following questions and return to:

Lois Taylor
Serenade Books
The Zondervan Publishing House
1415 Lake Drive, S.E.
Grand Rapids, Michigan 49506

1. Did you enjoy reading *Cries the Wilderness Wind*?

   ☐ Very much. I would like to see more books by this author!
   ☐ Moderately
   ☐ I would have enjoyed it more if ________________________

2. Where did you purchase this book? ________________________

3. What influenced your decision to purchase this book?

   ☐ Cover ☐ Back cover copy
   ☐ Title ☐ Friends
   ☐ Publicity ☐ Other ________________

4. Please rate the following elements from 1 (poor) to 10 (superior).

- [ ] Heroine
- [ ] Hero
- [ ] Setting
- [ ] Plot
- [ ] Inspirational theme
- [ ] Secondary characters

5. What are some inspirational themes you would like to see treated in future books?

____

____

6. Please indicate your age range:

- [ ] Under 18
- [ ] 18–24
- [ ] 25–34
- [ ] 35–45
- [ ] 46–55
- [ ] Over 55

Serenade / Saga books are inspirational romances in historical settings, designed to bring you a joyful, heart-lifting reading experience.

Serenade / Saga books available in your local bookstore:

#1 *Summer Snow,* Sandy Dengler
#2 *Call Her Blessed,* Jeanette Gilge
#3 *Ina,* Karen Baker Kletzing
#4 *Juliana of Clover Hill,* Brenda Knight Graham
#5 *Song of the Nereids,* Sandy Dengler
#6 *Anna's Rocking Chair,* Elaine Watson
#7 *In Love's Own Time,* Susan C. Feldhake
#8 *Yankee Bride,* Jane Peart
#9 *Light of My Heart,* Kathleen Karr
#10 *Love Beyond Surrender,* Susan C. Feldhake
#11 *All the Days After Sunday,* Jeanette Gilge
#12 *Winterspring,* Sandy Dengler
#13 *Hand Me Down the Dawn,* Mary Harwell Sayler
#14 *Rebel Bride,* Jane Peart
#15 *Speak Softly, Love,* Kathleen Yapp
#16 *From This Day Forward,* Kathleen Karr
#17 *The River Between,* Jacquelyn Cook
#18 *Valiant Bride,* Jane Peart
#19 *Wait for the Sun,* Maryn Langer
#20 *Kincaid of Cripple Creek,* Peggy Darty
#21 *Love's Gentle Journey,* Kay Cornelius
#22 *Applegate Landing,* Jean Conrad
#23 *Beyond the Smoky Curtain,* Mary Harwell Sayler
#24 *To Dwell in the Land,* Elaine Watson
#25 *Moon for a Candle,* Maryn Langer
#26 *The Conviction of Charlotte Grey,* Jeanne Cheyney

#27 *Opal Fire,* Sandy Dengler
#28 *Divide the Joy,* Maryn Langer
#29 *Cimarron Sunset,* Peggy Darty
#30 *This Rolling Land,* Sandy Dengler
#31 *The Wind Along the River,* Jacquelyn Cook
#32 *Sycamore Settlement,* Suzanne Pierson Ellison
#33 *Where Morning Dawns,* Irene Brand
#34 *Elizabeth of Saginaw Bay,* Donna Winters
#35 *Westward My Love,* Elaine L. Schulte
#36 *Ransomed Bride,* Jane Peart
#37 *Dreams of Gold,* Elaine L. Schulte

Serenade/Saga books are now being published in a new, longer length:

#1 *Chessie's King,* Kathleen Karr
#2 *The Rogue's Daughter,* Molly Noble Bull
#3 *Image in the Looking Glass,* Jacquelyn Cook
#4 *Rising Thunder,* Carolyn Ann Wharton
#5 *Fortune's Bride,* Jane Peart

Serenade / Serenata books are inspirational romances in contemporary settings, designed to bring you a joyful, heart-lifting reading experience.

Serenade / Serenata books available in your local bookstore:

#28 *Shadows Along the Ice,* Judy Baer
#29 *Born to Be One,* Cathie LeNoir
#30 *Heart Aflame,* Susan Kirby
#31 *By Love Restored,* Nancy Johanson
#32 *Karaleen,* Mary Carpenter Reid
#33 *Love's Full Circle,* Lurlene McDaniel
#34 *A New Love,* Mab Graff Hoover
#35 *The Lessons of Love,* Susan Phillips
#36 *For Always,* Molly Noble Bull
#37 *A Song in the Night,* Sara Mitchell
#38 *Love Unmerited,* Donna Fletcher Crow
#39 *Thetis Island,* Brenda Willoughby
#40 *Love More Precious,* Marilyn Austin

Serenade/Serenata books are now being published in a new, longer length:

#1 *Echoes of Love,* Elaine L. Schulte
#2 *With All Your Heart,* Sara Mitchell
#3 *Moonglow,* Judy Baer
#4 *Gift of Love,* Lurlene McDaniel
#5 *The Wings of Adrian,* Jan Seabaugh
#6 *Song of Joy,* Elaine L. Schulte

Watch for other books in both the *Serenade/Saga* (historical) and *Serenade/Serenata* (contemporary) series, coming soon.